Baker Towers

ALSO BY JENNIFER HAIGH

Mrs. Kimble

Baker Towers

JENNIFER HAIGH

DOUBLEDAY LARGE PRINT HOME LIBRARY EDITION

WILLIAM MORROW

An Imprint of HarperCollins*Publishers*

This Large Print Edition, prepared especially for
Doubleday Large Print Home Library, contains the
complete, unabridged text of the original Publisher's
Edition.

This book is a work of fiction. The characters, incidents,
and dialogue are drawn from the author's imagination and
are not to be construed as real. Any resemblance to
actual events or persons, living or dead, is entirely
coincidental.

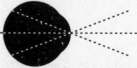

This Large Print Book carries the
Seal of Approval of N.A.V.H.

In memory of my father,

Jay Wasilko

If grief could burn out
Like a sunken coal,
The heart would rest quiet.

PHILIP LARKIN

All the brothers were valiant, and all the
sisters virtuous.

INSCRIPTION ON A TOMB
IN WESTMINSTER ABBEY

The family is the country of the heart.

GIUSEPPE MAZZINI,
THE DUTIES OF MAN

My sincere thanks to the MacDowell Colony and Vermont Studio Center, where portions of this book were written.

I am deeply grateful to Dorian Karchmar, Claire Wachtel, Michael Morrison, Lisa Gallagher, and Juliette Shapland, who make all things possible.

Love and thanks to my mother, Elizabeth Wasilko, and to Dan.

Baker Towers

ONE

Softly the snow falls. In the blue morning light a train winds through the hills. The engine pulls a passenger car, brightly lit. Then a dozen blind coal cars, rumbling dark.

Six mornings a week the train runs westward from Altoona to Pittsburgh, a distance of a hundred miles. The route is indirect, tortuous; the earth is buckled, swollen with what lies beneath. Here and there, the lights of a town: rows of company houses, narrow and square; a main street of commercial buildings, quickly and cheaply built. Brakes screech; the train huffs to a stop. Cars are added. In the passenger compartment, a soldier on furlough clasps his duffel bag, shivers and waits. The whistle blows. Wheezing, the engine leaves the station, slowed by the extra tons of coal.

The train crosses an iron bridge, the black water of the Susquehanna. Lights cluster in the next valley. The town, Bakerton, is already awake. Coal cars thunder down the mountain. The valley is filled with sound.

The valley is deep and sharply featured. Church steeples and mine tipples grow inside it like crystals. At bottom is the town's most famous landmark, known locally as the Towers, two looming piles of mine waste. They are forty feet high and growing, graceful slopes of loose coal and sulfurous dirt. The Towers give off an odor like struck matches. On windy days they glow soft orange, like the embers of a campfire. Scrap coal, spontaneously combusting; a million bits of coal bursting into flame.

Bakerton is Saxon County's boomtown. Like the Towers, it is alive with coal. A life that started in the 1880s, when two English brothers, Chester and Elias Baker, broke ground on Baker One. Attracted by handbills, immigrants came: English and Irish, then Italians and Hungarians; then Poles and Slovaks and Ukrainians and Croats, the "Slavish," as they were collectively known. With each new wave the town shifted to make room. Another church was constructed. A new cluster of company houses appeared at the edge of town. The work—mine work—was backbreaking, dangerous and bleak; but at Baker Brothers the union was tolerated. By the standards of the time the pay was generous, the housing affordable and clean.

The mines were not named for Bakerton; Bakerton was named for the mines. This is an important distinction. It explains the order of things.

Chester Baker was the town's first mayor. During his term Bakerton acquired the first streetcar line in the county, the first public water supply. Its electric street lamps were purchased from Baker's own pocket. *Figure the cost of maintaining them for fifty years,* he wrote to the town bosses, *and I will pay you the sum in advance.* After twenty years Baker ceded his office, but the bosses continued to meet at his house, a rambling yellow-brick mansion on Indian Hill. A hospital was built, the construction crew paid from a fund Baker had established. He wouldn't let the building be named for him. At his direction, it was called Miners' Hospital.

The hospital was constructed in brick; so were the stores, the dress factory, the churches, the grammar school. After the Commercial Hotel burned to the ground in 1909, an ordinance was passed, urging merchants to "make every effort to fabricate their establishments of brick." To a traveler arriving on the morning train—by now an expert on Pennsylvania coal towns—the hat shop and dry-goods store, the pharmacy and mercantile, seem built to last. Their brick facades suggest order, prosperity, permanence.

On the seventeenth of January 1944, a motorcar idled at the railroad crossing, waiting for the train to pass. In the passenger seat was an elderly undertaker of Sicilian descent, named Antonio Bernardi. At the wheel was his great-nephew Gennaro, a handsome, curly-haired youth known in the pool halls as Jerry. Between them sat a blond-haired boy of eight. The car, a black Packard, had been waxed that morning. The old man peered anxiously through the windshield, at the snowflakes melting on the hood.

"These Slavish," he said, as if only a Pole

would drop dead in the middle of winter and expect to be buried in a snowstorm.

The train passed, whistle blowing. The Packard crossed the tracks and climbed a steep road lined with company houses, a part of town known as Polish Hill. The road was loose and rocky; the coarse stones, called red dog, came from bony piles on the outskirts of town. Black smoke rose from the chimneys; in the backyards were out-houses, coal heaps, clotheslines stretched between posts. Here and there, miners' overalls hung out to dry, frozen stiff in the January wind.

"These Slavish," Bernardi said again. "They live like *animali*." At one time, his own brothers had lived in company houses, but the family had improved itself. His nephews owned property, houses filled with modern comforts: telephones and flush toilets, gas stoves and carpeted floors.

"Papa," said Jerry, glancing at the boy; but the child seemed not to hear. He stared out the window wide-eyed, having never ridden in a car before. His name was Sandy Novak; he'd come knocking at Bernardi's back door an hour before—breathless, his nose dripping. His mother had sent him run-

ning all the way from Polish Hill, to tell
Bernardi to come and get his father.

The car climbed the slope, engine racing.
Briefly the tires slid on the ice. At the top of
the hill Jerry braked.

"Well?" said the old man to the boy.
"Where do you live?"

"Back there," said Sandy Novak. "We
passed it."

Bernardi exhaled loudly. "*Cristo.* Now we
got to turn around."

Jerry turned the car in the middle of the
road.

"Pay attention this time," Bernardi told
the boy. "We don't got all day." In fact he'd
buried nobody that week, but he believed in
staying available. Past opportunities—fires,
rockfalls, the number five collapse—had
arisen without warning. Somewhere in Bakerton a miner was dying. Only Bernardi
could deliver him to God.

The Bernardis handled funerals at the five
Catholic churches in town. A man named
Hiram Stoner had a similar arrangement
with the Protestants. When Bernardi's black
Packard was spotted, the town knew a
Catholic had died; Stoner's Ford meant a
dead Episcopalian, Lutheran or Methodist.

For years Bernardi had transported his customers in a wagon pulled by two horses. During the flu of '18 he'd moved three bodies at a time. Recently, conceding to modernity, he'd bought the Packard; now, when a Catholic died, a Bernardi nephew would be called upon to drive. Jerry was the last remaining; the others had been sent to England and northern Africa. The old man worried that Jerry, too, would be drafted. Then he'd have no one left to drive the hearse.

"There it is," the boy said, pointing. "That's my house."

Jerry slowed. The house was mean and narrow like the others, but a front porch had been added, painted green and white. One window, draped with lace curtains, held a porcelain statue of the Madonna. In the other window hung a single blue star.

"Who's the soldier?" said Jerry.

"My brother Georgie," said Sandy, then added what his father always said. "He's in the South Pacific."

They climbed the porch stairs, stamping snow from their shoes. A woman opened the door. Her dark hair was loose, her mouth full. A baby slept against her shoulder. She was beautiful, but not young—at least forty, if Bernardi had to guess. He was like a timberman who could guess the age of a tree before counting the rings inside. He had rarely been wrong.

She let them inside. Her eyelids were puffy, her eyes rimmed with red. She inhaled sharply, a moist, slurry sound.

Bernardi offered his hand. He'd expected the usual Slavish type: pale and round-faced, a long braid wrapped around her head so that she resembled a fancy pastry. This one was dark-eyed, olive-skinned. He glanced down at her bare feet. Italian, he realized with a shock. His mother and sisters had never worn shoes in the house.

"My dear lady," he said. "My condolences for your loss."

"Come in." She had an ample figure, heavy in the bosom and hip. The type Bernardi—an old bachelor, a window-shopper who'd looked but had never bought—had always liked.

She led them through a tidy parlor—polished pine floor, a braided rug at the center. A delicious aroma came from the kitchen. Not the usual Slavish smell, the sour stink of cooked cabbage.

"This way," said the widow. "He's in the cellar."

They descended a narrow staircase—the widow first, then Jerry and Bernardi. The dank basement smelled of soap, onions and coal. The widow switched on the light, a single bare bulb in the ceiling. A man lay on the cement floor—fair-haired, with a handlebar mustache. A silver medal on a chain around his neck: Saint Anne, protectress of miners. His hair was wet, his eyes already closed.

"He just come home from the mines," said the widow, her voice breaking. "He was washing up. I wonder how come he take so long."

Bernardi knelt on the cold floor. The man was tall and broad-shouldered. His shirt was damp; the color had already left his face. Bernardi touched his throat, feeling for a pulse.

"It's no point," said the woman. "The priest already come."

Bernardi grasped the man's legs, leaving Jerry the heavier top half. Together they hefted the body up the stairs. Bernardi was sixty-four that spring, but his work had kept him strong. He guessed the man weighed two hundred pounds, heavy even for a Slavish.

They carried the body out the front door and laid it in the rear of the car. The boy watched from the porch. A moment later the widow appeared, still holding the baby. She had put on shoes. She handed Bernardi a dark suit on a hanger.

"He wore it when we got married," she said. "I hope it still fits."

Bernardi took the suit. "We'll bring him back tonight. How about you get a couple neighbors to help us? He'll be heavier with the casket."

The widow nodded. In her arms the baby stirred. Bernardi smiled stiffly. He found infants tedious; he preferred them silent and unconscious, like this one. "A little angel," he said. "What's her name?"

"Lucy." The widow stared over his shoulder at the car. "*Dio mio.* I can't believe it."

"*Iddio la benedica.*"

They stood there a moment, their heads bowed. Gently Bernardi patted her shoulder. He was an old man; by his own count he'd buried more than a thousand bodies; he had glimpsed the darkest truths, the final secrets. Still, life held surprises. Here was a thing he had never witnessed, an Italian wife on Polish Hill.

That morning, the feast of Saint Anthony, Rose Novak had gone to church. For years the daily mass had been poorly attended, but now the churches were crowded with women. The choir, heavy on sopranos, had doubled in size. Wives stood in line to light a candle; mothers knelt at the communion rail in silent prayer. Since her son Georgie was drafted Rose had scarcely missed a mass. Each morning her eldest daughter, Dorothy, cooked the family breakfast, minded the baby, and woke Sandy and Joyce for school.

Rose glanced at her watch; again the old priest had overslept. She reached into her pocket for her rosary. *Good morning, Georgie,* she thought, crossing herself. *Buongiorno, bello.* In the past year, the form of her prayers had changed: instead of asking God for His protection, she now prayed directly to her son. This did not strike her as blasphemous. If God could hear her prayers, it was just as easy to imagine that

Georgie heard them, too. He seemed as far away as God; her husband had shown her the islands on the globe. She imagined Georgie's submarine smaller than a pinprick, an aquatic worm in the fathomless blue.

Stanley had wanted him to enlist. "We owe it to America," he said, as if throwing Georgie's life away would make them all more American. Stanley had fought in the last war and returned with all his limbs. He'd forgotten the others—his cousins, Rose's older brother—who hadn't been so lucky.

Rose had resisted—quietly at first, then loudly, without restraint. Georgie was a serious young man, a musician. He'd taught himself the clarinet and saxophone; since the age of five he'd played the violin. Besides that, he was delicate: as a child he'd had pneumonia, and later diphtheria. Both times he had nearly died. If America wanted his precious life, then America would have to call him. Rose would not let Stanley hand him over on a plate.

For a time she had her way. Georgie graduated high school and went to work at Baker One. He blew his saxophone in a dance band that played the VFW dances

Friday nights. When the draft notice came, Stanley had seemed almost glad. Rose called him a brute, a braggart—willing to risk Georgie's life so he'd have something to boast about in the beer gardens. At the time she believed it. The next morning she found him gathering eggs in the henhouse, weeping like a baby.

He was strict with the children, with Georgie especially. Only English was to be spoken at home; when Rose lapsed into Italian with her mother or sisters, Stanley glared at her with silent scorn. Yet late at night, once the children were in bed, he tuned the radio to a Polish station from Pittsburgh and listened until it was time for work.

She left the warmth of the church and walked home through a stiff wind, wisps of snow swirling around her ankles, hovering above the sidewalk like steam or spirits. The sky had begun to lighten; the frozen ground was still bare. Good for the miners, loading the night's coal onto railroad cars; good for the children, who walked two miles each way to school.

At Polish Hill the sidewalk ended. She continued along the rocky path, hugging her coat around her, a fierce wind at her back. Ahead, a group of miners trudged up the hill with their empty dinner buckets, cupping cigarettes in their grimy hands. They joked loudly in Polish and English: deep voices, phlegmy laughter. Like Stanley they'd worked Hoot Owl, midnight to eight; since the war had started the mines never stopped. Rose picked out her neighbor Andy Yurkovich, the bad-tempered father of two-year-old twins. He had a young Hungarian wife; by noon her nerves would be shattered, trying to keep the babies quiet so Andy could sleep.

Rose climbed the stairs to the porch. The house was warm inside; someone had stoked the furnace. She left her shoes at the door. Dorothy sat at the kitchen table chewing her fingernails. The baby sat calmly in her lap, mouthing a saltine cracker.

"Sorry I'm late. That Polish priest, he need an alarm clock." Rose reached for the baby. "Did she behave herself?" she asked in Italian.

"She was an angel," Dorothy answered in English. "Daddy's home," she added in a whisper. She reached for her boots and glanced at the mirror that hung beside the door. Her hair looked flattened on one side. An odd rash had appeared on her cheek. She would be nineteen that spring.

"Put on some lipstick," Rose suggested.

"No time," Dorothy called over her shoulder.

In the distance the factory whistle blew. Through the kitchen window Rose watched Dorothy hurry down the hill, the hem of her dress peeking beneath her coat. People said they looked alike, and their features— the dark eyes, the full mouth—were indeed similar. In her high school graduation photo, taken the previous spring, Dorothy was as stunning as any movie actress. In actual life she was less attractive. Tall and round-shouldered, with no bosom to speak of; no matter how Rose hemmed them, Dorothy's skirts dipped an inch lower on the left side. Help existed: corsets, cosmetics, the innocent adornments most girls discovered at puberty and used faithfully until death. Dorothy either didn't know about them or didn't care. She still hadn't mastered the art of setting her hair, a skill other girls seemed to possess intuitively.

She sewed sleeves at the Bakerton Dress Company, a low brick building at the other end of town. Each morning Rose watched the neighborhood women tramp there like a civilian army. A few even wore trousers, their hair tied back with kerchiefs. What precisely they did inside the factory, Rose understood only vaguely. The noise was deafening, Dorothy said; the floor manager made her nervous, watching her every minute. After seven months she still hadn't made production. Rose worried, said nothing. For an unmarried woman, the factory was the only employer in town. If Dorothy were fired she'd be forced to leave, take the train to New York City and find work as a housemaid or cook. Several girls from the neighborhood had done this—quit school at fourteen to become live-in maids for wealthy Jews. The Jews owned stores and drove cars; they needed Polish-speaking maids to wash their many sets of dishes. A few Bakerton girls had even settled there, found city husbands; but for Dorothy this seemed unlikely. Her Polish was sketchy, thanks to Stanley's rules. And she was terrified of men. At church, in the street, she would not meet their eyes.

Rose laid the baby down. Every morning she carried the heavy cradle downstairs to the kitchen, the warmest room in the house. From upstairs came the sounds of an argument, the younger children getting ready for school.

She went into the parlor and stood at the foot of the stairs. "Joyce!" she called. "Sandy!"

Her younger daughter appeared on the stairs, dressed in a skirt and blouse.

"Where's your brother?"

"He isn't ready." Joyce ran a hand through her fine hair, blond like her father's; she'd inherited the color but not the abundance. "I woke him once but he went back to sleep."

"Sandy!" Rose called.

He came rumbling down the stairs: shirt unbuttoned, socks in hand, hair sticking in all directions.

"See?" Joyce demanded. She was six years older, a sophomore in high school. "I have a test first period. I can't wait around all day."

Sandy sat heavily on the steps and turned his attention to his socks. "I'm not a baby," he grumbled. "I can walk to school by myself." He was a good-humored child, not prone to sulking, but he would not take criticism from Joyce. His whole life she had mothered him, praised him, flirted with him. Her scorn was intolerable.

Joyce swiped at his hair, a stubborn cowlick that refused to lie flat. "Well, you're not going anywhere looking like that."

He shrugged her hand away.

"Suit yourself," she said, reddening. "Go to school looking like a bum. Makes no difference to me."

"You go ahead," Rose told Joyce. "I take him." He couldn't be trusted to walk alone. The last time she'd let him he'd arrived an hour late, having stopped to play with a stray dog.

He followed her into the kitchen. Of all her children he was the most beautiful, with the same pale blue eyes as his father. He had come into the world with a full head of hair, a silvery halo of blond. They'd named him Alexander, for his grandfather; it was Joyce who shortened the name to Sandy. As a toddler, she'd been desperately attached to a doll she'd named after herself; after her brother was born she transferred her affections to Sandy. "My baby!" she'd cry, outraged, when Rose bathed or nursed him. In her mind, Sandy was hers entirely.

Rose scooped the last of the oatmeal into a bowl and poured the boy a cup of coffee. Each morning she made a huge potful, mixed in sugar and cream so that the whole family drank it the same way. In the distance the fire whistle blew, a low whine that rose in pitch, then welled up out of the valley like a mechanical scream.

"What is it?" Sandy asked. "What happened?"

"I don't know." Rose stared out the window at the number three tipple rising in the distance. She scanned the horizon for smoke. The whistle could mean any number of disasters: a cave-in, an underground fire. At least once a year a miner was killed in an explosion or injured in a rockfall. Just that summer, a neighbor had lost a leg when an underground roof collapsed. She crossed herself, grateful for the noise in the basement, her husband safe at home. This time at least, he had escaped.

She filled a heavy iron pot with water and placed it on the stove. A basket of laundry sat in the corner, but the dirty linens would have to wait; she always washed Stanley's miners first. Over the years she'd developed a system. First she took the coveralls outdoors and shook out the loose dirt; then she rinsed them in cold water in the basement sink. When the water ran clean, she scrubbed the coveralls on a washboard with Octagon soap, working in the lather with a stiff brush. Then she carried the clothes upstairs and boiled them on the stove. The process took half an hour, including soak time, and she hadn't yet started. She was keeping the stove free for Stanley's breakfast.

"Finish your cereal," she told Sandy. "I go see about your father."

She found him lying on the floor, his face half shaven. The cuffs of his trousers were wet. This confused her a moment; then she saw that the sink had overflowed. He had dropped the soap and razor. The drain was blocked with a sliver of soap.

She watched the hearse disappear down the hill. A neighbor's beagle barked. For three days each November it was taken rabbit hunting. The rest of the year it spent chained in the backyard, waiting.

She had prepared for the wrong death. A

month ago, before Christmas, a car had parked in front of the Poblockis' house to deliver a telegram. Their oldest son was missing, his body—tall, gangly, an over-grown boy's—lost forever in the waters of the Pacific. Since then Rose had waited, listened for the dreadful sound of a car climbing Polish Hill. Now, finally, the car had come.

In her arms the baby shifted. From the kitchen came a shattering noise.

"Sandy?" she called.

He appeared in the doorway, hands in his pockets.

"What happened?"

He seemed to reflect a moment. "I dropped a glass."

The baby squirmed. Rose shifted her to the other shoulder.

"Where are they taking Daddy?"

"Uptown. They going to get him ready." She hesitated, unsure how to explain what she didn't understand herself and could hardly bear to think of: Stanley's body stripped and scrubbed, injected with alcohol—with God only knew what—to keep him intact another day or two.

"They clean him up," she said. "Change

his clothes. Mr. Bernardi bring him back tonight."

The boy stared. "Why?" he asked softly.

"People, they want to see him." She'd been to other wakes on Polish Hill, miserable affairs where the men drank for hours alongside the body, telling stories, keeping the widow awake all night. In the morning the house reeked of tobacco smoke. The men looked unshaven and unsteady, still half drunk as they carried the casket into church.

Sandy frowned. "What people?"

"The neighbors. People from the church."

The baby hiccuped. A moment later she let out a scream.

"I go change your sister," said Rose. "Don't touch that glass. I be back in a minute."

Sandy went into the kitchen and stood looking at the jagged glass on the floor. He'd been filling it at the sink when it nearly slipped from his wet hand. A thought had occurred to him. *If I broke it, it wouldn't matter.* He turned and threw the glass at the table leg. It smashed loudly on the floor. He had knelt to examine it. It was dull green, one he'd drunk from his whole life. Now, laying in pieces, it had become beautiful, the color deeper along the jagged edges, brilliant and jewellike. When he reached to touch it, blood had appeared along his finger. Then his mother had called, and he'd jammed his hands in his pockets.

Now he looked down at his trousers. A dark spot in his lap, blood from his finger. He looked at the clock. School had already started; he'd heard the bell ringing as he ran across town for the priest. *Tell him to come right away,* his mother had said, tears streaming down her face. He'd seen her cry just once before, when Georgie left for the war. *Tell him your father is dead.*

Sandy straightened. The spot on his trousers was brown, not red as he would have thought. His mother would know he'd touched the glass.

He took his coat from its peg near the door. Joyce would know how to get rid of the spot. He ran out the back door, across the new snow, down the hill to the school.

They'd met standing in line at the company store on a summer day. Friday afternoon, miners' payday: men spending their scrip on tobacco and rolling papers, wives buying sugar and coffee and cheap cuts of meat. Behind the counter, McNeely and his wife filled the orders, writing down each purchase in a black book. Rose's mother had sent her with a block of fresh butter wrapped in brown paper. Rose churned it herself, to trade each week for cornmeal or sausages or flour for pasta. When her turn came, Mrs. McNeely would weigh the block on a scale. Scarponi, butter, four lbs, she'd write in her book.

Rose held the butter in her apron. Already it had begun to soften in the heat. Behind her two miners waited in line, speaking what sounded like perfect English. The taller man spoke quietly, low and resonant. The oak counter beneath her elbow vibrated with his voice. She sensed the closeness of him, his length and breadth; but it was his voice that thrilled her. Even before she turned to look at him, she had fallen in love with his voice.

He'd been a soldier, like all of them. From his size and his blondness she guessed that he was Polish. This explained why she hadn't seen him before. The Poles had their own church, their parochial school. They were hard workers, serious and quiet. Nothing like the Italian boys, handsome and unreliable; *disgraziati* who loitered in the town square, sharply dressed, smoking cigarettes and watching the people go by. The Italian boys called after her—after all the girls, she'd noticed: even the plain ones, the heavy, the slow. Rose did not respond. In these boys she saw her uncles, her brothers, her own father, who tended bar at Rizzo's Tavern and drank most of what he earned. He'd kept his hair and his waistline and his eye for women, while her mother grew hunched and fat, shriller and angrier with each passing year.

Rose looked for the Polish man everywhere: in the street, the stores, the windows of the beer gardens she passed on her way home from work. She lingered at the park where the local team played. Her uncles were crazy for baseball, and that year the Baker Bombers led the coal-company league. On Wednesdays, Saturdays and Sundays, the ballpark was filled with men.

When she had nearly given up hope, he appeared in the unlikeliest place: the seamstress's shop where she worked. He was getting married in the fall, he explained. He would need a new suit.

Rose measured his chest, his arms and neck. He did not speak to her, only smiled, bending his knees helpfully so that she could reach his shoulders. Kneeling before him, she took his inseam, then recorded the numbers on a sheet of paper: chest forty-four inches, waist thirty-three. For three weeks she worked on the suit, cutting the fabric, piecing together the jacket and vest. All the while she imagined his wedding, the lovely blond-haired bride—all the Polish girls were blond. Tenderly she assembled the dark wool trousers, the silky inner fabric that would lie against his skin.

The leaves changed color. The suit waited on its hanger. Still the Polish man did not appear. In November, after the American holiday, the seamstress wrote him an angry letter. Finally, on a snowy afternoon just before Christmas, he came.

"Forgive me," he said, handing the seamstress a check. "I forgot the suit. My plans have changed." His cheeks were red—from cold or embarrassment, Rose couldn't tell.

Her fingers shook as she handed him the hanger. He covered her hand with his. That

Friday he took her to a Christmas dance at the town hall, and a month later he wore the suit to their wedding. The reception, a raucous affair at his uncle's house, lasted three days and two nights. For reasons Rose didn't understand, a pig's trough had been brought into the house, and Stanley's older brother had danced a jig in it. Her wedding night was spent in the uncle's attic. By the end of the festivities she was already pregnant.

She gave birth in the house on Polish Hill, helped by a neighbor woman trained in the old country as a midwife. Stanley considered his own name too Polish, so they called the baby George: the name of the first president, the most American name they knew. Like all company houses, theirs had three upstairs rooms; from the very beginning, the baby had one to himself. To Rose, raised in a cramped apartment above Rizzo's Tavern, the place seemed cavernous. Her mother had shared an icebox and a clothesline with two other families. The narrow yard had been worn bare by her own chickens and children, and those of the Rizzos and DiNatales.

Dorothy was born a year later, shocking

the neighborhood. Nobody had guessed Rose was pregnant; she had gained only a few pounds. For months she'd felt consumed from within and without: the girl baby growing inside her, the boy baby hungry at her breast. Later a neighbor took her aside and explained what all the Polish women knew: secret ways of delaying pregnancy; times in the month to push a man away; special teas that brought on bleeding if a woman was late. The Polish children were nursed for years; in some mysterious way, this delayed the return of a woman's monthly bleeding. Without such precautions, Rose was told, she'd give birth once a year, until she turned forty or dropped dead from exhaustion. Some women took these methods to extremes. May Poblocki nursed her sons until they started school, for reasons obvious to all: she was a handsome woman, and her husband drank. The women joked that May's son Teddy, stationed overseas in England, came home on furlough just to nurse.

Rose followed the advice strictly, and her babies came at longer intervals. Three years after Dorothy, she miscarried; the baby dissolved quietly, a soft mass of tissue and blood. Two years later, Joyce was born. Sandy was to be her last child; nursing him, she waited for forty, the age of freedom. Each new baby required time she couldn't spare, space and money they didn't have. The mines were slow then; at times Stanley worked only three days a week. In summer the children went barefoot. In winter they lived on dumplings made from stale bread, peppers and tomatoes she'd canned in September. The girls wore petticoats she sewed from flour sacks. Each day after school, Stanley took the older children to pick coal at the tipple; when the shuttle cars were unloaded, there was always some scrap coal that fell by. At suppertime they came back with a wagonload, enough to heat the house for a day.

By her fortieth birthday she had four children—a small family, by the standards of Polish Hill. She and Stanley celebrated her freedom. By then he was working Hoot Owl; each morning he washed up in the basement while she sent the children off to school. Afterward, the house empty and quiet, they climbed the stairs to their bedroom.

She'd been surprised when her cycles

stopped. "It's the change," said May Poblocki, who'd gone through it herself. The heaviness in her breasts, the strange dreams, the waves of sadness and joy—according to May it was all part of the change. Then, one afternoon as she staked tomatoes in the garden, Rose felt a stirring inside her and knew she was pregnant again.

The baby was born in November, a month after her forty-third birthday. The labor lasted an entire day. Rose scarcely remembered it; later the midwife told her she'd nearly died. Finally Stanley had called the company doctor, who cut her and took the baby with forceps. By then Rose was barely conscious. She remembered light in the distance, the angels coming to get her. When she awoke, the midwife brought her Lucy.

Miss Viola Peale ate lunch at her desk. She disliked the noise of the faculty lounge, its lingering odor of coffee and tobacco smoke. A few of the younger teachers ate in the student lunchroom, a fact Miss Peale found astonishing. Each day she brought the same lunch to school: celery sticks, a tuna sandwich and a boiled egg, prepared each morning by her sister Clara. The prospect of revealing to a pupil the contents of her lunch bag—the distinctive odors of fish and egg—was, to her, unthinkable. It struck her as exposing too much of herself, like coming to school in her slip.

Until that fall she hadn't so much as sipped a glass of water in the presence of a pupil. Then Joyce Novak asked permission to stay in the classroom during lunch period. She had a chemistry test that afternoon, she said, and she needed a place to study. The boys in the lunchroom made too much noise.

The request took Viola by surprise. Chemistry was a subject few girls studied, one she herself had avoided at the state teachers' college.

"Please?" said Joyce. She was a fair-haired girl with narrow shoulders and a sharp, birdlike face. The other sophomore girls wore lipstick and tight sweaters—in Viola's opinion, outfits entirely too sophisticated for girls of fifteen. Next to them Joyce Novak was slender as a child; yet her intelligent gray eyes were oddly adult.

"But what will you eat?" Viola asked.

"I'm not hungry. I'm too nervous to eat."

"All right," said Viola. "Just this once."

Joyce returned to her desk and opened her textbook. Viola reached into her lunch bag and nibbled timidly at her celery. Finally she'd unwrapped her sandwich. The fishy odor seemed especially strong. She wondered if Joyce noticed.

She ate in silence until the final bell. When it rang, Joyce closed her book. "Thank you, ma'am," she said politely.

"You're quite welcome." Viola had stopped short of peeling her egg, but she had eaten the sandwich and disposed of its wrapping in the dustbin. As far as she could tell, the child hadn't once looked up from her textbook.

"Joyce," she said as the girl rose to leave. "I know chemistry is a difficult subject. You're welcome to spend the lunch period here whenever you need to study."

Joyce, it turned out, was always studying—chemistry, history, plane geometry. Soon she spent nearly every noon hour in Viola's classroom. To Viola's relief, she never asked for help with her lessons. Viola could play the piano; she read and wrote French and commanded a vast mental catalog of memorized poems, but math and science were impenetrable to her. At normal school she'd graduated near the top of her class, but she'd never possessed the acumen she saw in Joyce Novak. She wondered where it came from; in nineteen years of teaching coal miners' children she had never encountered such an intellect. Often, watching her pupils struggle with Latin declensions or subjunctive tenses, she sensed the worthlessness of what she offered them, the cruelty of teaching geography to children who would never leave Saxon County. And what use was Latin grammar a hundred feet underground?

Joyce Novak was that rare pupil who stood to make use of what she'd been taught, who might do something more with her life than marry a coal miner and raise his children. Viola had witnessed it a hundred times: promising young girls (without Joyce's ability, but promising still) who married the week after graduation and were never heard from again. Their hard lives— the brutish husband, the endless succession of babies—seemed to swallow them completely; and those, everyone knew, were the success stories. No one spoke of the girls who stood at the altar six months pregnant, or the young mining widows left with more children than any sane woman could have wanted in the first place. Once, in the corridor between classes, Viola had glimpsed Joyce in conversation with a boy. *Be careful,* she wanted to say. Someone, she felt, ought to offer the girl some guidance. But guide her toward what, exactly, Viola couldn't imagine.

Her own path in life had been set from the beginning. Her father, a cousin of Chester and Elias Baker, had worked as their bookkeeper. When the mine prospered, the Peales had prospered, too. Viola's older sister was simpleminded and hadn't finished school, so Viola received an education for both of them. At twenty she graduated from normal school, returned to Bakerton and was hired as a primary teacher in a one-room schoolhouse in a rural township. She rose each morning at dawn and walked the five miles to school, where she fired the furnace and, in winter, shoveled a path from the unpaved road to the door. She taught all eight grades in a single room, to children whose first language was often Hungarian or Polish or Italian. Later she'd transferred to the high school, hoping to teach the literature and art history she'd learned at normal school. She'd been astonished to find that half the pupils quit before junior year, when elective courses could be taken; that those who remained chose home economics and metal shop rather than French. Each day Viola taught one section of Latin and five classes of English grammar. She delivered the grammar lessons with an urgent sense of mission, like Florence Nightingale dressing a wound. The children's English was deplorable. Nothing could be done about their diction—*dolwers* for *dollars, far hole* for *fire hall.* A victory was breaking them of *ain't* and the ghastly *yunz,* the Appalachian equivalent of the Southern *you all.* Their reading skills were poor; they could barely sound out the words on the chalkboard. Pupils who might someday, at most, read the Sunday paper or the United Mineworkers' monthly newsletter.

Then came Joyce Novak.

Viola made inquiries. According to Edna O'Shane, who taught art and music, Joyce could neither draw nor sing; but otherwise she was gifted in all subjects. She had a brother in the service and an older sister Viola vaguely remembered, a shy, dark-haired girl who'd watched her with terrified eyes and wouldn't speak in class. That the older Novaks had shown no special promise confounded her; she'd long observed that intelligence ran in families. (Her own excepted: her sister's slowness had a medical cause, a high fever she'd suffered as a child.) But like all the others, Joyce Novak was a coal miner's child. Her aptitude could not be accounted for.

That afternoon they sat in their usual spots—Viola at her desk, Joyce at her smaller one in the front row—eating slices of a lemon cake Viola's sister had baked. Viola had forgotten to pack forks. Giggling a little, she and Joyce ate the cake with their fingers.

"It was a cinch," said Joyce, when Viola asked about her geometry test. She sat erect in her chair, a white handkerchief spread across her lap; someone had taught her excellent table manners. "The first proof I wasn't sure about, but I got the others right."

They ate in companionable silence. Through the closed door Viola heard the hum of voices from the lunchroom down the hall. Most pupils went home at noontime. The few who remained were farm children who lived miles away.

"We had a letter from Georgie," said Joyce. "He's coming home on furlough." She spoke often of her older brother; indeed, he was the only family member she mentioned. The war seemed to fascinate her. She was better informed about the latest battles and casualties than Viola was.

"How wonderful," said Viola. "Your parents must be pleased."

Joyce didn't respond. She never spoke of her mother or father; when Viola asked after them, she answered in monosyllables. Still, Viola tried.

"Your mother must be busy with the new baby," she said.

"I guess so."

Viola waited for more. She wouldn't have known about the baby at all if, a few months back, Joyce hadn't missed several days of school. When Viola asked if she'd been ill, Joyce said she needed to be on hand in case the baby came. "But this could go on for weeks," said Viola. Her cheeks burned; she felt slightly ridiculous. *As if I know anything about childbirth.*

"Can't your mother simply phone the school when the time comes?" she asked. Joyce had blushed a deep red, and only then did Viola understand that the Novaks didn't have a telephone.

"His ship stopped in the Philippines," said Joyce. "The people there eat raw fish and seaweed. It's a very healthy diet. Some of them live to be a hundred. That's what Georgie says." She finished the last bite of cake. "That was delicious, Miss Peale. Thank you very much."

"You're quite welcome." Viola crumpled up the waxed-paper wrapping and tossed it in the dustbin. At that moment there was a knock at the door. *My word,* she thought, her heart racing. She felt instantly foolish. There was no rule against eating lunch with pupils.

She opened the door. A towheaded boy stood in the hallway—hatless, in a shabby winter coat. His hands were crammed in his pockets.

"Can I help you, young man?" she asked.

"Sandy! What are you doing here?" Joyce

rushed to the door. "This is my brother, Miss Peale. He's supposed to be in school."

Viola studied the child with interest. Curly blond hair, eyes unnaturally blue. His delicate mouth looked painted on, like a doll's. She glanced at Joyce: the wan complexion, the sharp plain face. It wasn't fair, the family beauty wasted on a boy.

Sandy took his hand from his pocket. "I cut myself," he said, showing it to Joyce. "I broke a glass."

Joyce examined the cut. "It's not so bad. You came all the way over here because of that?"

"I didn't go to school," he said, eyeing Viola. "I had to go find the priest."

"What for?" said Joyce.

"Come on," said the boy, his eyes filling. "We have to go home."

They drove across town in Viola's car, an ancient Ford her father had left her. Joyce had protested when Viola offered to drive them.

"It's a long way," she said. "I couldn't possibly accept."

"Nonsense," said Viola. "Of course I'll drive you."

They rode in silence, their breath fogging the windows. The boy rode in the rear seat. Joyce sat next to Viola, staring out the window. Her face was perfectly blank.

As it turned out, the Novaks lived just across town, in a company house in the Polish section. "You can leave us at the bottom of the hill," said Joyce, but Viola wouldn't hear of it. When she parked in front of the house, Joyce opened the door almost before she could engage the brake.

"Wait," said Viola. "I'll come in with you."

"Oh, no. That's all right." Joyce stepped out of the car, red-faced. She glanced quickly at the house. *Why, she's ashamed,* Viola thought.

"Thank you for driving us. It was very kind of you."

"You're quite welcome." Viola hesitated. "Joyce, I'm so very sorry about your father."

"Thank you, Miss Peale." Joyce took her brother's hand and climbed the steps to the porch.

*   *   *

All day long the food came. The neighbors sent chicken and dumplings, kielbasa and sauerkraut, almond cookies, loaves of bread. May Poblocki brought stuffed cabbage. Helen Wojick sent three kinds of pirogi: potato, cabbage and prune. Years before, when Rose's mother died, the donated food had surprised her. Downtown, in the Italian neighborhood, the bereaved were given nickels and dimes to buy masses for the soul of the deceased, votive candles to burn in church.

They ate the pirogi for supper; the other dishes Rose packed into the icebox. Stanley had bought it secondhand from a butcher in town. He'd paid in installments, a dollar from each paycheck; whether he'd yet paid it off, Rose wasn't sure. Every week he gave her money for groceries; the other bills he paid by check, from a ledger he kept in his bureau. Rose had never written a check, herself. It was yet another thing she'd have to learn.

In the evening the men came, carrying bottles: beer and whiskey, elderberry wine. Some had worked the day shift; they came shaved and showered, in Sunday vests and dark trousers. The Hoot Owl crew brought their dinner buckets; from Rose's house they would go straight to work. They sat in the parlor with the casket, drinking and speaking in low tones. Rose kept busy in the kitchen. Through the wall she heard their deep voices, hushed and somber, speaking a language she didn't understand.

"Here," she said, handing Dorothy a plate of sandwiches. "Take these to the parlor. They shouldn't drink on a empty stomach."

Dorothy took the plate, wiping her eyes with her sleeve. She'd come home from the factory at noon; since then she'd wept more or less constantly. Her eyelids looked raw and swollen, her nose shiny and red.

"What about you, Mama? You didn't touch your supper."

"Maybe later." Rose sipped a cup of tea, the only thing she'd managed to keep down all day. She detested tea but kept it on hand for such occasions, as her mother had. Coffee was for normal times, happy times. Tea was for miscarriages, mine accidents, measles, the grippe, a husband's philandering, the death of a family pet. In the Scarponi household, miseries of all kinds had been swallowed with tea.

At the table Sandy looked up from his history book. "Can we eat the cake?" It had arrived in the afternoon, a fancy hazelnut torte that Andy Yurkovich's Magyar wife had baked for her twins' birthday. When she saw the hearse parked out front, she'd sent it over to Rose.

"Later, *bello.* When you finish your schoolwork."

Sandy opened his mouth to protest, but said nothing. He had no homework to do, having missed the entire day of school. His father, he knew, would have found this excuse unacceptable. He'd made Sandy study every night after supper, spelling and history, whether he had homework or not.

He sat staring at his textbook, the letters blurring on the page. He closed his eyes and remembered the feeling of riding in the undertaker's car: the rumble of the engine, houses and storefronts flying past at a speed that seemed magical. The teacher's car had been slower, and he had told her so. He was proud of knowing this—just yesterday he wouldn't have known the difference—but Joyce had given him a dirty look. "You were terribly rude," she told him later. "After Miss Peale was nice enough to drive us." Alone, he'd taken his sled into the woods behind the reservoir, something his father would never have allowed. His mother hadn't even noticed. Except for the homework she seemed to have forgotten him entirely.

"Do I have to go to school tomorrow?" he asked.

"Not tomorrow," said Dorothy.

"The next day?"

"The next day is the funeral." She swiped at the table with a dishrag. "Why don't you go upstairs and study? We need the table. Mama wants to set out some food."

Sandy closed his book and climbed the stairs to his room. Outside the snow was falling. His sled waited in the backyard. He would have the hill to himself while the other boys were in school. In a day the world had become larger. Twice he had ridden in a car. Now, if he was quiet—if he was careful—he might never have to go to school again.

In the parlor the men drank. They lowered their voices when Joyce came into the room. Mr. Wojick switched in midsentence from English to Polish. She avoided looking at the casket. Instead she cleared the empty bottles from beside the chairs. In the morning she would carry them to the Italian market, where the storekeeper paid a dime a dozen. She used the coins to buy Defense Stamps, which cost a quarter apiece. It took her months to collect enough stamps to buy a War Bond, an exercise in patience.

She rarely had money of her own. At the end of each term, her friend Irene Jevic got a quarter for her report card. Joyce's parents gave her nothing, even though she earned all A's and Irene never got higher than a B. Once, timidly, Joyce had suggested to her father that her report card was worth a quarter. For a moment he'd considered this.

"No money," he said, kissing her forehead. "I give you credit."

Completely by accident, he had taught her to read. She was tiny then; every night after supper he'd sat between her and Dorothy, the newspaper spread out on the table. He had pointed at the headlines, waiting for Dorothy to sound out the words. His fingernails were black with mine dirt. He was gentle at first, but Dorothy read so slowly that he lost patience. Meanwhile

Joyce—so tiny he barely noticed her—learned to read almost without effort.

Only once had she made him angry. That fall she'd decided it was time the family got a telephone; knowing he'd object, she'd gone to the Bell Telephone office herself and ordered the service. When a letter came in the mail asking for a deposit, her father was furious.

"How dare you?" he roared. He had a powerful voice, like a bear's cry. "You humiliated me in front of those English people." She had always been his favorite child; he never scolded her as he did Georgie and Dorothy. Even when he was angry, she knew how to make him laugh.

But not that day. "Daddy," she said. She could barely speak; she willed herself not to cry. "We need a telephone. Times are changing."

"This is my house," he thundered. "The times change when I say."

For days he'd ignored her, refused even to look at her across the dinner table. "Daddy hates me," she told her mother one night after supper. "He'll never speak to me again." Sure of this, she'd left her report card on top of the radio, where he was sure to see it. In the evening he passed it around the table to Len Stusick and Ted Poblocki, who sat with him in the kitchen on Saturday nights, smoking cigars and listening to the radio. Joyce had laughed the next morning when her mother told her this. She appeared on the steps dressed for church and kissed her father's cheek.

"Good morning, Daddy," she said sweetly, as though nothing at all had happened.

Now she approached the casket. His face had changed, softened in a way that made him less handsome. *Oh Daddy,* she thought. *Where did you go?* It seemed impossible that he couldn't hear her. That he was simply gone.

His hands lay folded across his chest, holding a string of rosary beads. His skin looked smooth and waxy, but his fingernails were still black. Every morning after work, and every night before supper, he had scrubbed his hands with a stiff brush; but it never made any difference. His hands would never be clean.

* * *

The clock struck midnight, then twelve-thirty, then one. Rose lay curled on Stanley's side of the bed. She had done this for years when he worked Hoot Owl, as if keeping it warm for his return.

She lay awake, listening. Outside a dog barked. The baby breathed loudly in the cradle. Rose's stomach twisted inside her, and she remembered she had not eaten.

She crept downstairs in her bare feet, an old coat thrown over her nightgown. She needn't have bothered. The men in the parlor were passed out cold.

She turned on a kitchen light. Joyce or Dorothy had returned the casseroles to the icebox. Rose considered heating some dumplings or sauerkraut, a plate of gray, heavy Polish food. Then she noticed the glass dome sitting on the counter: Madge Yurkovich's hazelnut torte. She removed the cover. The cake was dusted with powdered sugar, the effect somehow formal, like a bride on her wedding day. She cut herself a slice and sat at the table.

She had never enjoyed sweets. It was Stanley who'd craved desserts, who was always after her to bake a pie or lemon custard. To please him she'd learned to make

prune kolacky and apricot horns; his Polish
aunts had taught her to pinch the dough
and fill the horns with jam. He'd loved her
pizzelle cookies, flavored with anisette; he
bragged that her cinnamon rolls were the
best in the neighborhood. Whether it was
true, Rose couldn't say. She rarely tasted
her creations. She baked only to please
him, to fill his house with sweetness.

She took a bite of the torte. The powdered sugar hit her palate first. Beneath it
was a subtler sweetness, not sugar but
cream. She counted six, seven thin layers of
cake, one soaked in a dark liquor. She ate
quickly, licking her fingers; then stared at
her empty plate. The cake was gone before
she'd really tasted it. Before she'd identified
its components, understood each sweet
miracle inside.

She went to the counter and cut a second
slice. The complexity amazed her. Between
the cake layers, more sweetness: crushed
hazelnuts, grainy dates, a smear of honeyed
cheese. She cut a third slice, and then a
fourth. Finally she brought the entire cake to
the table.

She'd been hungry before—as a girl of
eleven, on the sixteen-day boat ride from

Palermo to New York; in the first weeks of pregnancy, when her stomach kept emptying itself no matter what she ate. Yet she had never felt such appetite.

She would remember the feeling for the rest of her life, the intense sweetness of the hazelnut torte, the tears running down her cheeks, her wild hunger and shame and grief. Later she would wonder what had possessed her. It seemed to her that Stanley was responsible, her husband who lay dead in the next room entering her one last time, to enjoy this glorious cake through her. She felt his presence inside her, his need for sweetness, the appetite she had never felt before.

She ate until the cake was gone.

From that night onward Rose craved sweets. She baked cakes and pies and ate them daily, grateful for what seemed to be a whole new sense, as essential and pleasurable as hearing or sight. She considered her new hunger for sweetness a supernatural gift, a final pleasure left to her by her husband.

TWO

Years later, when her time in Washington had receded from memory, when her youth was like a faraway place she'd visited but could scarcely recall, Dorothy Novak would remember the Chinese woman.

She remembered a gray Saturday in early March: a wet breeze blowing in from the Potomac, cars crashing through puddles on Nineteenth Street, spraying water onto the sidewalk. Dorothy was heading downtown under her old black umbrella; in her pocket was a dollar she would not spend. It cost nothing to wander the department stores: Hecht's, Garfinkle's, Woodward and Lothrop, the brick buildings flanking F Street like majestic ships at port. Her Saturday entertainment was Domestics, Ladies' Shoes, Better Dresses. She was no fashion plate; she simply loved touching the fabrics, the wartime rayon that felt to her like silk. She lingered at the perfume counter, inhaling Shalimar or Chanel No. 5, trying to memorize the scent. Later she'd be unable to re-create it; the fragrance would hover at the edge of her memory, just beyond her reach.

She was standing under the canopy in front of Garfinkle's, tying a scarf under her chin, when a limousine stopped at the curb. A driver stepped out and opened the rear door; then a woman emerged, a tiny thing in a long mink coat. Her gloves were red, her hair twisted into a chignon, dark and glossy as the mink. She wore high-heeled slippers, a strand of pearls at her throat. Dorothy hugged her old coat around her, her hair flapping in the wind, fuzzy from the permanent wave her sister had given her back home.

The woman leaned in and spoke to the driver. She paused a moment, as if waiting to be photographed, then stepped delicately around a puddle and disappeared inside the store.

Dorothy blinked. For a moment the scene had seemed orchestrated, composed like a painting: pedestrians rushing past, heels clicking on the sidewalk; the cloud of smoke rising from the car's tailpipe; the Chinese woman standing at the center of it all, exquisite and improbable.

"What do you think of that?" she asked her friend Mag Spangler that night at the Federal Diner, where they'd each had a slice of pie.

"The Chinese embassy is close by. It must have been the ambassador's wife." Mag said this casually, as though she often rubbed shoulders with diplomats. In fact she spent each day typing government paychecks in a crowded office at Treasury, just as Dorothy did.

Dorothy finished her pie. They'd seen the early show at the Capitol Theater, John Wayne in *The Fighting Seabees.* Mag had vetoed *Lady in the Dark.* She considered musicals frivolous.

"A mink coat." Mag sniffed, horselike, a burst of air through her nostrils. "It hasn't snowed all winter, for Pete's sake."

Dorothy smiled. The impracticality of the coat hadn't occurred to her; it wasn't why she'd told the story. Since arriving in Washington she had witnessed remarkable things. Her first day in the city she noticed a Negro deliveryman standing on a street corner, singing deeply and carrying an armload of orchids. Seeing the Chinese woman step out of the car had given her the same feeling, as though at any moment something extraordinary might happen.

"We'd better go," she said. Customers stood three deep at the front of the diner. "People are waiting."

They each left a nickel on the table. Mag slid out of the booth, removing the napkin from the neck of her sweater.

"A mink coat," she said again. "For Pete's sake."

They were working girls, typing for the war. Dorothy had answered an ad in her hometown newspaper. A government recruiter had come to interview girls in the junior high cafeteria. The only requirement was a high school diploma.

Mag had come to Washington two years earlier and had acquired a jaded air. Dorothy hadn't known her back home—in school Mag was several grades ahead—but their

mothers were acquainted; Mag's father
owned the hat shop in town. In the way of
small towns, their mothers had put them in
touch.

When Dorothy arrived in Washington,
Mag had come to meet her train. Dorothy
recognized her immediately on the crowded
platform—a sturdy girl with a wide bosom
and a determined mouth, the type who'd always seemed older than everyone else, like
a chaperone at a dance. She wore stout
boots and a brown tweed coat, a hat
Dorothy recognized from the Spanglers'
shop in Bakerton. "Don't worry about a
thing," Mag had said, leading her through
the crowd: soldiers in uniform, WACs and
WAVEs in their navy blues. "Leave everything to me."

She took Dorothy to Straub's, a women's
boardinghouse on Massachusetts Avenue:
a shared room, breakfasts and dinners for
ten dollars a week. (Mag paid nine dollars
for a similar room across town; but such
bargains were a thing of the past, she as-
sured Dorothy.) At one time Straub's had
been a showplace. Now the upper floors
were divided into tiny rooms, just big
enough for two twin beds. Each floor had a

bathroom; every morning a line formed at the door, girls waiting with towels and dishes of soap. Meals were served downstairs—most nights, potatoes with stew. Breakfast was half a grapefruit and a bowl of oatmeal. On Sundays they each got a strip of bacon.

Mag walked Dorothy to work her first morning at Treasury. She pointed out the watercooler and powder room, and indicated with a look which girls Dorothy should avoid: the snooty ones who thought they were God's gift, the two-faced ones who'd smile to your face and cut you behind your back. They met each day for lunch, nickel sandwiches and orange sodas at Peoples' Drug Store. Saturday nights they saw a movie. In this way, months passed. At first Dorothy was grateful for Mag's company. Only later did she realize that she hadn't made any other friends. The girls at the boardinghouse remained strangers to her. She knew them by their sounds and smells: the middle-aged, slightly deaf schoolteacher who played her radio at high volume; the blond stenographer who monopolized the lavatory, leaving a trail of rose

perfume and a few golden pubic hairs clinging to the rim of the bathtub.

Dorothy had a roommate, Jean Johns, a
timid, dark-haired girl from Kentucky who
ran a switchboard at the Pentagon. Jean
slept in flowered nightgowns and was always cold. Every night after supper she'd
climb into bed, pull the blankets around her
and listen to the radio. They liked the same
programs: *Theater of Romance* at eight-
thirty, *Famous Jury Trials* at nine. At ten
o'clock they turned out the lights; a few
minutes later Jean would begin to snore.
Eyes closed, Dorothy imagined herself back
in her own room, her sister Joyce asleep
next to her. In this way she learned to ignore
the traffic noise, the hissing radiator. She
was not alone.

From their beds they monitored the war.
Europe was quiet that March. Hitler hadn't
been seen in months, and people specu-
lated that he was dead or dying. Reports
came instead from the South Pacific, a part
of the world no one had heard of until soldiers—Dorothy's brother Georgie among
them—were sent there. Los Negros, Ta-
lasea, Bougainville: pronounced, always, in
the American way, in a firm male voice that

made them seem familiar and knowable.
Dorothy's geography was hazy; she imagined each place the same way: a tiny ver-
dant island, the immense surrounding sea.
She had seen the ocean only in photographs. In her mind it was brilliant and calm,
a vast expanse of blue.

She hadn't seen Georgie in a year. He had
missed the funeral, hadn't even known their
father was dead until several days afterward. He wrote her often, if not consistently.
Once she'd received six letters in a single
week. At other times he didn't write for
months. Once Jean asked what he'd written, a question Dorothy couldn't answer.
Whole sentences had been blacked out by
the censors; all that remained were detailed
descriptions of the weather. She didn't
mind the lack of content. What mattered
was the familiar handwriting, the letters
drawn by Georgie's own hand. The sheer
volume of his communication delighted her.
For years—her entire adolescence—he'd
seemed embarrassed by her presence. At
school he'd ignored her. In the corridor,
walking with Gene Stusick or another of his
silent, awkward friends, he would not meet
her eyes.

He'd been a frail child, prone to fevers. At seven he caught diphtheria and was pronounced contagious; Dorothy was forbidden to enter his room. He slept poorly; she could hear him on the other side of the wall, his feverish tossing, his guttural cough. Carefully, so as not to wake Joyce, she climbed out of bed and crept into his room. She sat at the foot of his bed and told him a story—about what, she could no longer recall. She invented the stories as she went along, until his eyelids began to fall.

"Good night," she whispered as she rose from the bed.

"Come back tomorrow," he answered as she closed the door behind her.

Now she listened to the reports, her heart racing, her hands moist. The navy bombarding the Palau Islands; ships moving into Hollandia and Aitape. Whether his was among them was impossible to tell.

She typed all day in an office filled with women. The supervisor was a gray-haired man named Howard Leland, whom the typists rarely saw. Nearly every week a new girl came, from Pennsylvania or North Carolina or Ohio; a girl with bangs or pin curls, her sweater dyed to match her skirt. One by one they disappeared into the flock of Mr. Leland's girls, like ingredients folded into a cake batter.

Mag disliked the new girls uniformly, without regard to their abilities or personalities, their friendliness or lack of it. "We don't have room for them," she complained, as if she'd been charged personally with finding them desks and typewriters. "That last one is still sitting at a card table, for Pete's sake."

"I suppose we need the help," said Dorothy.

"Some help. That what's-her-name from Youngstown types twenty words a minute."

The quality of the new hires was a sore subject with Mag, who'd taken the commercial course in high school and scored well enough on the Civil Service exam to land what was then a coveted job at Treasury. Since then the government had lowered its standards. The exam was no longer required. Dorothy, who hadn't taken the commercial course, was paid the same as Mag, twenty-eight dollars a week. Feeling

wealthy, she'd sent home half her first paycheck. Later she realized she'd sent too
much, that she'd left herself barely enough
to live on; but it was too late. She could not
send less. Since her father's death, the family got a monthly check from Social Security.
In warm months it would be enough. But
this was March; the jarred vegetables from
last summer's garden had all been eaten.
Her mother still owed Baker for the winter
coal.

At night, in dreams, Dorothy returned to
the dress factory where she had worked:
the gloomy, airless upstairs room, the windows covered with dark paint to keep the
fabrics from fading; heat rising up through
the floorboards, from the dozen large press
irons on the level below. The ancient machines had malfunctioned as often as they
worked; five, ten times a day her machine
had snapped the cheap cotton thread,
chewing the fabric into an unusable mess.
When the foreman fired her she felt relief,
then terror. The job at Treasury had seemed
a godsend; but now her mother counted on
her paycheck. She would never be able to
go home.

*   *   *

One night she came back from work to find Jean Johns packing a suitcase.

"Where are you going?" she asked.

"Home." Jean tucked a flowered night-gown into the space between her sweaters.

"How'd you get the vacation time?" Dorothy had accumulated none yet, herself. She hadn't even gone home for Easter.

Jean met her gaze. Her eyes were red. "I quit."

There was, she explained, a boy back home. They had gone together all through high school. That morning he had asked her to marry him.

"Back home?" said Dorothy. "He isn't overseas?"

His number hadn't been called yet, Jean explained. It could happen any day.

"When's the wedding?" Dorothy felt the envy in her stomach, squeezing her insides like sickness. Not because Jean was getting married. Because Jean was going home.

"As soon as possible," said Jean. "A week or two, at the most."

"So fast!" said Dorothy, though of course she understood. Jean's fiancé could be called up at any moment. Naturally they would be in a hurry, not knowing how much time they had left.

"Can you imagine?" she asked Mag the next day at lunch. "A week from now she'll be married." It seemed an incredible feat. Washington in those days was a city of women; you could go weeks without seeing a man older than eighteen or younger than fifty. Though according to Jean, the Pentagon was different. At the Pentagon you were surrounded by men.

"He proposed in a letter," said Dorothy. "She had a fellow all this time and never said a word about it."

"That's an awfully quick engagement." Mag bit into her sandwich—the same kind she ordered every day, chicken salad on toast. "Sounds like she got herself in trouble."

"That's a terrible thing to say." Dorothy thought of Jean's eyes, swollen as if she'd been crying. Then she remembered a morning when Jean had left the breakfast table suddenly, her hand over her mouth.

"Believe what you want," said Mag.

When Dorothy returned to her room that night, Jean Johns was gone.

*   *   *

Empty of Jean's possessions, the room
seemed hollow and drafty. One afternoon
Dorothy covered the walls with photos she'd
clipped from Screen Stars: Veronica Lake,
Tyrone Power; a close-up of Hedy Lamarr,
whom people said she resembled. She
caught herself glancing at Hedy each morning before she left for work, a more confident, more glamorous version of herself.

Sundays were the longest days. In the
morning she went to mass at St. Matthew's
Cathedral. Then, for hours afterward, she
walked. Up Massachusetts Avenue past the
grand embassies; the whole length of Connecticut Avenue, from Rock Creek Park to
the White House. She walked for distrac-
tion, for warmth. Some days she wandered
the elegant neighborhoods around Dupont
Circle. She knew the owners' names from
the society pages: Cissy Patterson, the
newspaper heiress; Mrs. Sumner Welles,
the diplomat's wife. One Sunday evening
the Welleses had thrown a party; Dorothy
had joined the small crowd on the opposite
corner, gathered to watch the guests arrive: men in white jackets, bare-shouldered

women in dark silk. Oddly, it was the men's hair that most impressed her: long enough in back to touch their collars, slicked with something to make it shine. In a time when most fellows wore army cuts, the curling forelocks seemed more extravagant than jewels.

In the spring a new girl came. Looking back, Dorothy would remember it as the beginning of everything, a door swinging open, a dark room filling with light.

She arrived on a Sunday night. Dorothy returned from her walk to find the bedroom door ajar. A girl sat on Jean's old bed, polishing her nails. A radio played in the background; the girl hummed along with it, her voice low and husky. A cigarette burned in an ashtray near the window.

"Hi there," said Dorothy. "I'm Dorothy Novak."

The girl started. "Good Lord, you scared me. Patsy Sturgis." She offered her hand, then withdrew it. "Wet," she explained, blowing on her nails. "Sorry about the mess." On the bed lay a suitcase, half unpacked; an open steamer trunk stood in the corner, trailing scarves and sweaters.

"I brought too many things." She was small and blond, with a perfect rosebud mouth. "Lord knows where I'll put it all."

"Here. It's for us to share." Dorothy opened the flimsy metal armoire. The cupboard was already crammed full of dresses. Her own skirts and blouses had been shoved to one side.

Patsy laughed, a trilling sound. "Sorry, Dottie. Looks like I hogged all the closet space."

Dorothy smiled. Nobody had ever shortened her name before. She liked the sound of it.

"That's okay. You have more clothes than I do." She fingered the sleeve of a dress, embroidered with tiny flowers. The fabric was sheer and light, soft as a person's skin. "This is beautiful."

"Oh, that. I've had it for ages. I can't squeeze into it anymore, but I hate to part with it. Lord knows when I'll get another silk dress." Patsy butted her cigarette. "You can borrow it, if you like."

"Really?"

"Try it on."

"Now?" She had never undressed before a stranger. She and Jean Johns had waited until the other left the room, or gone down the hall to change in the washroom.

"Go on," said Patsy.

Dorothy turned away and unbuttoned her blouse. Her brassiere was yellowed from too many bleachings, the elastic of her girdle puckered and worn. She stepped quickly out of her skirt, then pulled the dress over her head.

"Well, look at you," said Patsy.

Dorothy approached the mirror. The dress fit perfectly, close at the waist and hip. The rose color flattered her complexion. She looked like someone else entirely. *Like Dottie,* she thought.

Patsy helped her with the zipper. "God, I'd love to be so slim. In my family we're all top-heavy. Turn around." She frowned. "Fits like a glove, but it hangs a little funny."

"It's my posture. My mother's always after me to stand up straight."

"Tall girls! You make me sick. When you're five-one you can't afford to slouch." Patsy glanced at the photo on the bureau. "Is that your fellow?"

"My brother Georgie. He's in the South Pacific."

Patsy leaned close to examine it. "He's nice looking. Does he have a girl?"

"Back home he went with Evelyn Lipnic. Now, I don't know."

"I'll bet he does." Patsy straightened. "This room isn't much. I thought it would be bigger." She squinted at the photos on the wall. "Are those yours?"

Dorothy flushed. "The other girl put them up," she lied. "The one who lived here before. You can take them down, if you want."

"Whew." Patsy wiped an imaginary bead of sweat from her brow. "That's a relief. I'd get the willies looking at Errol Flynn all day. He's queer, you know." She giggled, seeing Dorothy's look. "You didn't know? He likes boys."

Dorothy thought of a Sunday afternoon, months ago, when she'd seen two blond-haired fellows walking hand in hand in Lafayette Park. At the time it had given her a strange feeling. Now she put it aside to think about later, how such a thing was even possible.

"My sister lives in California," said Patsy. "Everyone out there knows about it."

"California!" Dorothy repeated, impressed. "Is she in the pictures?"

"Lord, no. She lives near an air-force base in San Diego. Her husband's a pilot. She's just a regular girl. Dottie, you're a stitch." She blew at her fingernails. "I guess I'm dry." She peeled a photograph from the wall. "You don't want to keep these, do you?"

She crumpled the photo and tossed it into the wastebasket. Later, following her downstairs to supper, Dorothy recognized the dark eyes of Hedy Lamarr staring up at her from the trash.

After supper they sat on Dorothy's bed, eating caramels Patsy had produced from her suitcase. Dorothy ate one candy to Patsy's three, savoring the rare sweetness of rationed sugar. Laughing, Patsy unpacked a bottle of bourbon. "From my daddy," she said. "So we'll be stocked when he comes to visit."

She was a Southern girl, raised in Charleston; the baby in a family of girls. Her daddy was a lawyer for the local school dis-

trict. He had taught her to ride and shoot, to
tack in a windstorm, to drive a car. That
morning he'd slipped her an emergency
twenty dollars at the train station in
Charleston. " 'Don't fritter it away on perfume and bonbons,' " Patsy said, imitating
his voice. " 'Use it for bail money, or not at
all.' " She loved Charleston but lately found
it depressing: the girls working in the ship-
yards, like Communist women. "It's a different place now," she said, lighting a cigarette. "It won't be the same until the boys
come back. Then look out, Lucy! I'm going
home."

"Do you have a fellow overseas?"
Dorothy asked.

"Actually," said Patsy, "I have two." It
wasn't two-timing, she explained; she
hadn't seen either of them in a year, and
that was barely one-timing in her book. The
boys, Fred and Ted, were like night and day.
Fred had been her beau in high school, a
tall, serious boy who planned to become a
doctor. Ted had kept her occupied after
Fred left. He had no plans for the future that
Patsy knew of. He was just after a good
time.

"He's a lot of fun," she admitted. "I went

with Fred for two years, so we were like an old married couple. No more surprises. You know how that is."

Dorothy had no idea how that was, but she was pleased that Patsy thought she did.

"What happens when they come back?" she asked.

"I'll jump off that bridge when I come to it," said Patsy.

The next day they met Mag Spangler for lunch.

"Lord, it's crowded," said Patsy. She and Dorothy had arrived late. Every table in the drugstore was taken.

"Well, no wonder. It's nearly ten past." Mag shot Dorothy a look. *Where've you been, for Pete's sake?*

They sat at the counter: Dorothy in the middle, Mag and Patsy on either side. "Patsy works at the CAS," Dorothy told Mag.

"Central Administrative Services," said Patsy. "We're the ones who scare up desks and file cabinets for all your new girls."

Dorothy glanced nervously at Mag, who knew perfectly well what the CAS was. She'd been complaining about it for months.

Patsy scrabbled in her pocketbook for a cigarette. "The funny part is, I don't have a desk yet, myself. Or a typewriter."

"Then what do you do all day?" Mag asked.

"Yesterday I read the paper."

"You're joking," said Mag.

"No, really. It's a piece of cake. I can't complain."

Mag snorted. "I think *I'd* complain. I'd feel terrible, getting paid for nothing when the boys could use that money overseas."

Patsy smiled sweetly. "Do you have a fellow in the service, Mag?"

"No," said Mag. "Do you?"

"Patsy has two. One in England and one in Italy." *Why am I telling her this?* Dorothy marveled; but she couldn't help herself. Mag's frown delighted her. In some way it made her proud.

That week Mag's schedule was changed, her lunch break pushed back by an hour so that another girl could use her typewriter. After that Dorothy and Patsy ate lunch without her, at a different drugstore near the Treasury.

Every sunday night Dorothy wrote a letter to her mother.

"Why don't you just call her on the phone?" Patsy asked. There was a pay phone downstairs in the lobby. Dorothy often saw her standing next to it with a handful of coins.

"I like writing," said Dorothy. "Can you hand me another sheet of paper?" She didn't explain that to receive a phone call, her mother would have to walk a mile to town and wait at the booth in Meeghan's Drugstore.

"I ought to do the same," said Patsy. "I haven't written Fred in ages." She took a sheet of paper from a drawer and handed it up to Dorothy. A week before, in a burst of inspiration, Patsy had proposed stacking their beds like soldiers' bunks. The two bed frames were identical, she pointed out; the square end posts would fit together perfectly. They spent a rainy afternoon struggling with the beds. Patsy bought a hammer at the dime store and tapped in a few nails for good measure. Dorothy took the top bunk, Patsy the bottom. The idea was a good one; the room seemed doubled in size.

They installed themselves on their beds. Dorothy glanced at the letter her mother had sent. Cold weather in Bakerton, a rainy spring. Georgie was still waiting to hear about his furlough. *With everything happening,* he'd written Dorothy, *don't hold your breath.*

She filled her pen and began to write. Beneath her Patsy sighed loudly. Dorothy heard her crumple up her letter and toss it into the trash.

"I'm out of smokes," she said, rising. "I'll be right back."

"It's Sunday. The store is closed."

"I'll bum one from the gray lady."

"Mrs. Straub smokes?"

"Drinks, too. I can smell it on her breath."

Dorothy blinked. She had known the landlady for months and had never suspected. More and more, the people around her seemed mysterious, impenetrable, their lives governed by secret desires visible to everyone but her. She wondered what else she had failed to notice.

At the end of her letter she added a post-script: *I haven't seen Mag in ages, not since Mr. Leland moved her lunch hour. But we have not had a falling-out. I can't imagine why Mrs. Spangler would think such a thing.*

She climbed down from her bed and reached into the bedside table, where Patsy kept a supply of stamps. At the bottom of the drawer she found the box of stationery and a leather-covered Book of Common Prayer, its gold-edged pages perfectly crisp, as though it had never been opened. She took a stamp from the box. The corner of a photograph peeked out from beneath the prayer book.

She hesitated a moment, then withdrew the photo. Patsy and a tall, thin boy stood before a gleaming automobile. The boy's face was long and handsome. He wore rimless eyeglasses. To Dorothy he looked like a young Franklin Roosevelt. *Fred and Pat* was written on the back. *May 1942.*

She replaced the photo and closed the drawer. She'd never had a beau; she'd never even gone on a date. That any girl did these things filled her with wonder. She remembered clearly the moment when her classmates had begun to pair off, early in the tenth grade. It had seemed then that she'd missed a crucial lesson, one that would not be repeated. Girls like Mag Spangler had missed the lesson, too; for years they'd been Dorothy's only friends, keeping her company as they all fell further behind. Patsy, clearly, hadn't missed anything. Dorothy watched her closely, feeling privileged to share her dresses, her secrets. For the first time in her life, it seemed she might actually catch up.

Noon, a rainy monday. The luncheonette was noisy and crowded, the windows steamed with the diners' breath. Dorothy and Patsy took seats at the counter. Next to Patsy was a lone man in uniform, looking into a bowl of soup. He sat with his right hand flat on the counter, his sleeve rolled to the elbow. His left hand was tucked into his trouser pocket.

"Excuse me," he said (to which of them, Dorothy would later wonder). "Can one of you girls give me a hand with my soup?"

The soldier, Chick Rowsey, treated them to a boyish smile. His eyes were blue, his mouth full-lipped and adult.

"What's wrong with your hand?" said Dorothy.

"This one's fine," he said, showing his right. "But I'm a lefty, so that doesn't do me much good."

Laughing a little, Patsy dipped the spoon into the soup; she leaned close and lifted it to his lips. The soldier opened his mouth to accept it. A rivulet of broth dribbled down his chin.

"You girls work for the government?"

"The CAS." Patsy dabbed at his chin with a napkin. "I'm a file clerk."

"You're lucky." He reached for a packet of saltines and tore it open with his teeth. "I'm looking, myself. Before the war I was a carpenter. Guess I need a new line of work."

Dorothy watched him crumple the crackers in his suntanned hand. If another man had done it, she reflected, you'd call his manners atrocious; but a wounded soldier was different.

Rowsey looked up from his soup and saw her watching him. She looked away, embarrassed.

"What about you?" he asked. "You're a file clerk, too?"

"Typist," said Dorothy. "At the Treasury."

"Good for you." He took a cigarette from the pack on the table. "That's a good skill for a girl to have."

"Awfully noisy, though. You should hear the racket in Dorothy's office. I'd lose my mind." Patsy tilted the bowl and spooned up the soup. "I'm happy filing, thank you very much." If she and Dorothy had been alone, she'd have launched into an angry monologue about why the filing clerks made five dollars less per week than the typists did; but now she only smiled.

"Down the hatch," she said, lifting the spoon to his lips. "Oops!" Giggling a little, she dabbed his chin with a napkin.

"So," Rowsey said after he'd finished. "What are you doing this weekend?"

Dorothy felt her face flush. He seemed to be talking to her. She glanced quickly at Patsy, who smiled and shrugged.

"Me?" she said finally.

He waved a hand carelessly, as though it made no difference.

"Both of you," he said. "I want to take you out on the town."

*   *   *

They lay stretched out on the imported sand, the soldier in bathing trunks, the two girls in bright nylon suits, one green, the other red. Substantial suits, reinforced with darts and seams and sewn-in undergarments; yet Dorothy felt unprotected, uncomfortably exposed. The borrowed suit fit closely at her hips. It would have fit anyone. She'd never worn one before and was surprised by the fabric—curiously elastic, like a balloon.

The park, Glen Echo, sat on forty acres south of Washington. From May to September, the city trolley stopped there six times a day. The park had a swimming pool, two carousels and a Ferris wheel. There was a casino for gambling, a bandstand and a dance floor.

Dorothy leaned back on one elbow and shielded her eyes. Light danced on the surface of the Crystal Pond—the largest swimming pool on the East Coast, built to hold three thousand swimmers. Purple-lipped children crowded the shallows at the perimeter. Mothers in sunglasses clustered along the edge. The water at the center was a deeper blue; a few swimmers crossed it with smooth strokes. Lawn chairs dotted the half-acre beach, sand brought in by the truckload from the eastern shore of Maryland. There were girls in Bermuda shorts, smoking cigarettes, flipping through magazines; girls under umbrellas, in straw hats, in bathing caps. Under a tree, a few grandfathers drank cans of beer from a cooler. Otherwise there were no men at all.

Beside her Patsy stretched in the heat. She examined her plump shoulder. "I'm red as a beet." She reached for the bottle of oil.

"Let me," said Rowsey.

"You'd like that, wouldn't you?" She handed the bottle to Dorothy.

"Just trying to help." His eyes went to Dorothy. "Look at this one. She's not burned at all. Gypsy blood, am I right?"

"My mother's Italian."

"No kidding." He grinned. "I spent four months in Sicily. Those girls were something. Wouldn't give us the time of day, most of them, but they were something to look at."

Dorothy spread the oil over Patsy's shoulders. The skin was moist and freckled, hot to the touch.

"Hey, you know who you look like?" said Rowsey. "It just hit me. Hedy Lamarr."

Dorothy's cheeks warmed. "No, I don't."

"Sure you do. It's been bugging me. The first time I saw you, at the lunch counter, I thought, 'This girl looks like someone.' The eyes, the mouth. Doesn't she?" he demanded.

"Hedy Lamarr isn't Italian." Patsy raised her head, shrugging Dorothy's hands away. There was an edge to her voice. "She's Austrian."

"What's the difference?"

Patsy glared at him. "What's the *difference*?"

Rowsey frowned, aware he'd made an error. Girls were forever getting mad at him. He accepted this fact cheerfully, as he accepted bad weather.

"I'm going for a swim," he said, pulling off his shirt. "Anyone want to join me?"

"Too crowded," said Patsy.

"No thanks," said Dorothy. She stared up at him, her eyes drawn toward the thick scar at his shoulder.

"Suit yourselves." He loped easily toward the pool.

The girls sat back on their blanket. Patsy

reached for the oil and spread it thickly over her shins. Dorothy squinted into the sky— a faded blue, streaked with high clouds. A bell clanged in the distance, the streetcar stopping to let off passengers. A breeze blew the sweet, burned aroma of roasted peanuts.

She closed her eyes. The trip to the park had been Rowsey's idea. The girls had met him that morning at Union Station and they had ridden the streetcar together. He had chosen a seat in the middle of the car. The girls had sat on either side.

Dorothy picked him out of the crowd, watching as he lowered himself to the edge of the pool.

"I'm surprised he can swim," she said. "With his bad arm." He'd taken a bullet in the shoulder at Salerno, which had severed a bundle of nerves. His hand hadn't worked properly since.

"I hope he drowns," Patsy snapped, then laughed. "Oh, don't look so shocked. I didn't mean it."

"I thought you liked him."

"I like him fine. But sometimes I'd like to jerk a knot in him."

"What do you mean?"

"Oh, for God's sake." Patsy studied her pink-tipped toes. "Doesn't it bother you, the way he plays cock of the walk? It's unnatural for a man to have so many women falling all over him. It turns everything backward."

She stretched out on her back. Her skin glistened with oil; her plump legs looked smooth and boneless, like a roast. At the edge of the pool, Rowsey stood talking to a woman in a striped bathing suit. A fussy toddler squirmed in her arms. Smiling, Rowsey took the baby from her. The child quieted, hanging easily over his good shoulder.

"Look at that," said Dorothy.

Patsy opened one eye, then snorted. "I'm taking a nap. Wake me if something interesting happens."

She rolled over onto her stomach and covered her head with a towel.

They were both sleeping when Rowsey returned to the blanket. He leaned over them and shook his wet head, like a dog drying itself. The girls shrieked, outraged.

He stretched out on the blanket between

them, his skin radiating cold. Dorothy avoided looking at him. She sensed rather than saw his long blond legs, his belly matted with darker hair.

Patsy sat up, rubbing her eyes. "Who were you talking to?"

"Some girl. Her husband's over in England."

"Does he know she's back here flirting with half-naked men in swimming pools?"

"Who's flirting?" He studied her. "You're jealous."

"Oh, that'll be the day." Patsy gathered her things and rose. "Don't flatter yourself."

"Where are you going?" said Dorothy.

"I need some shade. Come find me when you're ready to go." She turned and headed toward the pavilion. The suit rode up on her pink thigh, revealing a slice of white skin.

"What's eating her?" Rowsey asked.

"The heat, I guess."

"It's awfully hot," he agreed. "You ought to dive in and cool off."

Dorothy hesitated a moment. "I can't swim."

"You're kidding." He sat up, studying her. "How come?"

"I never learned. Back home there was no

place to go. Not for girls, anyway. There was a swimming hole in the woods where the boys went." Every sunny day her brother had hiked there with his friends—Gene Stusick, two or three of the Poblocki boys. Once, the summer she turned fourteen, she had followed behind, stepping carefully along the rugged trail. Screened by trees, she had stood a long time watching. A thick branch of cherry hung low over the water. The naked boys dropped from it like monkeys. Tenor shouts, Tarzan cries, a flash of skin.

"Come on," said Rowsey. "I'll teach you."

"Really?"

"Sure." He got to his feet. "It's time you learned."

She followed him across the expanse of sand, stepping between blankets and lawn chairs. A wind had started. The pool was emptying out. Mothers crouched on the cement walkway, wrapping children in beach towels.

The lifeguard gave Rowsey a wave. "There's a storm coming. If you see any lightning, get out quick."

Dorothy approached the edge and

dipped her toe in the water. A chill traveled up her leg.

"You can't do it like that. You've got to go all at once. Watch." He backed up a few paces and took a running leap into the water, landing with a loud splash. Dorothy stepped back, startled.

His slick head reappeared at the surface. "See?" He swam toward her. "Your turn."

"Don't splash," she cried. And quickly, before she could change her mind, she scrambled down the ladder. The water was very cold, a shock to her heart.

"That's not so bad, is it?"

"It feels good," she admitted.

"Come on." He led her by the hand toward the center of the pool, until the water reached her chest. Before she realized what was happening, he reached behind her and swung her into his arms.

"Don't be scared," he said. "Just lie back. All you have to do is float."

She exhaled slowly, aware of his arms beneath her. She felt perfectly weightless.

"What about your shoulder?" she asked.

"Don't worry. I've got you."

She stared up at him: the rough stubble at his throat, the thick scar on his shoulder.

Alien textures, hinting at the vast difference between him and her.

"Hang on," he said. He spun her gently in a circle, his hands gripping her waist, the outside of one thigh. She laughed, delighted.

"Good," he said. "Now kick."

She did. A thrill rose in her stomach.

"I could have you swimming in no time," he said. "You're a natural."

Water filled her ears; her heartbeat rose in volume. Dreamily she closed her eyes. The sensation was like nothing she could name; so why did it feel familiar? Heat above her, cold below; herself suspended perfectly between them. His body seemed to be everywhere around her. No man had ever touched her before. Yet that, too, felt familiar.

"Did you hear that?" said Rowsey.

"What?"

"Thunder."

The lifeguard's whistle sounded.

"We should get out," said Rowsey. "Hang on. I'll float you in."

A flash of lightning tore across the sky. He drew her in close to his chest.

"Here we are, madam," he said, releasing her into the shallow water.

Dorothy got to her feet. The pool had emptied out. Patsy was standing at the edge. She wore a terry-cloth romper over her swimsuit. "Where have you been?" she asked sharply.

"Chick was giving me a swimming lesson."

"The trains are packed," said Patsy, ignoring her. "We'll be stuck waiting in the rain."

He climbed up the ladder, holding his left arm to his side. "Take it easy," he said, touching Patsy's shoulder.

"Keep away from me," said Patsy. "You're stinking wet."

They walked to the train station in the rain. Patsy lagged behind; her shoes were giving her blisters. Once, twice, Rowsey stopped so she could catch up.

"For God's sake, I'm right behind you."

"Suit yourself." He fell into step next to Dorothy. "How'd you like your swimming lesson?"

"It was wonderful," she said, suddenly shy. "Thank you."

They approached the platform. The crowd was oddly silent.

"What's going on?" said Rowsey.

"Hush," said an old woman. "We're trying to hear."

Dorothy peered through the crowd. At the center of the platform stood a teenage boy—a redheaded, pockmarked boy with a transistor radio.

"What is it?" said Dorothy. "Did something happen?"

Chick made his way through the crowd. People stepped aside, for reasons that were not clear. His height perhaps, his deep voice, the simple fact of his maleness. He stood a moment, listening intently. Then he called out.

"They did it! They landed in France."

Afterward she would wonder how it had happened. Had she approached him, or had he come to her? Later this would seem tremendously important; but in that moment there was only his damp shirt, the chlorine smell of his skin, the warm pressure of his mouth on hers. She had seen hundreds of kisses in the movies, but they had not captured the complete feeling: heat, breathing, the movement of another heart. He lifted her high into the air and she was again floating.

Around them the world roared.

*   *   *

It was all a mistake.

The Allies had not landed in France. In London, an English girl named Joan Ellis, newly hired as a Teletype operator by the Associated Press, had tapped out the message as a practice exercise: AMERICANS LAND IN FRANCE. Within minutes it was relayed to New York. At the Polo Grounds, where the Giants were up in the third inning, the crowd observed a moment of silence. At the Pentagon, Jean Johns's old switchboard was besieged with calls.

When the real invasion happened three days later, the celebration wasn't nearly so grand. Dorothy did not join in the excited chatter at the breakfast table, Mrs. Straub and the deaf schoolteacher and the blond stenographer huddled around the *Washington Post.* She sat eating the last of her grapefruit, thinking of Chick Rowsey and the day she had nearly learned to swim.

That day, on the streetcar platform at Glen Echo, the pockmarked boy with the radio had shouted in vain; all around him strangers wept and laughed and embraced.

Finally he stood on a bench to make himself heard.

"It's a mistake," he cried. "They made a mistake." His eyes tearing, he held the radio close to his ear.

"Quiet!" a young woman cried.

"I can't hear a thing," said another, her face streaked with tears.

The voices hushed. Again the crowd gathered around the radio.

"I don't understand," said Dorothy. "How do you make a mistake like that?"

When the streetcar came they piled into it, along with the mothers and babies, the girls in straw hats, the wet-haired children and aging grandparents. A lucky few found seats; the rest stood pressed against one another, uncomfortable in their sodden clothes. The rain had stopped, and with it the breeze. Heat rose off their damp bodies, the vinyl seats stuck to damp thighs. No one spoke. Strangers again, they avoided one another's eyes.

"I can't believe it," Dorothy said. She and Patsy sat shoulder to shoulder in the crowded car. Rowsey stood at the other end, smoking.

"Will you stop saying that?" Patsy

snapped. "And ask your boyfriend if he can spare a cigarette."

"He's not my boyfriend," said Dorothy, delighting in the words. Even the denial gave her a thrill.

"I know his type," said Patsy. "He had a good time with you today, but I'll be surprised if you ever hear from him again."

Later, at home, she apologized. The heat made her cranky, she said. She was getting the curse.

"I understand," said Dorothy, her cheeks flushing. Her own periods were unpredictable: sometimes twice in the same month, sometimes three months apart. As a girl, she'd feared bleeding in school, in church, blood running down her leg as she crossed the street. On certain days of the month she could think of nothing else as she sat in class, a fear that paralyzed her when Miss Peale called her to the chalkboard.

The next morning they both had cramps. Patsy complained; Dorothy felt secret relief. She hadn't bled since coming to Washington. She was shocked and delighted that her body still worked.

For a week nothing happened. In the evenings Dorothy listened to the radio and waited. Another week passed, and she knew that Patsy had been right. She would never see Chick Rowsey again.

Most of these evenings she spent alone. Patsy had a new friend at the CAS, a pretty redhead with a sharp laugh. One Saturday afternoon Dorothy saw them come out of the fitting room at Hecht's loaded down with dresses. She hid in Housewares until they left the store.

In July a letter came. Her brother Georgie was coming home on furlough. He would spend two weeks in Bakerton, then a final night with Dorothy in Washington before shipping out from Norfolk. Mrs. Straub offered the attic bedroom, a dark little corner outfitted with a narrow cot. "He can have it all to himself," she said—grandly, as though it were a luxury suite at the Watergate Hotel.

He planned to arrive on a Friday evening. Dorothy would meet his train; afterward they would eat dinner at a restaurant near the station. Already she'd chosen a dress from Patsy's closet, a dark blue silk she'd admired for weeks. That day she splurged and took the bus home from work. For once there was no line at the bathroom door, and she took her time setting her hair—she'd borrowed Patsy's foam rollers to smooth out her fuzzy perm. She wrapped herself in a housecoat and headed back to her room. She was surprised to find Patsy there, standing before the armoire in her slip.

"I thought I'd come to the station with you." Patsy rifled through the closet. "You don't mind, do you?"

Dorothy hesitated. For weeks she'd imagined showing Georgie around Washington—a city she'd walked end to end, the first place that had ever belonged to her.

"Of course not," she said. "You're welcome to come along."

They dressed in silence. When Patsy picked the navy blue silk off its hanger,

Dorothy nearly spoke: *I was hoping I could wear that one, if it's all right with you.* Instead she slipped into a dress of her own, a plain green one she'd brought from home. She waited as Patsy arranged her hair and dabbed perfume at her wrists.

Outside it had begun to rain. They stood on the front step, tying scarves over their hair. A gray Plymouth slowed at the curb, flashing its lights. The driver rolled down the window. It was Chick Rowsey.

"Hey, dreamgirls!" He wore a white shirt and a tie.

Dorothy felt flushed, agitated. She remembered the long years of high school, a hundred Friday nights reading magazines, listening to the radio, waiting for something to happen, for her life to begin. *Why now?* she wanted to say. *What took you so long?*

"Hey, yourself," said Patsy. "What are you doing here?"

"Looking for you girls." He nodded toward Dorothy. "How's the swimmer?"

"Where did you disappear to?" said Patsy.

"Baltimore. I had to see a doctor up there."

"We must have missed your phone calls."

"I'm here now, aren't I?" He stepped out of the car. "I was hoping you'd be home. I just got my check from Uncle Sam, and I wanted to take you girls out for a steak dinner." He smiled broadly. "Where are you off to?"

"None of your business," said Patsy.

"Come on. Don't be like that."

Dorothy glanced at her watch. "I'm sorry, Chick, but we really should be going."

"Where to? I can give you a lift."

She glanced at the sky, heavy with dark clouds. She felt her hair wilting under the thin scarf. "Union Station. My brother's coming in on the six-thirty. I'm afraid we'll miss him."

"Well, hop in, then." He opened the passenger door with his good hand. Patsy, sulking, stepped inside. Dorothy followed him around to the driver's side and got into the backseat.

"This is so nice of you," Patsy said as he pulled away from the curb. "We'd never have gotten a taxi in this weather."

"It's my cousin's car. I borrowed it special to take you out." Rowsey glanced over his shoulder at Dorothy. "I'm sorry about dropping off the face of the earth. I want to make it up to you."

Dorothy hesitated. "My brother ships out in the morning. We have plans for tonight."

"Just my luck." He pulled in front of the station. "At least let me wait for you. I'll drive the three of you back to the boardinghouse. I can't let a GI walk across town in the rain."

At the station Rowsey went in search of parking. The girls stared up at the electrified sign that announced arrivals and departures. "We're late," said Dorothy, her voice quavering. "We missed him. Now what will we do?"

"There he is!" said Patsy.

Dorothy turned. A man in uniform stood on the platform. She had looked directly at him, but hadn't recognized him.

"Georgie!" she called, her heart quickening. "Over here!"

He loped toward them, a knapsack over his shoulder. "Hiya, kid," he said, clasping her briefly. Except for the day he'd left for boot camp, he had never embraced her before. He was taller than she remembered, bigger through the shoulders. His dark hair had thinned at the temples; his face looked

long and thin. He reminded her of their father.

"I can't believe it's you," she whispered.
He let go first.

"Who's this?" he asked, grinning.

"Patsy Sturgis." She gave him a dazzling
smile. "I recognized you right away."

"How's that?"

"I wake up every morning looking at you."
She giggled at his expression. "Dottie keeps
a photo of you on the bureau."

"Patsy's my roommate," Dorothy explained.

"No kidding." His eyes rested on her a
moment.

"Hey!" Rowsey called from across the
platform.

Patsy ignored him. "How was your train
ride, George?"

"No complaints." He glanced at Rowsey,
who was hurrying toward them. "That guy a
friend of yours?"

"That's Chick Rowsey. He drove us here."

"Are you hungry?" Patsy asked.

"There's a place nearby that makes great
hamburgers." Dorothy had never eaten
there herself, but Jean Johns had once
gone there on a date.

"You mean Morrison's? That's pretty tame for a returning hero." Patsy cocked her head at Rowsey. "Hey, big spender. Didn't you say something about steaks?"

He grinned sheepishly. "It's Friday night. A table for four might be tough to swing."

"I'm sure you can do it." Patsy turned to Georgie. "When's the last time you had a Delmonico steak?"

"A long time," he admitted, grinning. "A coon's age."

"Then it's settled." Patsy took his arm. "We're going to Patrick Henry's."

They crowded into a booth near the kitchen, a cozy semicircular one meant for a couple. Georgie sat in the middle, the girls on either side. A waiter brought an extra chair for Rowsey. Drinks were ordered: beers for the men, Coca-Colas for the girls. When the waiter disappeared, Rowsey produced a flask from his pocket. He took a swig and handed the bottle to Georgie.

"What is it?" said Patsy.

Rowsey grinned. "It's not suitable for ladies."

"That's not fair," she said. "It's rude not to share."

Rowsey clapped Georgie's shoulder. "Two weeks' leave, huh? How'd that happen?"

"Don't ask me, pal. How does anything happen?"

Patsy leaned forward. "Dorothy says you have a girl back home. Evelyn, isn't that right?"

Georgie shot Dorothy a look. "Not anymore. That's finished now."

"What do you mean?" said Dorothy.

"Ev's marrying Gene Stusick."

"Gene? I can't believe it!" Their fathers had worked on the same crew. From school, from church, the six Stusick children were as familiar as cousins. "You two were always such good friends."

"It's no big deal." Georgie drained his glass. "I don't mind. I wish them the best."

"Women," said Chick. "You can't count on them."

Georgie lit a cigarette.

"You smoke now?" said Dorothy.

"Off and on." He grinned. "I haven't had one all week. Not with Mama around. It wouldn't have been worth the grief."

"All GIs smoke," said Patsy, reaching for his pack. "Isn't that so?"

"Most of them. But it's a bad habit." George nudged her. "Especially for a girl."

"It's worse for a girl," Rowsey agreed solemnly. "Makes her look fast."

Patsy giggled. "Watch it, buster."

"You're a bad influence," said Georgie. "You didn't get my sister started, did you?"

"Not Dorothy," said Rowsey. "She's not that kind of girl."

Dorothy felt a flush creep across her cheeks. The conversation embarrassed her, but it was delightful to be out with her brother. He was glad to see her; he looked handsome in his uniform. They had not laughed together in years.

Rowsey raised his glass. "They say it's almost over."

"They said that a year ago," Georgie said.

The car wound slowly through the dark streets. Dorothy sat up front next to Rowsey, Georgie and Patsy in the rear. The rain had stopped. A dense fog blanketed the warm night. Dorothy's watch showed two-thirty. She'd never seen Washington at this hour. She was surprised by how much activity there was.

They stopped at a light on Sixteenth Street. At the corner two men stood smoking cigarettes. Across the street, a soldier and his girl leaned against a low wall, kissing.

"Lively neighborhood," Georgie observed.

"There's an officers' club up ahead," said Rowsey.

In the backseat Patsy murmured something to Georgie, and he answered in a low voice. She giggled shrilly. Dorothy glanced in the rearview mirror, wondering what was funny.

Rowsey turned onto Massachusetts Avenue and stopped in front of the boardinghouse. The engine idled loudly in the quiet street. In an upstairs window a light came on.

Patsy stepped out of the car, adjusting her skirt. "Good Lord, I'm tired."

"Rowsey," said Georgie, hefting his duffel to his shoulder. "Good to meet you, pal."

"Good night," Dorothy added, but Rowsey seemed not to hear her. He shook Georgie's hand.

"Aren't you coming?" Dorothy called from the stoop. Patsy had reseated herself in the car.

"In a minute." She tucked her legs up under her. "Go ahead. I'm right behind you."

Dorothy led Georgie up the steps. Her heels clicked loudly on the cement.

"What's the story with those two? She seems mad at him about something." Georgie glanced toward the car. Rowsey had cut the engine; he and Patsy seemed deep in conversation.

"She's always mad about something," said Dorothy.

"She's a funny girl."

Dorothy unlocked the door. His curiosity irritated her, mainly because she knew Patsy would interrogate her later: *What did your brother say about me?* Patsy, who already had two fellows overseas, who at that very minute was sitting in Chick Rowsey's front seat. It occurred to her that Patsy wouldn't be satisfied until every boy in the world was thinking about her.

She led Georgie to the attic room and switched on the light, a single bare bulb hanging from the ceiling. A cot had been made up with sheets and a blanket. "I hope it's not too uncomfortable."

"Are you kidding?" Georgie set down his duffel. "You should see the places I've slept the last couple years. You wouldn't believe me if I told you." His eyes were bleary in the harsh light, shot through with red.

"Sleep well," she whispered, forgetting all about Patsy and Chick Rowsey. "I'm so glad you're here."

Quietly she closed the door.

She was nearly asleep when Patsy came into the room, dropping her pocketbook loudly on the floor. Dorothy could smell her across the room, perfume and cigarettes, the fried-food odor they'd breathed all night. She switched on the lamp. "Is everything all right?"

"Fine." Patsy kicked off her shoes.

"What were you talking about with Chick?"

"Oh, nothing interesting." She sat heavily on the bottom bunk. "He isn't all that fascinating when he's sober. Never mind with a few drinks in him." She stretched out on the bed. "Your brother's a dreamboat. A real gentleman. Where did he run off to?"

"Upstairs, to bed. He was exhausted."

"He's a nice fellow."

Dorothy waited for more—*Did he ask about me?*—but the question never came. When she reached down to turn off the light, she saw that Patsy was asleep.

He had been dreaming of the ocean. The sickening lurch, the eternal smell, briny and dank, like rotting fish. As always in his dreams, on his way to somewhere. The destination secret at first, revealing itself later in a terrible moment of clarity and dread. The same dream, always with some small variation. This time Gene Stusick was there—his old buddy Eugenius—now, somehow, the ranking officer on board. They had been hit; men wounded on deck, pandemonium below. George was bleeding from the back, his shirt wet with blood.

A sound woke him. He lay on the cot, still dressed; his throat raw, his shirt reeking of cigarettes. His undershirt was soaked with sweat. He glanced around the room and re-membered where he was. Someone was knocking at the door.

"Who's there?" His head throbbed. Un-clear how much he had drunk. A steady stream of beers, furtive swigs from the flask when Rowsey remembered to pass it.

The door creaked open. The blonde stood in the hallway, still wearing her blue dress. She held something behind her back.

"Whatcha got there?"

Smiling broadly, she produced a bottle. "Kentucky bourbon. I keep it for when my daddy comes to visit."

"Where's Dorothy?"

"It's past her bedtime. But I knew you'd be awake." She closed the door and sat on the cot beside him. "I only had the one glass. You don't mind sharing, do you?"

He shook his head to clear it. The room was very hot. Outside, he heard rain, the civilized hum of traffic. "What happened to Rowsey?"

"Oh, him." *Glug-glug-glug* as she filled the glass. "I sent him home. I had enough of his company for one night."

"What's the problem? He seems like a nice fellow."

"He's not my type." She handed him the glass. "It's your sister he's after."

"No kidding." George considered this. For two years he'd carried a certain picture of Dorothy in his mind, the way she'd looked the morning he'd left: bare-legged, in short cotton socks, hunched and shivering in her old coat. Earlier, at the station, he'd barely recognized her. It seemed odd that Rowsey had chosen her over the blonde, but only a little. Odd, but not impossible.

Patsy reached for the glass. For a moment her breasts fell forward, offered like pastries on a plate.

"Cheers." She tucked a leg underneath her. He caught a flash of skin, a white glimpse of thigh.

"They're fake," she said, following his gaze.

He frowned.

"My stockings. Look at the seams." She stood and turned her back to him. She lifted her skirt a few inches. The dress clung to her backside. "It's Magic Marker."

He ran a finger down her leg. The flesh was smooth and warm.

"Pretty good. They're almost straight."

She laughed. "I can't take any credit for that. Dottie drew them on."

Dottie. For a moment he wondered who she was talking about.

The blonde set down her glass and turned to face him, her skin pale in the low light. He saw that she was dead sober.

She knew exactly what she was doing.

The next morning Dorothy and Georgie took a cab to the station. They rode in silence; the easy warmth of the night before had vanished. She felt the old awkwardness between them. Still, she tried.

"I had fun last night," she said. "Didn't you?"

"Sure." He stared out the window. "It was a kick to meet your friends. Rowsey and—" He pretended to grope for her name. *Nice try,* he thought. *That's some slick acting, pal.*

"Patsy," said Dorothy.

"Where is she, anyhow?" He avoided Dorothy's eyes. "I figured we'd see her at breakfast, so I could say good-bye."

"It's the strangest thing. She got up at the crack of dawn. She's spending the day in

Richmond with her father. I guess he's there on business." Dorothy frowned. "She didn't say a thing about it until this morning. That's not like her."

"You two seem pretty tight," said Georgie.

"She's my best friend."

There was something girlish in her voice, a childish pride. *She's still a kid,* he thought.

"We tell each other everything," she said.

Good Christ, he thought, *let's hope not.*

"Well, tell her good-bye for me." He stared out the window, thinking of her body in the darkened room, her buttocks compact and round, small enough to fit in his hands. He'd been stunned when she reached for him. *Let me,* she said. She would not allow him inside her. Instead she finished him off expertly with her hand.

I won't see you tomorrow, she told him, dressing before the window. *I'm tied up all day.* She leaned over and kissed him. *Don't worry, I can keep a secret.* The door closed silently behind her.

It wasn't right; he knew it wasn't. But a part of him felt he deserved those few moments of pleasure, a single happy memory to fortify him in the dark months—maybe years—to come. Evelyn had thrown him

over, and he was still smarting. Gene
Stusick's betrayal had wounded him deeper
still. Under the circumstances a painkiller
was in order, a stiff shot of something to get
him through. If he'd used Patsy for this purpose, she certainly had consented. More
than that: she'd sought him out, come to his
room of her own volition. She was not a
conscript, but an enlisted girl, an enthusias-
tic volunteer.

"Chick liked meeting you," said Dorothy.

George thought of Rowsey and Patsy in
the front seat of the Ford, their blond heads
inclined toward each other. Had she volunteered for him, too? Oddly, the possibility
did not trouble him. Rowsey had been
wounded; he'd taken his licks. He, too, deserved a little comfort. At that moment
George would have loaned the guy his shirt.

"Rowsey's a good guy," he said.

"I think so," said Dorothy.

George eyed her closely. He took her
hand.

"Be careful," he said. "Guys like Rowsey,
they're a little mixed up when they first
come back. They need time to sort it all
out."

She stared at him, wide-eyed. She looked utterly perplexed.

"It's none of my business," he added, reddening. "Just be careful, is all. I don't want you to get hurt."

The cab pulled in front of the station. Georgie reached for his wallet. "Take her back where we came from," he told the driver.

"But I'm coming with you," she protested. "To see you off."

"What's the point? It's pouring rain." He embraced her quickly. "It was good to see you, kid."

She clung to him. *Too fast,* she thought, feeling sick. *Too fast.* She had deliberately not thought about him leaving, or what he was returning to.

"Georgie, be careful," she whispered.

"Don't worry," he said. "It's almost over."

Summer settled over the city. Electric fans hummed in every window. Pedestrians moved listlessly: office girls with shiny faces, men sweating through their shirts. The streetcar passengers fanned themselves with newspapers. The outdoor air smelled burned and tarry, as though the avenues were melting. Women languished on stoops and porches, listening to the radio, waiting for a breeze.

In August Dorothy went home to Bakerton for a visit. She had worked at Treasury six months, entitling her to five days of leave. Tack a weekend to either end, and that made nine luxurious days at home.

She slept in her old room, on the soft, sagging mattress next to her sister. Joyce was fifteen that summer, a slight, pale-faced girl, not shy but reserved, with a quiet certainty that made people treat her like an adult. She planned to enlist after graduation and worried that Hitler would surrender before she had the chance. She kept the room bare and orderly, as though an inspection were imminent. Above the bed hung a recruitment poster, wheedled out of a clerk at the post office: ARE YOU A GIRL WITH A STAR-SPANGLED HEART? JOIN THE WAC NOW!

The family had changed since Dorothy left, but they seemed not to have suffered. Her mother had grown plump and healthy. Lucy had begun to crawl. Sandy had turned into a little savage. He spent the days playing in the woods and refused to have his hair cut. That and his strange coloring—brown face and arms, hair bleached white by the sun—gave him an odd, aboriginal look.

Dorothy envied his freedom. For months she had dreamed of home; but now that she was there, the time weighed upon her. She took walks to fill the afternoons. Once, walking down Main Street, she'd spotted Mag Spangler's mother arranging hats in the shop window. Dorothy waved but didn't stop to chat.

She returned to Washington a day early, Saturday instead of Sunday. It was only sensible, she told her mother; the trains being what they were, she'd be crazy to travel on the busiest day of the week, with all the soldiers returning from furlough.

The boardinghouse was quiet when she arrived. "Everyone is on holiday," Mrs. Straub told her. The blond stenographer had gone to the shore for the weekend. The deaf schoolteacher spent summers with her people down south.

"What about Miss Sturgis?" Dorothy asked.

"In and out. I haven't seen her all day."

Upstairs, the girls' room was a wreck. Ashtrays overflowed. Both beds were draped with Patsy's clothes. Dorothy folded them and placed them on the bureau: sunsuits and Bermuda shorts, the red bathing suit she'd borrowed to wear at Glen Echo. She wondered where Patsy had worn it, if she, too, had gone to the shore. She thought of the long, eventless week in Bakerton and wondered what she had missed.

At ten o'clock she climbed into bed. The night was close; she expected to toss and turn, but the trip had tired her. With her eyes closed, the world seemed to rush past, as though she were still on the train. In minutes she was asleep.

Low voices, a whisper. "Hush. The old lady hears like a bat."

Dorothy opened her eyes. She had been dreaming of home. Her baby sister had crawled away, and Dorothy had found her under the porch steps. The room was dark. The bed seemed to shift slightly. Too late, she realized the voices were beneath her, and one of them belonged to Patsy.

"Don't hit your head." Giggles, a stifled laugh.

The bed rocked softly. It was a moment before she understood. *No,* she thought. *It can't be.*

There was a smell in the room, liquor and cigarettes; they had been out drinking. Dorothy stared at the ceiling, grateful that she hadn't spoken. She wished herself invisible. If they saw her, she would die of shame.

The movement quickened. Someone breathed loudly. She had no idea how long the act would take. Minutes? Hours? She thought of the three-penny nails they had used to secure the beds.

Underneath a kind of sigh, deep and guttural. Abruptly the movement stopped. The breathing slowed, as though an animal were sleeping.

She wondered if it was over.

"Don't get too comfortable," Patsy whispered. "You can't stay here."

The bedsprings creaked. Dorothy squeezed her eyes shut. *Don't see me,* she prayed. Dressing sounds, a zipper closing. Then the doorknob turned.

She opened her eyes a crack. A man stood at the door, his back to her. His left hand was tucked in his pocket.

"Sleep tight, dreamgirl," he whispered, opening the door.

Beneath her Patsy rolled over in bed. " 'Night, Chick."

Dorothy rose early Sunday morning. Quietly she dressed for church, stepping around the stockings and underpants on the floor.

Patsy lay on her side, snoring softly, facing the wall.

When Dorothy returned, Mrs. Straub was setting the table for breakfast. The blond stenographer complained about the crowds at the shore. Dorothy ate in silence, forcing down the oatmeal. She left the bacon on her plate.

After breakfast she climbed the stairs to her room. Both beds had been made. Patsy sat on hers, fully dressed, smoking.

"Hey there," she said, butting her cigarette.

"Hey, yourself." Dorothy stood at the mirror, removing her hat.

"When did you get back? I saw your suitcase when I woke up." Patsy reached for her pack and lit another, her hands shaking.

"Yesterday afternoon."

"I wasn't expecting you until today." Patsy's voice quavered. "I didn't see you when I came in last night."

"Well, I saw you."

"Honey, I'm sorry." Patsy rose from the bed. "I'm so ashamed. I don't know what to say."

The girls stared at each other, their eyes tearing.

"Patsy," said Dorothy, her voice breaking. "How could you?"

The question held a hundred others, none Dorothy was able to ask, none Patsy was prepared to answer. Yet she struggled an instant, as though she might try.

"I don't know what you heard, or thought you heard," she said finally. "But boys are different when they come back. Chick, your precious brother. All of them."

My brother? Dorothy thought. *What does this have to do with my brother?*

"What about Fred?" she asked instead. Her breath felt unreliable; she wondered if she would faint. "And Ted? What are you going to do when they come back?"

"Oh, please. What do you think Fred's been doing over there for two years?" Patsy sucked viciously at her cigarette. "You're a child, Dottie. It's about time you grew up."

In September a letter came. Dorothy spotted it on the hall table and placed it on Patsy's pillow. When she returned to the room that night, Patsy was packing a suitcase.

"Fred's been wounded." Her face was flushed, a smack of red on each cheek. "They're sending him home." Carelessly, angrily, she tossed garments into the suitcase: sweaters, underthings, the blue silk dress.

"Oh, Patsy." Dorothy sat. "Is it serious?"

"He lost a leg." She stopped a moment and looked around, as though she, too, had lost something. "He says he's going to be fine. Can you beat it? 'Don't worry, Pat. They're setting me up with a fake one. By the wedding I'll be good as new.' "

"Wedding?"

"That was the plan, remember?" She shut the case and tried to fasten it; overstuffed, it refused to close. "Damnation." She sat on the bed and leaned forward, her head in her hands.

"Here." Dorothy opened the suitcase and repacked it, folding the slips and blouses. Her hands moved quickly over the soft fabrics. For a moment she thought of the women in the dress factory. She'd never imagined her own hands could move so fast.

"I'm a mess," said Patsy. "An ugly mess."

"Don't say that." Dorothy stroked her hair,

stiff with hair spray. She hesitated. "What about Chick?"

Patsy lifted her head sharply. "What about him?" They hadn't mentioned his name in weeks.

"Have you told him?"

Patsy laughed bitterly. "Don't worry about him. He'll take it fine. It'll save him the trouble of getting rid of me." She clicked the suitcase shut. "Don't worry about me, Dottie. I always land on my feet."

Again she ate lunch alone, nickel sandwiches and orange sodas at Peoples'. On
Saturdays she wandered the stores; Sundays she went for a walk. It amazed her,
how quickly life reverted to its old order, as
if there had never been a Patsy at all.

One day, as she was eating lunch at the
counter, someone tapped her on the shoulder.

"Hi, stranger," said Mag Spangler. "Mind
if I join you?" She took the stool next to
Dorothy's.

"I thought you had lunch at one-thirty,"
said Dorothy.

"Mr. Leland moved me back. I'm his personal assistant now. I keep the same hours
he does." Mag removed her coat. She wore
a brown skirt and blouse Dorothy remem-

bered, the same feathered hat from her parents' shop in Bakerton.

"That's wonderful, Mag. I'm glad for you."

Mag looked around. "Are you alone?
What happened to that roommate of
yours?"

"Patsy. She moved back home to get
married."

"That figures."

How? Dorothy wondered. *How does anything figure?*

"Certain girls, you can tell right away
they're not serious. That one—" Mag
paused.

"What about her?"

"Some girls always need to be the center
of attention. She was one of those. Spoiled
rotten, is my guess." She lowered her voice.
"Oversexed, too, if you want to know what I
think."

Dorothy flushed.

"I suppose it's not her fault," said Mag.
"Some girls can't help themselves."

A waitress came to take their order, two
creamed chickens on toast.

"*Oriental Dream* is playing at the Capitol,"
said Dorothy. "Held over for one more week,
if you want to go."

"And listen to that German voice? No thanks." Mag snorted. "She may be pretty, but as far as I'm concerned she's not much of an actress."

In the end they settled on *The San Antonio Kid,* a sensible western. It was just the sort of thing Mag liked.

THREE

They came back in the summer, weighed down with treasures. A scarf or a ring for one kind of girl; for the other kind, silk stockings and French perfume. The best loot went to fathers and little brothers: weapons picked from enemy corpses, the grisly mementos of war.

They came home to girls who'd forgotten them and girls who hadn't, parents aged and sickened, or like George Novak's father, simply gone. The lucky ones found garage apartments, cramped quarters above shops downtown. Gene and Evelyn Stusick spent their wedding night on a roll-away cot in his parents' attic, a cramped space redolent of mothballs, crowded with bicycles and Flexible Flyers, the junk of his youth.

They came home to the mines: Baker

Brothers, Concoal, Eastern Coal & Coke. After the surrender came a flurry of bidding, the operators scurrying to acquire new land. There were five Baker mines, then seven, then ten. In the summer of 1945, a huge parcel of land was purchased, thirty thousand acres just across the Susquehanna; and the son of Elias Baker broke ground on Baker Twelve.

Crews were hired, equipment purchased. Coal was mined seven days a week. Paychecks in hand, the men turned their attention to other things. Tryouts were held, a team assembled. In April 1946, the Baker Bombers returned to the field. On Wednesdays, Saturdays and Sundays, Bakerton played ball.

The town didn't wait for Georgie, for the navy boys still at sea. A month after V-E Day Bakerton held a parade. Chester Baker himself appeared—resurrected from the dead, some said—to welcome the soldiers home.

"This town belongs to you," the old man boomed from the dais. He had grown frail and leaned heavily on a cane; he wore long whiskers in the old style, a mane of silver hair. "We have done our best to keep it sound in your absence, and we hand it over to you with every confidence that you will make us proud."

Some, of course, did not come home. Polish Hill had its casualties. Two of the Wojicks had debarked at Normandy. James was killed at Omaha Beach; John landed at Utah and survived, not knowing his brother lay bleeding to death twenty miles away.

Three of May Poblocki's sons returned. One night, drinking and carousing at the Vets, the youngest suffered a strange seizure and died before the ambulance arrived. Epilepsy, some said; the family called it a heart attack. He was twenty-three years old.

Across town in Little Italy, the four Bernardi boys—Angelo and Jerry, Victor and Sal—came back with stripes. The older cousins worked at Baker and played for the Bombers. Jerry returned to driving the hearse.

George and his new bride drove into Bakerton in a 1948 Chevy Fleetline sedan, a wedding gift from Marion's father. They'd been driving for seven hours, the last two on a narrow country road that wound north, more or less, from the highway. "That's impossible," she'd protested when he told her how long it would take. But his estimate—allowing for dirt roads and rugged hills, farm equipment and sluggish coal trucks—turned out to be correct.

"Almost there," he said. "It's just over this hill." He accelerated and was rewarded by an exquisite sound, the mellifluous roar of the ten-cylinder engine.

At the top of Saxon Mountain he slowed, looking down on the town: the bustling main street with its six traffic lights; the eight church steeples; the railroad tracks that cut the valley in half. A whiff of sulfur hung in the air. From this vantage point you could see all of Saxon Valley: Polish Hill, the old mine camp known as Swedetown, the Number Five tipple just beyond. Baker Towers loomed above the train tracks; behind them, rows of identical shingled roofs. If Marion had asked, George would have told her what they were: *Bony piles. Company houses.* But his wife, bless her, did not.

He rolled down his window. It was a clear Saturday in late June; at every church in Bakerton, someone was getting married. A warm breeze blew up from the valley, carrying the sound of bells. A riot of bells, circling and discordant: the stately carillon at St. John's Episcopal, the twelve tones of the Angelus, the soaring refrain of "Ave Maria." George had heard the bells his whole life; each set was distinct, recognizable, its voice as familiar as a relative's. Intermingled now: the chorus crazily beautiful, festive as a circus organ.

Home, he thought.

They drove through the town. Bridesmaids posed on the steps of St. Brigid's, waiting to be photographed. A full parking lot at St. Casimir's, Fords and Oldsmobiles decorated with tissue-paper flowers. A gasping Studebaker idled out front, a string of empty beer cans trailing from its bumper.

"My goodness," said Marion, removing her dark sunglasses. She was unaccustomed to early mornings; the skin beneath her eyes looked slightly blue. "What is that all about?"

"They hang a lot of junk on the groom's car. When the newlyweds drive away, it makes a real racket."

She smiled uncertainly. "Is that a—Polish tradition?"

"A Bakerton tradition." He grinned. "Aren't you sorry we missed out on that?"

He took the long way through town, imagined the sun glinting off the Chevy's chrome bumpers. The car was baby blue; in four weeks he'd already waxed it twice. The interior was white leather, the backseat wide as a sofa.

He stopped at the traffic light next to Bellavia's Bakery. One of the Bernardi boys, Vic or Sal, stopped in the street to stare. George gave him a wave. They crossed the railroad tracks and climbed Polish Hill. A barefoot boy ran in the street. The

Poblockis' chickens pecked quietly at the front yard. Fingering her rosary, Mrs. Stusick rocked back and forth on her porch swing, a babushka tied under her chin.

"The houses are all the same," Marion observed.

"Company houses," he said matter-of-factly. *There,* he thought. *That wasn't so bad.* He pulled in front of his mother's house and engaged the brake. "Here we are."

"I hope they like me," she said.

"They'll love you," said George, who had loved her the moment he saw her. "How could they not?"

They'd met on Thanksgiving at her parents' house in Haverford, a wealthy suburb on Philadelphia's Main Line. George had been invited by her brother, Kip Quigley, whom he knew from a chemistry class at Temple. Quigley had hired George as his tutor, which meant that he sat behind George during exams and copied with impunity from his paper. For this privilege he paid ten dollars a week, enough to keep George's second-hand Ford in gas and lube. The car trailed oil all over Philadelphia; George had never managed to find the leak. When he could afford to, he simply added another quart.

The two were friendly, but not friends; their lives were too different. Quigley was nineteen and lived with his parents; he took classes when he felt like it, in between hangovers and tennis. George worked in a hardware store to pay for textbooks, clothes and other necessities the GI Bill didn't cover. He studied at night, early in the morning and in the student union between classes. He was pressed for time, for cash; most days his body felt hungry for sleep; yet when exam results were posted, he was always at the top of the class. A clerical error, he thought the first time it happened. Somebody had made a mistake.

In high school he'd been an indifferent student; if not for his father's constant prodding, he would never have opened a book. He worked one summer at the tiny music store in town and took his pay in merchandise: a beat-up saxophone, a secondhand clarinet. His band played the school dances; onstage, he imagined himself Woody Herman or Jimmy Dorsey, enthralling audiences with the silky sound of his clarinet. School was his buddy Gene Stusick's department. His high marks had earned him the nickname Eugenius: a boy who could name all thirty-two presidents in their proper order, who'd dazzled their sixth-grade teacher by adding long columns of figures in his head. George was no Eugenius. A grown man now, he simply studied harder than anyone else—galvanized by his dread of the coal mines, a life spent slaving underground like his father.

Mining had killed Stanley Novak. George didn't know how, exactly, but he was sure that it had. A big man, he'd spent much of his life crammed into tight, damp spaces; from the way he walked you could tell he was in pain. His breathing was labored. As a boy George had fallen asleep to the sound of it. The jagged rasp was audible through the floorboards, louder than the Polish radio station in the parlor downstairs. His father had given his life to Baker Brothers. The mines had given him a heart attack at fifty-four.

For six months after graduating high school, George had worked as a greaser in the machine shop at Baker One—a sweetheart job, by mine standards. Before the

war, the shop had been staffed by Baker's
star ballplayers, to save their knees and
backs and lungs for the playing field. The
shop was cold and filthy, the noise deafening; but George didn't mind. He was grateful to be working aboveground.

His first day at work, he'd ridden the
mantrip with a dozen other men and felt his
heart race as they entered the shaft. The
memory still haunted him: the echoing
dampness, the sulfur smell. The dark shaft
was narrow and airless, no wider than the
beam of his headlamp. Here and there, a rat
scuttled. A few times, water fell from the low
roof like a thundershower, soaking his
shoulders. The One was a wet mine, the
foreman explained; but where the water
came from, or what kept it from flooding the
mine completely, no one seemed to know.
That single day had been enough for
George; at the end of his shift he handed in
his helmet. Luckily the foreman took pity on
him and got him the job lubing shuttle cars.
He was almost relieved when his draft notice came.

He would never go back. He'd made up
his mind long ago, when he was still in the
navy, and this resolution had guided his

every decision. One of his navy buddies had grown up in Philly; after their discharge they'd shared an apartment on Broad Street. When the other fellow moved out to get married, George found a tiny studio in a rooming house downtown. He worked a series of jobs: deliveryman, butcher's assistant, night janitor at a pet store, scrubbing down cages and shoveling dog shit. He worked and studied. His hair thinned. In the mirror he saw his father.

Meanwhile letters came from home. His boyhood friends had returned to Bakerton like boomerangs, to hometown girls and good-paying jobs. No one else had even tried to leave. As a boy, George had idolized a local ballplayer, Ernie Tedesco, who was picked from the coal league and signed to the majors. He'd played six seasons with the St. Louis Cardinals—as far as George knew, the only guy ever to escape Bakerton. As examples went, it wasn't much help. George was no athlete, never had been. His dream was to become a surgeon, to fix what was broken. In three years as a medic, he'd glimpsed what was possible. Time was the problem; time and money. The years of training stretched before him, rigorous and expensive. He was a twenty-five-year-old sophomore, keenly aware of the years he had lost.

Later, after he and Marion were married, he was struck by the unlikelihood of their union, how incredible it was that he had won her, how easily they might never have met. He pictured the lackluster unfolding of his life without her, the ordinary girl he might have married—the first of many banal and pragmatic choices, all adding up to a life without distinction. By all rights it was the life he'd been born to, a fate he'd escaped through hard work and persistence and sheer stubborn will.

He'd refused Quigley's invitation at first. He had planned to drive to Bakerton to spend the day with his family; but on Thanksgiving morning the Ford wouldn't start. He called Quigley at the last minute, unwilling to face the holiday alone in his rented room, his usual dinner of sandwiches and canned soup.

He'd dressed carefully for dinner—pressed trousers, his only sport coat. He

knew that Quigley came from money.
Quigley's department store was a Philadelphia institution. George had never bought
anything there—the prices were too steep—
but he passed the store each day on his
way home from the bus stop, stepping
around well-dressed matrons with their
green-and-white shopping bags. He saw
Quigley's bags all over the city, miles away
from the actual store. Merely carrying such
a bag was a status symbol. That alone
should have tipped him off.

The opulence of the house astonished
him. Seated between two elderly aunts, he
tried to be sociable but was flummoxed by
the many forks and glasses. The Quigleys
had invited a crowd. George counted sixteen heads at the long table, not including
the woman who appeared to serve each
course. At the far end, Marion sat with her
chin in her hand, leaning on her elbow, vio-
lating everything George had been taught
about table manners. Beside her an old
man railed loudly against Truman. Marion
nodded occasionally, her eyes glazed with
boredom. She seemed to feel George's
gaze; she looked directly at him and tipped

one eyebrow, a skill he admired. Then she
drained her wineglass in a single gulp.

After dinner George took Kip aside.
"Who's that? In the blue."

"My sister. I'd introduce you, but I like you
too much."

"Come on," George said, laughing.

"You'll see. Don't say I didn't warn you."

When the guests moved to the living
room, George spotted Marion alone on a
sofa and introduced himself.

"Marion Baumgardner," she said, offering
her hand.

He paused for a moment, confused. A
sick feeling in his stomach: she was married. The intensity of his disappointment
surprised him.

"You're a friend of my brother's?" she
asked.

"We're in a class together."

"I suppose I can't hold that against you."

He laughed uncertainly. "Oh, Kip's all
right."

"I think he's an ass." She leaned forward
and took a cigarette from a case on the
table. Her hand was long and white, slender
as a fish.

"Where were you stationed?" she asked.

He grinned. "How'd you know I was a vet?"

She shrugged languidly, as if to ask what else he could be.

"In the South Pacific," he said. "I was a medic on a navy minesweeper."

"Good God."

For a moment he was dumbfounded. Most girls were impressed by this fact, or pretended to be. Marion looked utterly horrified.

He leaned over to light her cigarette. When she raised her hand he saw that she wore no wedding ring.

She seemed to read his mind. "I'm a widow," she said. "My husband was a paratrooper. His glider was shot down over Sicily." Her voice was flat, her face still as a mask.

"Oh," he said stupidly. And then, recovering: "I'm sorry."

"So tell me, George Novak: What brings you to this part of the world? You're not from here." It wasn't a question.

Is it that obvious? he wondered.

"You've got to be somewhere," he said.

She seemed amused when he asked for her phone number, but gave it to him anyway. When he called her the very next night, she invited him to her apartment.

She lived alone, on the top floor of a brick row house off Rittenhouse Square, a grand place with two fireplaces and twelve-foot ceilings. One room held a wide bed, the only furniture she owned. In the living room were an easel and several unfinished canvases: bright colors in jagged patterns that seemed perfectly random, like the scrawlings of an angry child. The place smelled of coffee and turpentine. The refrigerator held tonic water, vodka and gin.

Their first date lasted the entire weekend. George emerged from her apartment on a Sunday afternoon, exhilarated and slightly dizzy. He hadn't eaten, and his temples ached with hangover. Her paint-dappled rug had left a crisscross pattern on his back.

Sexually, she was more experienced than he, a fact apparent to them both. She did things to him no girl had done, and she made it clear, with words and gestures, that he was to reciprocate. Her frankness shocked and thrilled him. Her movements were expert. He hadn't expected a virgin; yet she had lived with her husband for only a month. She had been fitted for a diaphragm; when exactly, George didn't ask. If she'd had other lovers, she never mentioned them. For this he was grateful.

He proposed after three months. Her father took the news calmly. *He gave up on me long ago,* Marion had told George. *When I ran off and married a Jew.*

"Novak," said the old man. "What kind of name is that?"

"Polish, sir. My father came over from Poland."

Quigley raised his bushy eyebrows. "A lot of Jews came from Poland."

"My family is Catholic, sir."

George knew from Marion that this wasn't welcome news either, but her father received it stoically. In the end he gave his blessing, and Marion Baumgardner became Marion Novak—one youthful indiscretion expunged by another, less egregious one.

They were married that spring, in a quiet ceremony at the Quigleys' church in Haverford. George's family did not attend; he didn't tell his mother until afterward. She would have insisted on a Catholic wedding, and that was a conversation George didn't wish to have. Later it would seem a cowardly decision, but at the time he deemed it practical. To him one church was as good as another. Any sort of ceremony would suffice, as long as it made Marion his wife.

His little sister greeted them as they climbed the porch steps. She wore a ruffled pink dress with a stiff petticoat, a ribbon tied in her hair.

"Hi, Georgie," she said shyly, peering through the screen door. She was four years old, timid with strangers. He hadn't visited since Christmas and was amazed at how she'd grown.

"Hi, honey." He opened the door and lifted her into his arms. "Isn't she a doll? My baby sister Lucy."

He was prepared to hand her over so Marion could hold her, but his wife only smiled. He put Lucy down and went inside.

"Hello!" he called, heading for the kitchen.

His mother stood at the sink rinsing dishes. He was relieved to see that she was wearing shoes. Not only that: she had put on lipstick. It was the first time in years he'd seen her without an apron.

He embraced her. She was stouter than
he remembered; her hair smelled of garlic. A
wonderful aroma filled the kitchen, a strawberry pie cooling on the windowsill. "Mama,
this is Marion."

"How do you do." Marion offered her
hand. Next to Rose she looked slim as a
whippet, tall and elegant in her pale blue
suit.

"Please to meet you," Rose said carefully,
as though she'd rehearsed it.

They sat. His mother took plates from the
cupboard and set about slicing the pie.

"Mama, come sit down."

"In a minute. First I make coffee."

She bustled about the kitchen, putting
on water, measuring the grounds. Marion
glanced around the room. "Is that a coal
stove?"

"Yep," said George.

She studied it with naked fascination, as
though she'd never seen such a thing. It hit
him that she probably hadn't. The stove, the
Last Supper hanging on the wall, the Lenten
palm leaves tucked behind it to ward off
lightning strikes. All the familiar objects of
his childhood were curiosities to her.

"Where does it go, the coal?"

He indicated the compartment at the side of the stove.

"You fill it every day?"

"Every few hours. Depends on how much cooking you do. That was my job when I was a kid. Filling the coal bucket."

"Who fills it now?"

"Sandy, I guess. My little brother. Mama, where is he?"

"Outside someplace. I don't know. Me, I never know." She spoke softly, as if not wanting to intrude on their conversation. She brought cups and saucers to the table.

"Mama, please sit down." He regretted the edge in his voice. He only wanted her to sit and talk like a regular person, instead of behaving like a waitress.

Finally she sat, hands folded in her lap.

"It smells delicious in here," said Marion.

"I been cooking all day." Her eyes met Marion's. "You like to cook?"

Marion laughed, a low, bubbling sound. "Heavens, no. I'm a disaster in the kitchen. George is still teaching me to fry an egg."

Rose frowned. "What you eat, then?"

"Oh, I don't know." Marion crossed and uncrossed her long legs. "We go to restaurants, or make sandwiches. I don't have much of an appetite."

George avoided his mother's gaze. He knew what she was thinking. *What kind of girl you marry, she don't know how to fry an egg?*

"You still working, Georgie?" Rose asked. "With the hardware?"

"I quit that job. I'm working for Marion's father now. He has a store."

"What about the school?"

"I'm taking the summer off," he said. "We're saving up for a house."

"Mrs. Novak," said Marion. "George tells me your family is Italian."

Rose looked down at her lap, smoothed the fabric of her dress over her knees. "That's right. We come over when I was a little."

Marion leaned forward in her chair, smiling warmly. "Have you ever considered going back?"

Rose glanced uncertainly at George, confusion written on her face. *Your wife, she want to send me back.*

"What for?" she asked.

"Oh, just for a visit." Again Marion smiled. She was not a smiler by nature; George sensed her effort. "It's a different world since the war. It would be interesting, wouldn't it, to see how things have changed? The way of life, the political situation . . ." Her voice trailed off.

"Me, I got nobody there." His mother rose and dipped a dishcloth in the sink. She wrung it out and passed it over the counter.

"My grandparents lost touch with their relatives when they left," George explained.

"That's too bad." Marion stirred her coffee, though she hadn't added any sugar. "I'd like to go one day. My husband died there during the war."

George felt his face warm.

"Your husband?" his mother repeated

"George didn't tell you? I'm a widow."

"He don't tell me." Again Rose wiped at the counter with the rag.

A long silence in which Marion sipped her coffee. George swallowed bite after bite of strawberry pie, which seemed to be piling up on the way to his stomach. Finally Marion got to her feet.

"Would you mind if I lay down for a while?" she asked. "I've got a bit of a headache."

*   *   *

George led her upstairs to Joyce's bedroom, where they would be sleeping. The
room was immaculate, the walls bare. When
he'd last visited, a recruiting poster had
hung above the bed. It had been removed
for their visit and replaced with a crucifix.
Two folded towels, bleached and threadbare, had been placed on the bureau.

"You shouldn't have told her that," said
George.

"Told her what?"

"That you were married before."

She stared at him. "I assumed she already knew."

"Why would I tell her a thing like that?"

"Because it's true. It's what happened."
She frowned. "Should I be ashamed of it?"

"Of course not," George said hastily. He
couldn't bring himself to explain it, that his
mother had expected what every mother
expected: for her son to marry a virgin,
sweet and uncomplicated. An altogether
different sort of girl.

"Mama is old-fashioned, that's all. It's
hard enough getting used to a daughter-in-
law."

Marion shrugged as though the matter were hardly worth discussing. "I'm exhausted," she said, stripping down to her panties.

He watched her undress. Her casual nudity still startled him. Her habit was to sleep late, skim the newspaper and paint for an hour or two, all without putting on a stitch of clothing. In their own apartment, with the shades drawn, it excited him. Here in his mother's house it seemed wrong.

"What's the matter?" Marion asked.

"Nothing." The truth—that he wished she'd put some clothes on—seemed foolish and neurotic. She certainly would have thought so.

She climbed under the covers and rolled onto her side. "I won't sleep. I'll just close my eyes."

He closed the door softly and went downstairs. The kitchen was empty. At the doorway to the parlor he paused. His father's chair stood in the corner, the old console radio beside it. Since his death George had visited a half-dozen times, but he'd never seen his mother sit there. He wondered if anyone ever did.

He went out the front door and sat on the

porch swing. His sister Joyce was coming up the hill, a pocketbook over her arm.

"Hey there," he called.

She shielded her eyes from the sun. "Georgie! When did you get here?"

She hurried up the porch steps and accepted his kiss on her cheek. Unlike his mother and Dorothy, who nearly smothered him with affection whenever he visited, Joyce did not like to be touched. He sensed she'd be perfectly happy with a handshake, but that offended his sense of correctness. She was his sister, after all, and a girl.

"Holy cow," she said. "Is that your car?"

"Yep." He couldn't keep the pride out of his voice. "It's a forty-eight. Brand-new." He looked her up and down, a mousy little thing in a gray skirt and blouse. Her blond hair was set in tight waves. "You did something to your hair."

She waved her hand dismissively, as if the topic were of no interest.

"Sorry to kick you out of your room," he said.

"I don't mind. I'm happy bunking on the couch." She peered through the screen door. "Where's your wife? Jeepers, I can't believe you're married."

"She's upstairs resting."

Joyce seemed confounded, as if only an invalid would sleep in the middle of the day. "Is she sick?"

"A little headache, is all."

They sat on the swing. "What's the big idea, running off and getting married? We didn't even know you had a girl."

George smiled. "How did Mama take it? She didn't answer my letter."

"How do you think? She had a bird. And Dorothy had ten fits. Why the big secret?"

"It wasn't a secret. It just happened very fast."

"Love at first sight?"

"Something like that." He lowered his voice. "Look, don't say anything to Mama, but we didn't exactly get married in the church. Marion's family is Presbyterian, and I didn't want to rock the boat. Keep it to yourself, okay?"

Joyce gave a low whistle. "Oh, boy. I see why you did it on the Q.T. Don't worry, I won't breathe a word."

He grinned. "Where've you been all afternoon? Have you got a secret, too?"

"I enlisted."

He laughed appreciatively. Too late, he saw her flinch.

"You're serious? Enlisted in what, for God's sake? Haven't you heard? The war's over."

"There's a women's unit in the air force." Her voice was calm but firm, as though she were explaining it to a child.

"Joyce, are you crazy? Why would you do a thing like that?"

"I don't know why you're so surprised. I've only been talking about it for five years. Remember all those letters I wrote you?"

"Sure I remember. I thought it was cute. I figured you'd outgrow it."

"I'm eighteen." An edge crept into her voice. "Same as you were, when you went."

"That was different," said George.

"Because you're a boy?"

"Because I was drafted, for God's sake! There's no way in hell I would have gone if I'd had a choice." Across the street Mrs. Stusick looked up from her rosary. He lowered his voice.

"You don't know what you're getting into. Trust me, the military is no place for a girl."

"Well, the air force disagrees." She rose. "I expected this from Mama and Dorothy, but not you. I thought you of all people would understand." She went into the house, the screen door slamming behind her.

George hesitated. He ought to go in and talk to her, but what more could he say? What would his father have said? *You can't go. I forbid it.* Except that George wasn't her father. He wasn't even much of a brother. He fumbled in his pocket for a cigarette, then remembered where he was. There'd be hell to pay if his mother smelled smoke on his clothes.

He'd met WAVEs in the navy—stateside, before he shipped out. He remembered a particular dance at Norfolk that seemed to be crawling with them. He had tagged along with a couple of buddies, flush with beer and springtime and weekend freedom. They were green then, unaccustomed to drinking. It had struck them as comical to see girls in uniform; they'd complained loudly that the uniform skirt was too long. He thought of Joyce's skinny legs, her bony knees covered with childhood scars, like a little girl's.

He went around to the back of the house. The small yard was in need of mowing. His brother Sandy sat on the back steps, bouncing a ball off the sidewalk, his skinny arms burned brown by the sun.

"Whatcha doing?" said George.

Sandy turned. His hair was pale as corn-silk, his blue eyes startlingly clear. *Like Daddy's,* George thought.

"Come on." He fished in his pocket for his keys. "Let's go for a ride."

They drove through the center of town and out the other side. George accelerated at the bottom of Indian Hill. A stand at the top sold frozen custard. It was a good-enough excuse for a drive.

Sandy fiddled with the radio, pressing the dial tabs. Each tab corresponded with a jazz station in Philadelphia; in Bakerton they yielded only static. Finally he located KBKR, the town's AM station. The Benny Goodman Orchestra was playing "Moonglow."

George wanted to laugh. *Nothing happens here,* he thought. *Nothing ever changes.* Years had passed, the world had been transformed by war, and still Bakerton was listening to "Moonglow."

"That's an oldie," he told Sandy. "I remember it from when I was in high school."

Sandy nodded politely.

"What grade are you in now? Seventh?" He was ashamed he didn't know.

"Sixth. I got left back."

"Nobody told me that." George glanced at him. "What happened? Did you fail a subject?"

"English and arithmetic. Miss Peale," he added, as though that explained it.

"That dinosaur? She must be a hundred years old."

Sandy laughed, pleased. "She's not so bad. Anyways, it wasn't her fault. I didn't try very hard," he said cheerfully.

At the top of the hill George pulled into the parking lot. He thought of his father, who'd drilled Dorothy on multiplication tables until she cried. He wondered who had taught Sandy the multiplication tables. Nobody, he guessed.

They got out of the car and stood at the window. George ordered two vanilla cones.

"Thank you," Sandy said politely. He ate quickly, like a dog gobbling its food.

"Sandy," George asked. "What do you remember about Daddy?"

The boy stared.

"Anything?"

Sandy pondered this a long time. "I remember the funeral," he said at last. "There was a big snowstorm. After church, Mama let me take out my sled."

They were standing there eating their custard when a woman approached, pushing an empty stroller, holding a baby on her hip. It was a moment before George recognized her. Her red hair was tied back with a kerchief, and she had filled out some. Her breasts were twice the size he remembered—the few times he'd worked up the nerve to touch them, they had barely filled his hands. Only her face was the same. She still looked eighteen years old.

"Ev," he called out.

"Georgie?" She looked stunned, flushed from the exertion of pushing the stroller up the hill. Her hand went to her hair. "I can't believe it's you."

They embraced briefly, an awkward moment as she shifted the baby to her other hip. The child wore a blue sailor suit. His mouth had left a wet stain on Ev's blouse. Their hair, George noticed, was the same shade of red.

"Who's this fellow?" he asked.

"Leonard." She smoothed the baby's hair. "We named him for Gene's dad. He was two in March."

"March," George repeated. Against his will he found himself counting off the months. Gene had come home from France in the summer. He and Ev hadn't wasted any time.

"What are you doing in town?" she asked.

"In for a visit." His custard was beginning to melt. He was aware of it dripping onto his hand. "How've you been?" And then: "How's Gene?"

Her blush intensified. "He's home sleeping. He's on Hoot Owl. At the Twelve." She smiled nervously. "I hear you're going to medical school."

"Not yet. There's a bunch more classes I have to take first. I have a long ways to go." He fumbled in his pocket for a napkin. "Where are you living these days?"

"We have an apartment over Bellavia's."

"No kidding," said George. His grandparents had lived on the same block, above Rizzo's Tavern.

"My dad had a fit," said Ev. " 'What are you doing over there with the Eye-talians?' "

she mimicked. "But honestly, Georgie, they couldn't be nicer. Well, *you* know."

He smiled. She had always made a special effort with his mother. He'd been grateful for it.

"Well, I should get going. He's a little fussy." She bent and placed the squirming child in the stroller. "It was nice seeing you, Georgie. I'll tell Gene you said hello."

He watched her push the stroller up the hill. Her broad behind was shaped like an upside-down heart. He'd spent his adolescence imagining her naked, or trying to; he'd come up with a picture that was part Ev, part Betty Grable—to his mind, exactly how a girl should look. The picture was hazy now; Marion had erased it with her long belly, her sleek thighs. Ev's small-town beauty was no longer what he wanted. She belonged in that apartment above Bellavia's, in the life she'd chosen when she picked Gene over him. He no longer blamed her for that. If anything, he was grateful. Whether she knew it or not, he owed his life to Ev. Her betrayal had allowed him to escape.

"Come on," he told Sandy. "Let's hit the road."

It wasn't until later, driving down Indian Hill, that a thought occurred to him. He hadn't even told her he was married.

He woke early the next morning, dressed and headed downstairs. His mother stood in the foyer, pinning a scarf over her hair. He went back upstairs. Marion lay on her side, breathing deeply.

"Honey," he whispered. "Honey." He touched her shoulder, gently at first. She gave a low moan.

"Marion, wake up."

She stirred slightly, then opened one eye.

"Get dressed, darling. It's time for church."

"Tired," she said.

"What's the matter? Did you take a pill?" He got up and rummaged through her overnight bag: cigarettes, cosmetics, her diaphragm in its blue plastic case. *Why'd she bring that thing?* he wondered. *Did she really think she would need it?*

Finally he found the bottle. For years she'd had trouble sleeping; her doctor had prescribed a sedative, which she took several times a week. She'd been awake at dawn; George had heard her in the bathroom. If she'd taken a pill at that hour, she might easily sleep half the day.

She rolled over onto her back, naked. A moment later she began to snore. George dressed and closed the door behind him.

"Marion's not feeling well," he told his mother in the kitchen. "She won't be coming to church."

Rose eyed him suspiciously. "Georgie, you want to tell me something?"

"What do you mean?"

"Your wife. She going to have a baby?"

He thought of the diaphragm in its case. His faced warmed. "No, Mama. Why would you think that?"

Rose shrugged elaborately. "How come you get married so fast? And now she don't feel good in the morning."

She's doped up on sleeping pills, he thought but didn't say. Having his mother think Marion was pregnant, while embarrassing, was preferable to the truth.

Rose smiled broadly, her face flushed with delight. "She don't eat enough. She got to eat more."

"I'll tell her," said George.

* * *

When they came home from church Marion was waiting for them on the porch swing.

She wore the same clothes as the day before, but at least she'd combed her hair and put on lipstick. Her eyes were puffy from sleep.

"Good morning," said George. "I thought you'd still be asleep."

"I am." Her skin looked slightly gray. Across the street, a car was parked in front of the Stusicks'. George wondered if it belonged to Gene, if he'd brought Ev and the baby to his mother's for Sunday dinner.

From inside came the metallic clang of pots and pans, Rose and Joyce bustling around the kitchen. Marion rubbed her temples. "Dear God, what is all that clatter?"

"Dinner." A Bakerton girl would have risen to help, but coming from Marion, the gesture would have been ridiculous. Her kitchen skills were limited to opening a wine bottle.

"I hope you're hungry," he said.

"At this hour? I couldn't eat a bite."

"Try," said George. "Please."

"Why on earth?"

"My mother thinks you're pregnant."

Marion hooted, a shrill laugh that ended in a cough. "Oh, that's delightful."

He felt his pulse in his temples. "What's so funny?"

"Oh, George. You're not serious, are you?" She stared. "For heaven's sake, do I look like the maternal type?"

George smiled uncertainly. He'd never given much thought to children, and Marion had seemed equally indifferent. Since the wedding she'd continued using her diaphragm, at least most of the time. He took that to mean her attitude was casual. *If it happens, it happens,* he'd told himself.

Now he thought—he couldn't help it—of Ev, the red-haired child she'd made with Gene.

"Come on," he teased. "Girls always say that. Then when the baby comes it's a different story."

Marion did not smile.

"Well, we don't have to think about it right now," he said carefully. "Let's just play it by ear." He pushed off with his feet; the swing rocked gently. "Oh, I forgot to tell you," he said, as though it had just occurred to him. "I ran into someone the other day. That girl

I told you about, who wrote me letters when I was overseas."

"Evelyn Picnic," said Marion.

"Lipnic."

"Lipnic." She rubbed at her temples. He knew what she was thinking: *Dear God, these names.*

"Don't you want to know what happened?" he teased.

Marion laughed. "Nothing happened. If something had, you wouldn't be telling me about it."

His smile faded. He'd hoped, for a moment, to make her jealous. Now he saw that she was only amused. As brief as it had been, as frenzied and passionate, their courtship had left him no time for reflection. Marion had bewitched him completely: her beauty and sophistication, her withering intelligence, the absolute self-containment that disappeared—ferociously, deliriously—in bed. She seemed a different species from his mother and his sisters, from Evelyn Lipnic; she was unlike any woman he had ever known. Yet now that she was his, a question had begun to nag at him: What did Marion see in him?

"You're right," he said. "There's nothing to

tell. She wrote me a few letters when I was overseas. I wasn't too good about answering. Then I came home on furlough and found out she was engaged." *To my best friend,* he could have added, but didn't. He still believed in keeping things simple.

"That's all?" She sounded disappointed.

"Yep. Half the guys in the navy could tell you the same kind of story." He rose. "I'm going to see if they need any help in the kitchen." He bent and kissed her cheek. "Try and work up an appetite."

George watched his mother pile Marion's plate: homemade macaroni with sardines and tomatoes, fried cauliflower breaded with cornmeal.

"Georgie, did I tell you?" his mother asked. "Your sister Joyce, she going to the air force."

George glanced quickly at Joyce. They hadn't spoken since their conversation on the porch. Last night at dinner, and this morning at church, she had avoided his eyes.

"You think it's okay?" his mother asked.

Joyce rose and filled her glass at the sink. "Mama, don't put him on the spot. It's got nothing to do with him." She turned to face him. "Let's just have a nice visit. Give him a chance to tell us about his wedding."

George met her gaze. The implication was clear: *Back me up, or I'll tell her everything.*

"It's a big decision," he said carefully. "There's a lot to consider."

His mother nodded agreement. "*Ecco.* I think maybe she wait a little while. If she want to, she could go next year."

"Next *year*? A whole *year*?" Joyce's face reddened. Her eyes met George's.

"Just a minute," he said hastily. "Let's look at this rationally. What's the alternative? Can she find a job here in town for a year?"

"She could go in the factory," said Rose.

"Mama! That place is a graveyard. Remember how miserable Dorothy was there? Georgie, tell her." Her voice vibrated with emotion, her desperation to get away. *Why should she have to stay?* George thought. *If I can leave, why not her?*

"Mama, it'll be okay," he said finally.

"Joyce is a tough girl. I'm sure she can handle whatever they throw at her."

He took his plate to the sink, squeezing her shoulder as he passed. A bony little shoulder, fragile as a cat's.

George and marion left early the next morning. His mother and Joyce stood on the porch, watching them go. He waved from the window as the Chevy rolled down the hill. Marion rummaged through her pocketbook for a cigarette.

"Oh, God," she said, inhaling deeply. "God, that's good."

"Don't be so dramatic," George said.

Her eyebrows shot up. "As if you haven't been craving one yourself."

"I'm fine. What's the big deal? It's just a couple of days."

Marion laughed, a throaty chuckle. "Oh, please. You don't fool me. You've been dying for one all morning." She handed him the pack; he flipped open a Zippo from his pocket. The sound was oddly soothing. He inhaled deeply.

They crossed the railroad tracks and continued on through the town: Mount Carmel Church, where his Scarponi cousins had been baptized; the apartment above Rizzo's Tavern, where his grandparents had lived. At the corner, the Baker Brothers bus—an old school bus painted dark green—had stopped to let off passengers. He watched them cross the street, black-faced men carrying dinner buckets, heading home to sleep off eight hours of Hoot Owl. He wondered if Gene Stusick was among them, coming home from the Twelve, climbing the fire escape behind Bellavia's Bakery to the apartment he shared with Ev.

He glanced over at Marion, smoking quietly, her long legs crossed at the knee, coolly elegant in her pale blue suit.

"Come on," he said, accelerating at a yellow light. "Let's get out of here."

FOUR

The town grew.

Baker Twelve was mined around the clock. By its third year it employed six hundred men, two hundred per shift. At dawn, and at midafternoon, and again late in the evening, cars idled at the new bridge that had been built across the Susquehanna. White-faced men in the westbound lane, heading toward the tipple. Black-faced ones in the eastbound lane, driving home from their shifts.

Baker Towers grew taller and broader, their shape softly conical, like a child's sand castle. In time they took over the old rail yard, where the coal cars had been loaded before the new depot was built. Rain eroded them. In winter they resembled alpine peaks. Each week they were fortified

with truckloads of black dirt, the rocky en-
trails of the One, the Three, the mighty
Twelve. In the summer of 1950, the Pennsylvania Department of Industry sent a field
technician to measure the piles. It was the
lead story in that week's *Bakerton Herald,*
the triumphant headline in two-inch letters:
SIXTY FEET!

On a good day the air smelled of match-
sticks; on a bad day, rotten eggs. When the
local thundered down Saxon Mountain, its
passengers held their breath. On breezy
days the whole town closed its windows,
but no one ever complained. In later years
this would seem remarkable, but at the time
people thought differently. The sulfurous
odor meant union wages and two weeks'
paid vacation, meat on the table, presents
under the Christmas tree.

The *Herald* increased its frequency to
twice a week. More was happening, and
more often, than a weekly paper could possibly report. The grammar school enrolled
its largest class ever; the children shared
desks and readers. A trailer was brought in
to handle the overflow. A year later, a second one was parked behind the school.

A few things did not grow. In 1951, the

Pennsylvania Railroad ended passenger service to Bakerton. After the war, business had dwindled. Nearly every family in town owned a car. Some people minded: those too young to drive or too old to learn, women like Evelyn Stusick whose husbands refused to teach them. Still, the coal trains continued to rumble through the town, reminding the old-timers of what had been lost.

A Town Improvement Committee was formed. They agreed at their first meeting that everything needed improving; the question was where to begin. A referendum was held to rank possible improvements in order of importance. The list included a water treatment plant, a public library, a job training center, housing for veterans, and a maternity wing for the hospital. Space was left for write-in suggestions, in case there was anything the committee had missed.

The referendum was held, the votes tallied.

That summer, a new baseball park was built.

Joyce Novak came home in September, in the last brilliant week of summer: hot afternoons fading early, the morning grass touched with dew. She had left on just such a day. The coincidence made the last four years of her life seem imaginary, the vivid dream of a late-afternoon nap.

But Joyce did not nap; for her, daylight made sleep impossible. On the train ride from Charlotte to Washington, the longer one from Washington to Harrisburg to Altoona, she stared out the window as the other passengers snored around her. With her she brought a hatbox and a suitcase full of civilian clothes, the skirts and blouses she'd worn as a teenager. In her pocketbook was a packet of letters from her friend Irene Jevic. Except for the letters and the hat, she'd acquired nothing in her years away.

Sandy met her train at the station in Altoona. They embraced awkwardly. He had grown four inches that year. His cheek felt rough against hers. *He shaves now,* she thought.

She followed him to where the car was parked. He had borrowed it from the Poblockis up the hill. "Does Mama know you're driving?" she asked. He was only fifteen.

He backed smoothly out of the parking space, one elbow hanging out the window. "Sure." He grinned. "It's fine by her. She doesn't even know you need a license."

They drove past the diocesan cathedral, the bus station, Gable's department store. Growing up, she'd considered Altoona a major city. Now she saw that it was just another town.

Sandy downshifted smoothly at a light. "Who taught you to drive?" she asked.

"Nobody. I just picked it up."

"Picked it up where? On whose car?"

"Everybody has a car. Everybody but us."

They rode in silence, the lights of the town disappearing behind them. The sky had begun to darken; the road wound narrowly. On either side of it the corn had been cut.

"I can't believe you're back," Sandy said. "You're not really going to stay, are you?"

"Mama needs me." She hesitated, not sure how much to tell him. She studied his handsome profile, the blond forelock curling over his forehead like some exotic plumage.

"You need a haircut," she observed.

Sandy shrugged. "I like it this way."

Twilight was falling as they came into town. A new traffic light had been hung at the corner of Main and Susquehanna, another at the bottom of the hill. A horn sounded in the distance. At the crossing they waited for the train to pass. A string of traffic formed behind them, headlamps bright in the rearview mirror.

"So many cars," said Joyce.

"It's quitting time." Sandy glanced over his shoulder. "They're going to West Branch. There's a bunch of new houses out by the Twelve."

They drove through the town and crossed the tracks to Polish Hill. A chorus of dogs announced their arrival: the tenor bark of beagles, the deeper baying of Ted Poblocki's hounds. Sandy parked and honked the horn. The house looked small and shabby. The grass hadn't been cut in weeks.

The front door opened. Rose appeared, barefoot, on the porch. She had grown fat; her hair was almost totally gray. She descended the steps carefully, as though her knees pained her. Joyce felt a weight in her stomach, as if she'd swallowed something heavy. *She's getting old,* she thought. Her mother had worn the same housedresses since Joyce was a child. Seeing her change in any way was deeply unsettling.

She got out of the car and filled her lungs with the cool air, then accepted her mother's embrace, an ordeal to get through as quickly as possible. Joyce had a horror of crying; tears caused her nearly physical pain. When she felt them coming—the warning ache in her throat—she rebuked herself with a single word: *Don't.* A bald command, suitable for a dog, but it generally worked. She hadn't cried in years.

"So thin!" her mother exclaimed. She'd said this every time Joyce came home on furlough, though her weight hadn't changed since basic training.

Sandy leaned out the car window. "I'm

going to drop this wreck off to the Poblockis. I'll be right back."

Joyce watched the car pull away, thinking, *He shouldn't be driving without a license.* But that—like the shaggy lawn, the cracked pane in the front window—could wait until later. There was already so much to fix.

Her little sister appeared in the front doorway. Her plaid jumper was tight across her belly. Her glossy black hair hung in a braid down her back.

"*Bella* Lucy," said Rose. "Come and say hello."

The girl hesitated a moment, then came down the porch stairs. She walked awkwardly, thighs touching, her calves slightly bowed.

"Hi, honey," said Joyce, clasping her briefly. The words sounded strange to her; she couldn't remember the last time she'd called someone that.

The house was smaller than she'd remembered; it seemed incredible that her entire family had once lived there. The first floor had three rooms: a parlor, a dining room—never used for dining—and a large kitchen. Upstairs were three bedrooms and a tiny bath. The summer before his death, her father had hauled away the outhouse and installed the tub and toilet himself.

Joyce glanced around the rooms, noticing everything. The parlor furniture was worn and threadbare. There was another cracked window in the kitchen, patched with electrical tape.

She sat at the kitchen table while her mother reheated a plate of spaghetti. She wasn't hungry, but refusing was more trouble than it was worth.

"How are you feeling, Mama?"

Rose's eyes darted in Lucy's direction. "Go and play, *bella,*" she said, handing her a macaroon from the jar.

Joyce waited until Lucy had disappeared into the parlor. "Did you make an appointment?" she asked.

Rose dismissed this with a wave, as though no doctor were worth the extraordinary bother of making a telephone call.

"I'll go uptown and call tomorrow." Joyce accepted the plate, twice as much spaghetti as she could possibly eat.

"And Mama," she said. "Isn't it time we got a phone?"

*   *   *

She slept in her childhood bed, the mattress bowed in the spots where she and Dorothy had slept. Sandy occupied Georgie's old room. Lucy—as she had her whole life—shared a bed with her mother. In the morning the house smelled of breakfast, scrambled eggs and fried toast. Her mother still kept hens, in the coop Joyce's father had built.

The mornings were damp, smelling of fall. From the front porch Joyce watched the neighborhood children walking to school, girls in loafers and plaid skirts, carrying stacks of books. A strange sadness filled her. Her own girlhood had passed too quickly. She felt older than she was, lost and depleted. Nothing had turned out the way she'd planned.

Each morning she slept late, then walked to town for the newspaper. *Reds Vote Japs Out of U.N. Senator Nixon Denies Wrongdoing, Admits Gift of Dog.* The world seemed very far away.

One morning she walked across town to the Bell Telephone office, paid a deposit, and brought home a telephone. She had dressed in her uniform; walking down Main Street, she felt the gaze of shopkeepers, old women, night miners coming home from the Twelve. A man watched her cross at the corner. He turned and spoke to his buddy in a low voice, and laughed. Later, at home, Joyce hung her uniform at the back of her closet. She never wore it again.

She'd been a girl when she left, barely eighteen; she had committed herself to military life with a certainty that now seemed childish. She'd tried to convince Irene Jevic to enlist with her. Like Joyce she had no money, no boyfriend, no prospects; they both seemed destined for the dress factory. Irene's sister worked there already. In a few years the place had transformed her into a stout matron with eyeglasses, broad in the behind from too much sitting, plagued by headaches and eyestrain. An example that should have persuaded anybody, in Joyce's view; but Irene was both timid and stubborn. Only one argument could convince her. "There must be a hundred boys for every girl in the air force," Joyce told her. "If you can't find a fellow there, you might as well give up."

Irene agreed, but lost her nerve, and in

the end Joyce rode the bus alone to the induction center halfway across the state. The ride itself was a revelation; except for a class trip to an amusement park near Pittsburgh, Joyce had never left Saxon County. In her small suitcase was a leatherbound copy of *Pride and Prejudice,* the only book she'd ever owned. It was a going-away present from Miss Peale, who'd inscribed the flyleaf in the careful loops of the Palmer method: *Good books are good friends. From your friend and teacher, Viola Peale.* Joyce had read it in a single day. The story itself—a convoluted tale of young women scheming to find husbands—did not impress her. Of all the books ever written, she wondered why Miss Peale had chosen this one for her.

Poor Miss Peale. She'd seemed stunned when Joyce told her the news. "The air force?" she'd repeated, as if she'd never heard of it. "Joyce, are you sure?"

"It's a fine opportunity for a young woman." She'd been told this by the recruiter and had repeated it to her entire family.

"But it seems so—*drastic.*"

"I've given it a lot of thought," Joyce as-sured her. The reaction disappointed but did not surprise her. Her mother, Dorothy, even her brother Georgie had failed to understand. There was no reason to think Miss Peale would be different.

Later, she saw that she hadn't explained it properly. She wasn't like Georgie, desperate to leave Bakerton; if she'd merely wanted to escape her hometown, any sort of job would have sufficed. File clerk or factory girl. Cleaning houses for money—or, if she managed to find a husband, for free. But Joyce longed to devote herself to something of consequence; of the paths open to her, only the military seemed meaningful enough. She was a Bakerton girl with no education and no prospects. Serving her country was her only chance, the only way her life could ever be important.

She'd considered herself, if not born to it, then raised for it. In every important way, the war had defined her childhood. Of all the Novak children, only Joyce had spent her evenings in the parlor with their father, listening to Lowell Thomas: the bombings and casualties, the daily movements of troops. As a youngster, she'd saved her gum wrappers, valuable sources of aluminum. Though she hated knitting, she'd made afghan squares for the Red Cross. Later, in junior high, she'd organized twice-yearly collection drives, gone door-to-door asking for old tires, used pots and pans, anything made of metal or rubber or tin. She was a proud girl, and begging was not in her character; but she had done the work gladly. Her small humiliation was nothing compared to the sacrifices of the soldiers. The same sacrifices she would make later, as an adult.

She was sixteen when the war ended, almost ready to enter the world. After the initial joy of the surrender, she was at a loss. Working in an office as Dorothy did, or in a store like Georgie, would have seemed a capitulation. Her whole life she'd imagined her future in uniform. She couldn't picture it any other way.

One afternoon, coming out of the butcher shop in Little Italy, Joyce glimpsed a short, stout figure in a familiar plaid coat.

"Irene!" she called.

The girl turned and broke into a grin. The two friends embraced, laughing and exclaiming. For the first time in weeks, Joyce felt at home.

"Good to see you, stranger," she teased. "Did you lose my address? I thought you fell off the planet." She linked her arm through Irene's. "Come on. Let's go have a pastry at Bellavia's. My treat."

"Joyce, I can't," Irene stammered. "I need to get home." Her watery blue eyes were bloodshot. There was a roll of extra flesh beneath her chin.

"Not even for a minute?" Joyce looked at

her closely, shocked by how she'd changed. Irene wore rimless eyeglasses, and the left side of her face looked swollen. To Joyce she looked forty years old.

"Irene," she said softly. "Is everything all right?"

"I have a toothache." Her hand went to her cheek. "It's driving me crazy. And I'm kind of in a hurry. I should have been home at four. My mother's going to wonder what happened to me."

"Are you still working at the station?" After graduation, Irene had been hired to answer phones at KBKR. The pay was lousy, she'd written, but it kept her in lipstick and movie tickets.

"Oh, no. I quit that ages ago. I'm at the factory now. Listen, I have to run." She gave Joyce's elbow a squeeze. "When do you head back to North Carolina?" She started down the street, not waiting for an answer.

"It's great to see you," she called over her shoulder. "I'll try and stop by the house before you leave town."

Joyce watched her go. *The factory,* she thought wonderingly. A few years ago, Irene had been as horrified by the place as Joyce was. Now she'd quit a perfectly good desk job and—if Joyce was any judge—would work in the factory for the rest of her life. Bakerton did this to people: slowly, invisibly, it made them smaller, compressed by living where little was possible, where the ceiling was so very low. Joyce thought of her father, a big man whom Bakerton had diminished. After thirty years of mining he'd walked with a stoop. Once, to show her how he spent his workday, he'd crouched on his hands and knees beneath the kitchen table, the contorted posture of a miner in low coal.

How can I stay here? Joyce thought. *How much smaller can I get?*

"Tell me what you see."

The doctor spoke in a deep voice. Joyce caught her mother's eye, nodding encouragement. Rose was shy around strangers, self-conscious about her accent. The gaze of a stranger, a man especially, could render her speechless.

"Flashes of light," Joyce interjected. "And her vision is blurred."

"It's like I look at everything through a veil," Rose added.

The doctor made a note in a folder.

"Does she need glasses?" Joyce asked.

"No," he said curtly. "That wouldn't help." He turned to Rose. "Have you been tired lately?"

"Sometimes," she said softly.

"Any unusual thirst?"

Joyce thought of her mother standing at the sink, drinking two tall glasses of water, one after the other. She had never considered this odd. Rose had done it for years.

"Have you gained or lost weight?"

Rose explained, haltingly, that she cooked too much since the children had left. If she'd gained a few pounds, that must be why.

In the end a nurse came to draw blood. "What's the problem?" Joyce asked the doctor.

"I won't know for certain until I see the test results, but I suspect that your mother is diabetic." Briefly he explained the nature of the disease: a problem with the pancreas, a hormone it failed to secrete.

"But what does that have to do with her eyes?"

He explained that diabetes puts stress on all the organs: the kidneys, the heart. The eyes were particularly vulnerable. "There's another doctor she should see." He wrote a name on a card. "His name is Lucas. He's an eye specialist in Pittsburgh."

Joyce took the card. She had never been to Pittsburgh in her life.

"One more thing," said the doctor. "Mrs. Novak, could you take off your shoes?"

Rose bent and unbuckled them. The doctor reached for her foot and held it in his lap. He took a wooden tongue depressor from the table behind him and ran it along the sole of her foot.

"Can you feel this?" he asked.

Rose nodded.

"What about this?" He prodded her skin with the end of the stick, then repeated the test on her other foot.

"Diabetes can affect sensation in the extremities," he explained. "Your mother might cut herself and not feel it, and the consequences could be serious. Diabetics are prone to infection, and their wounds don't heal normally. What would be a minor abrasion in a healthy person could become gangrenous. The patient could end up losing a foot."

"Is that common?" Joyce asked, horrified.

"It's not uncommon. I've seen cases." He turned to Rose. "I don't mean to scare you, Mrs. Novak. But it's important that you take care of your feet."

Rose leaned close to Joyce and whispered into her ear.

"My mother has a question," said Joyce. "Is there some kind of medicine she can take?"

"I'm afraid not. There are no easy treatments for diabetes. The most important thing is to keep an eye on her diet. No sweets. Cut back on bread and starches." He reached into a drawer and handed Joyce a printed leaflet. "If she lost some weight along the way, that certainly wouldn't hurt."

Joyce took the paper. It was a list of foods, with calorie counts.

"Diabetes is a serious illness," said the doctor. "Your mother will have to be very careful. If she can control her diet, it will add years to her life."

Later, at home, Joyce made a tour of the yard, a pad and paper in hand. Two broken windows. The back screen door was nearly off its hinges. The front porch had several rotten floorboards. Someone as heavy as her mother could easily step right through.

She went around to the cellar door, down the steps to the basement. Water pooled near a crack in the foundation, another item to add to her list. The shelves were loaded with canned peppers and tomatoes, boxes of empty Ball jars. Broken glass crunched beneath her shoes. She thought of Rose in her bare feet, placing the jars on the shelves. How easily, and how often, she might drop a jar.

Her father's toolbox was where he'd left it, on a low table in the corner. Joyce knew from her mother that Georgie seldom visited—he was busy with his fancy wife, his baby son, his job at the department store. When he did come to Bakerton, it clearly never occurred to him to fix anything. The toolbox was covered with dust.

She pried open the rusted latch. Inside, the tools were neatly stacked. One by one she lifted them out: hammers, wrenches, a framing square, several pairs of pliers. Exquisite, heavy tools, handmade by her uncle Casimir, who'd forged wheels for mining cars during the day and worked nights in his own blacksmith shop. The wooden grips were worn smooth from use. From her father's hands. Tears stung at her eyes. She closed the box.

The upstairs door squeaked open. She heard footsteps on the stairs.

"Joyce?" Her little sister stood in the doorway to the kitchen, a macaroon in her hand.

"Don't come down here. There's broken glass on the floor."

Lucy took another step. She peered into the dimness. "Why are you crying?"

"I'm not." Joyce turned away. "Go back upstairs."

The door closed. Joyce fumbled in her pocket for a handkerchief. Her hands were dirty from the tools. *I must look a sight,* she thought. Carefully she replaced the tools. She blew her nose and went out through the cellar door.

She had come home to help her mother. That was the explanation she'd given her superior officer, her few friends in the service; it was the story she'd told herself. Rose's letter—*I don't feel so good. Every day I get a headache. I think maybe I need glasses.*—had come at a convenient time. She hadn't asked for help. Joyce had simply volunteered. She was disillusioned with military life, fed up and furious; and here was an escape route, a way to save herself without losing face. A sick mother—she was ashamed to admit it, but she had even liked the sound of that. Explaining the situation to her CO, she'd felt noble and high-minded. She hadn't stopped to consider whether any of it was true.

She thought of the games she and Dorothy had played as children: hide-and-seek, blindman's bluff, duck-duck-goose. At the beginning of the game all players were equal, and anything was possible—every kid in the neighborhood running breathless and excited, like bees humming around a hive. Then someone found you, or pointed you out, or slapped your sweaty back, and like it or not, you were it.

Georgie and Dorothy had escaped the hand—whether through speed or calculation, or just the simple dumb luck of being older, Joyce couldn't say. But the hand had landed on her shoulder. She, apparently, was it.

Duck, duck, goose.

* * *

The eye specialist was booked until November. Joyce took the first appointment available, a Friday morning, the day after Thanksgiving. At the drugstore she bought a road map of Pennsylvania and spread it before her on the counter. She located Pittsburgh immediately, an agglomeration of bright yellow at the southwest corner of the state. Bakerton was harder to find, the name in faint italicized letters, the smallest typeface on the map.

She set out early the next morning, in sturdy shoes. In half an hour she had reached the edge of town, where a car dealership had just opened. She stood in the lot a moment, looking around uncertainly.

A boy in a suit approached her. "Can I help you, ma'am?" He was tall and gangly, his face studded with pimples. He looked barely old enough to drive.

"I need to buy a car." She pointed to a blue sedan at the edge of the lot. "How much is that one?"

"That Plymouth over there?"

"Yes," she said. "The Plymouth."

He named a figure that seemed impossible. She had a small savings account, where she'd deposited her last check from the air force.

"That's more than I can afford," she said, embarrassed. Her own discomfort irritated her. *Brush it off,* she thought. *He's just a kid. Who cares what he thinks?*

"Do you have one less expensive?"

He pointed to a smaller car. "That Rambler is four hundred dollars. It's second-hand, but it runs good. You want to take it for a test drive?"

She looked him in the eye. "I don't know how to drive."

He stared at her, mystified. "Then what do you need a car for?"

Mentally she ticked off a list: the Wojick boys, the half-bright Poblockis, her brother Sandy, who'd "just picked it up." Every male on Polish Hill knew how to drive. How difficult could it be?

"I'll learn," she said.

The bank was bustling that morning. Tellers stood at their windows, silently counting. A half-dozen customers waited in line. Joyce approached a window.

"I'd like to fill out a job application," she said.

The teller, a short round-faced man, eyed her briefly. "Hang on a second." He resumed counting, then wrote a figure on a scrap of paper. He placed the paper atop the stack and wrapped it with a rubber band.

"Stiffler," he said to the man at the next window. "This lady wants to fill out a job application."

Two men turned in her direction. One, Irving Stiffler, was her brother's age; he'd come back from the war missing a foot. Joyce had seen him around town and was amazed by how well he walked, with only a slight limp.

"Hello, Joyce," Stiffler said, nodding. "You'll have to talk to the manager. Have a seat, and I'll tell him you're here."

Joyce sat on the vinyl sofa near the window, aware of the silence in the room. In a moment the clerks resumed counting. Two men in overalls came in the front door. The bank opened early on Friday mornings to accommodate the miners, the Hoot Owl crews who stopped to cash paychecks on their way home from work.

Half an hour passed. Finally, a portly man in shirtsleeves came toward her. He eyed her uncertainly, then sat beside her on the sofa, hitching up his trousers to preserve their creases. "What kind of a job are you looking for?"

"Secretarial," she said. "I type seventy-five words a minute. I can do just about anything involved with running an office."

"Have you tried over at the factory?"

She blinked. He seemed not to have heard her. She tried again. "Actually, what I'm looking for is an office job. A teller position would be ideal."

He scratched his head. "The thing is, we generally don't hire girls for those jobs. We did years ago, during the war, but these fellows"—he gestured with a nod of his head—"are all veterans."

"I see." She wished, for a moment, that she'd worn her uniform. "I'm just out of the air force, myself."

A smile played at his lips. "Good for you," he said. "But these men are combat veterans—wounded, some of them. With families to support. You can understand that, can't you?"

"Perfectly," she said evenly. "I've got a

family as well, sir. My mother is a widow, and my younger brother and sister are still in school."

The man glanced at his watch. "Well, I can't help you. We aren't hiring right now." He rose. "Try over at the factory," he said again. "Good luck to you, Joyce."

On Saturday afternoon she left the house carrying a tin of macaroons. Her mother baked them every Friday. Unless Joyce watched her closely, she'd eat half of them herself.

The Jevics lived in a dilapidated frame house, a big, barnlike structure near the Number One tipple. Irene was the third of ten children; every few years, it seemed, her father built another bedroom onto the house. As a little girl, Joyce had been intimidated by the place, not just its size but its strangeness. All her other friends had lived in company houses—three rooms upstairs, three rooms down. It had never occurred to her that a house could be built any other way.

In the Jevics' backyard, boys ran and

shouted. Joyce climbed the porch steps and knocked at the front door. She sensed a flurry of activity behind it: a radio playing, a baby crying, tiny voices raised in anger or joy. Then Irene's mother opened the door, a dark-haired baby on her hip.

"Joyce Novak!" She held the door open. "For God's sake, I didn't know you were back."

Joyce stepped inside. Shrill voices in the next room, the excited chatter of little girls. "I brought you some macaroons. I remember how you liked them."

"You're a sweet girl. Those Eyetalian cookies are delicious." Mrs. Jevic shifted the baby to her other hip. She was a big, red-faced woman with wide, startled-looking eyes, the same watery blue as Irene's.

She led Joyce to the kitchen. "Irene's at the dentist, having that tooth pulled. She'll be back any minute. Sit down and have some tea."

Joyce sat at the table, its Formica top extended with a plywood leaf. Bottles and rubber nipples dried on a towel by the sink. Beside the back door was a metal washtub, overflowing with different-size shoes. The place was as chaotic as a kindergarten.

"Have you met little Susan?" Mrs. Jevic asked, smoothing the baby's hair.

"No," said Joyce. "She's adorable. How old is she?"

"A year next month." Mrs. Jevic filled the teapot with water. Susan squirmed and let out a squeal.

"Here we go again," said Mrs. Jevic. "You won't be quiet—will you?—until your mother comes home."

Your mother? Joyce thought.

Mrs. Jevic wiped her hands on a tea towel. Then she saw Joyce's face.

"You didn't know?" She spoke rapidly, in a low voice. "Heavens to Betsy, I thought the whole town knew. She's Irene's baby."

The kitchen seemed very warm. Sweat trickled down Joyce's back. "I had no idea." Her voice came out in a whisper. "Irene never said a word."

"Well, she's ashamed, of course. Can you blame her?" Mrs. Jevic sat heavily in a chair. "She's had a hard couple years. Don't get me wrong—I don't excuse what she did. But she's paid the price, I can tell you that."

Joyce swallowed. "What about—the father?"

"An Eyetalian boy. No offense." Mrs. Jevic checked the baby's diaper. "He skipped town the minute she told him. He could be anywhere by now. And his mother's a real witch. She won't have anything to do with Susan. She blames it all on Irene."

There were footsteps on the porch. Then the screen door slammed.

"Irene!" Mrs. Jevic called. "Joyce Novak is here."

Joyce's heart quickened. She wished, absurdly, for a place to hide. *What do I say to her?* she thought frantically.

They waited a moment.

"Irene?" Mrs. Jevic called.

She rose and glanced out the window.

"That's strange," she said. "Looks like she went back up the street."

Joyce walked home, her hands in her pockets. The air had turned cold. She'd waited another half hour, but Irene hadn't returned. "I'll come back another time," she told Mrs. Jevic, after they'd each had two macaroons. She walked quickly, grateful to leave the noisy, overheated house.

Her whole life she'd heard of girls who had to get married; less often, girls sent away to convents, or to live with relatives out of state. At one time she'd believed, childishly, that these girls were wicked. Later she decided they were merely stupid. A boy would try to talk you into anything; he had nothing to lose. It was the girl who took all the risks.

Experience had taught her that life was not so simple. Irene wasn't stupid, just a girl who'd seen too many movies—as Joyce had; as they all had. It was, she reflected, a dangerous pastime, mooning over the handsome, clever men on the screen. It doomed you to disappointment; it made you expect too much. Joyce had never been in love, but felt herself capable of it. She could love Fred Astaire or Clark Gable or Errol Flynn, an elegant, cultivated fellow who wore wonderful clothes and possessed all sorts of hidden talents, who sang and danced and even fought in a way that looked beautiful; who even when he drank was witty and articulate and gentle and wise. The harder job was loving what men really were—soldiers and miners, gruff and ignorant; drunken louts who communicated mainly by cursing, who couldn't tell you anything about life that you didn't already know. That was something Joyce wanted no part of. It seemed to her a waste of love.

Poor Irene. Joyce could imagine easily how it had happened. Stuck in Bakerton, answering phones at the radio station; Irene bored and boy-crazy, starved for attention. An easy mark for a fellow who wanted only one thing.

She crossed the tracks and began the hike up Polish Hill. Halfway up, the sidewalk ended; a narrow path wound alongside the road. The path was safer than the road, quicker than hiking through the woods. Still, it was a rough climb, narrow and winding and littered with red dog. One false step and you'd easily twist an ankle, trip and fall headlong down the steep hill.

Irene, Joyce reflected, had taken a false step, one nobody would let her forget: *I thought the whole town knew.* She herself had stuck to the path. As far as she could tell, it was the only logical route, even though it didn't take her anywhere she wanted to go.

The days grew shorter. By suppertime it was nearly dark. The family ate at the big table in the kitchen. Lucy chattered about her day at school. Sandy hunched silently over his plate. Rose cooked enough for ten: huge vats of minestrone, piles of macaroni, pounds of eggplant baked with cheese. She herself took seconds and sometimes thirds. Joyce reminded her, gently at first: A serving of noodles is two ounces. She had saved the leaflet from the doctor's office and pasted it to the refrigerator door. Finally she bought a scale at the drugstore and meted out the portions herself.

In the evenings they sat together in the parlor: Joyce reading, Lucy doing homework, Rose hemming skirts or trousers by hand. A tailor in town paid her a half-dollar per item. She sewed for ten, twenty minutes at a time, then stopped to rest her eyes.

Years later, looking back, Joyce would try to remember where Sandy spent those evenings. Often he barricaded himself in his room. "Homework," he said, when Joyce asked what he did in there for hours on end. He said it with a twist to his lips, a smart-aleck tone that made her feel foolish. He seemed to be laughing at her.

Some nights a car would park in front of the house and honk its horn. Then Sandy would rumble down the stairs.

"Where are you going?" Joyce would call after him.

"Uptown," he'd answer, slamming the door behind him.

A few times she had gone to the window. Each time a different car—a green Plymouth, a Studebaker sedan—and a different girl. Sandy hopped inside, and the car tore away, scattering gravel. Music from the open windows, a silly song that had been popular that summer: *Rag mop, rag mop.*

* * *

Joyce filled out applications at the phone company and the post office, the grocery store and the five-and-ten. She could run a cash register or serve customers at the candy counter. It wouldn't be ideal, but she could do it. Still nobody called.

A month passed. The weather turned cold. The winter coal was delivered and paid for. Lucy's parochial school tuition came due.

"She could try the public school," Rose said hesitantly, but Joyce disagreed. She herself had graduated Bakerton High and considered her own education lacking. Unlike Sandy, Lucy was a good student. If the town had a better school, she deserved to go there.

In November Joyce went to work at the dress factory.

She was placed on the second floor, collars and facings. In the same department were two of her classmates from high school, Sylvia Fierro and Frances Scalia. Irene Jevic followed the other two like a lost child. Her first day on the job Joyce noticed them in the lunchroom, Sylvia and Frances chattering loudly, Irene chewing silently at her sandwich.

"Hi there," said Joyce, pulling up a chair.

Irene looked stunned. "What are you doing here?"

"Collars and facings. I started this morning."

"Holy cow."

For a long time neither spoke. *"Holy cow" pretty much covers it,* Joyce reflected. There was nothing more to say.

"Sorry I missed you on Saturday," Irene said. "I left my glasses at the dentist's. I had to run back and get them."

"That's okay. I had a nice visit with your mother."

Irene chewed silently at a thumbnail. Her fingernails, Joyce noticed, were bitten to the quick.

"I guess you met Susan." She spoke very quietly; Joyce had to strain to hear her. "My baby sister."

"Yes," said Joyce. "I did."

"The last of the Mohicans." Irene smiled wanly. "With ten brothers and sisters she'll be spoiled rotten. You can imagine."

Joyce thought of the Punnett squares she'd studied in high school biology; then of Irene's parents, with their watery blue eyes. Irene hadn't taken biology. No one had told her that two blue-eyed parents couldn't produce a brown-eyed baby.

"She's a beautiful child," Joyce said.

"I think so, too," said Irene.

Joyce's task, at first glance, was a simple one. She was assigned to a machine and given two piles of fabric—one pile of collars, one pile of facings. She was to stitch a collar to the underside of a facing, then pass the pieces on to Mrs. Purdy, who fitted them into the bodice of a dress at a speed that seemed supernatural. One after another Joyce stitched together the curved bits of fabric, cursing her slowness. Around her the machines roared. The foreman, a big sullen man named Alvin Blick, watched her from the door. Twice she attached the collars backwards. Criminy, she thought. I'll go crazy doing this.

By the end of her second day she had developed a system, a way of laying out the pieces on her table and folding the edges together so that the fabric fed smoothly into the machine. After that the work became automatic, and her mind began to wander.

She remembered the interminable trip to Lackland Air Force Base in San Antonio, three days by train. Basic training; the heat a constant presence, like a sleeping beast. Maneuvers at noon: the malevolent sun, girls collapsing on the parade grounds. The air force had provided salt tablets; the briny water turned her stomach, but still she kept drinking. It was impossible to drink enough. At night she slept deeply, the night loud with bugs. Sometimes, when the factory whistle roused her, she felt she'd traveled a hundred miles. Then she looked up from her machine and saw she hadn't been anywhere at all.

She worked as part of a team. There were four girls who fused collars and facings, three older women who attached the collars to the bodices. To Joyce's left sat Mrs. Purdy's daughter, a big, slow-witted girl named Betty. Though she'd worked there for months, she was clumsier than Joyce. At least twice an hour her thread would break. Several times a day the fabric became caught in her machine. When this happened, Mrs. Purdy would get up from her own machine and lumber over to Betty's. She moved slowly, rheumatism in her knees and back. Only her fingers were fast.

Blick, the foreman, began to notice. "You're getting backed up," he'd yell, and it was true: a pile of collars and facings would accumulate each time Mrs. Purdy left her machine. At those moments Joyce thought of her sister Dorothy, who'd lasted eight months before Alvin Blick fired her. Dorothy was as timid as Betty Purdy; Joyce imagined her trembling like a child whenever Blick glanced in her direction.

He's a bully, she thought. She had strong opinions about bullies. The air force was full of them. She'd spent four years at their mercy.

One day after lunch she returned to her machine early and showed Betty her method for laying out the fabric. "It's quicker this way," she said. She felt Alvin Blick watching them from across the room.

The whistle blew; the women settled at their machines. Later, when Betty's thread broke, Joyce reached over and quickly rethreaded the machine. Mrs. Purdy looked up, surprised.

"Thank you, dear," she whispered.

Joyce became so skilled at rethreading

Betty's machine that she barely rose from
her chair; most times Alvin Blick, busy barking orders at the cutters or glaring at one of
the other girls, didn't even notice. Over time
Betty's thread broke less often; only rarely
did the machine gobble up her fabric. Free
of interruptions, Mrs. Purdy attached collars
to bodices at her usual blistering speed.
Joyce was nearly as fast. In this way their
section became the most efficient on the
floor. The women downstairs, who assembled the bodices before sending them up to
Mrs. Purdy, could scarcely keep up.

Lucy loved all holidays, but Halloween was her favorite. The festivities combined candy and compliments, her two favorite treats. Each year her mother sewed her a special costume. At different times she had been a fairy, a gypsy, a kitten with whiskers and a tail of fake fur. This year she would be Pocahontas, the Indian princess. Her sister Dorothy would come home from Washington especially for the occasion, to braid her long black hair.

In the past her costumes had gotten only two wearings: trick-or-treat in the neighborhood, and the children's costume party in the fire hall uptown. But this year the third grade had an especially nice teacher. A Halloween party would be held Friday morning at school.

On Thursday afternoon Lucy sat at the kitchen table, flattening cookie dough with a rolling pin. Her mother padded around in bare feet, singing along with the radio: "Come on-a My House," in a funny voice that sounded like her aunt Marcella. The song always made Lucy laugh. They were singing together when the back door opened.

"Mama, what are you doing?" Joyce stood in the doorway, her coat over her arm, a pinched expression on her face. A draft filled the kitchen.

"Making cookies." Her mother stood with her back to the oven. "Your sister need them for school."

Joyce sighed.

Lucy stared down at her floury hands, the circle of dough she had rolled flat on the counter. They had cut the dough into different shapes—a witch, a jack-o'-lantern—and dusted them with colored sugar. In between they nibbled at the sweet, buttery dough, which tasted better than the finished cookies.

Her mother took a pan from the oven. "I leave the sugar off these. See? They're not so bad."

"Mama."

"Me, I just bake them. I don't eat none."

Lucy's heart quickened. It was a lie; they had each eaten five or six. Her mother turned on the faucet and scraped at the bar of soap, to clean the black-and-orange sugar from beneath her fingernails.

Joyce turned to Lucy. "Honey, go upstairs and wash your hands. You're all sticky." She smiled then—an afterthought, it seemed to Lucy. Joyce was usually too busy to smile. Busy reading something, cleaning something, folding laundry with more energy than seemed necessary. When she picked clean sheets from the clothesline, the fabric made a whipping noise, like a flag flapping in the wind. She expected Lucy to be busy, too: to red up her room and set the table every night for supper, to gather the eggs each morning before school.

"After that you can start your homework," Joyce called after her. "I'll be up in a minute to see how you're doing."

At the top of the stairs Lucy listened.

"Mama, you can't," said Joyce. "The doctor told you. No more sweets."

"I make for your sister. That school cafeteria, they cut corners. She don't get
enough to eat."

"She doesn't need them either. Lucy is
overweight. She can barely fit into her uniform."

Lucy's hands went to her belly, swollen
now with raw cookie dough.

"She still growing," said Mama.

"We have to do something. It's not bad
now, but what happens when she gets
older? She could have a weight problem for
the rest of her life."

Lucy backed away from the railing. A
coppery taste in her mouth, from gnawing
the inside of her cheek.

"Lucy is beautiful," said Mama. "She'll always be beautiful."

She *was* beautiful; Lucy knew this as she
knew her eyes were brown. She'd been told
it her whole life—by her mother and
Dorothy, her Italian aunts, the Polish ladies
who lived in the neighborhood. An Indian
princess: this was how Lucy had come to
think of herself. She was no blond, bland

Rapunzel, cooped up in the tower; but a warrior in the wild, fast and strong. Born in November, just past the cutoff date, she'd been kept back a year and was the oldest in her class. She was also the tallest. She could run faster and throw farther than any boy in the third grade. At the noon recess they played stickball, dodgeball, frenzied games of tag and Red Rover. She came back to the classroom soaked with sweat, her blouse sticking to her back. If the other girls ignored her, she didn't care. Pocahontas had no girlfriends either. Her braves were the only friends she needed.

Now, standing before the bedroom mirror, she examined the swell of her belly. She was getting bigger; lately her school uniform cut her under the arms. Each night after supper, she undid the top button of her dungarees. Her mother had always changed into her nightgown after supper, removing her girdle with a great sigh of relief. Lucy could see that the girdle hurt her, leaving angry red marks across her belly. Now she wore the girdle all the time. Since Joyce's return, they had all suffered.

There was a knock at the door.

"How's the homework coming?" Joyce called.

Lucy buttoned her dungarees.

"Fine," she answered. Her mother never asked about homework; neither, when she visited, did Dorothy. Instead they listened to the radio after supper: first the news, then *Gunsmoke* or *The Red Skelton Show*. Fridays were the best nights, because of Mario Lanza. He sang in a deep voice, like a priest; his show was her mother's favorite, a special occasion. Friday nights they shared a big bowl of buttered popcorn and a plate of macaroons.

Joyce came into the room and sat on the bed. "What are you learning in arithmetic?" she asked, peering over Lucy's shoulder. "Times tables?" She took the book from Lucy's hands. "Let me quiz you."

Lucy felt sick. "That's okay."

"I don't mind. What's three times eight?"

Joyce led her through the threes and fours. By the fives she was struggling. By the sixes it was clear that she hadn't studied at all.

"We just started the sixes today," said Lucy, taking back her book. This was a lie.

They'd already been assigned the elevens and twelves.

"Just the same, you don't want to fall behind. If you're not sure of the sixes, you'll get all confused with the sevens." Joyce glanced at the clock. "Give it another half hour."

"But my program is starting." Every Thursday she listened to *Tom Corbett, Space Cadet*. She had never missed an episode. "Can't I study after that?"

"At nine o'clock? You'll fall asleep on your math book." Joyce rose. "Twenty minutes on the sixes. I'll quiz you again tomorrow night."

Lucy lay in bed, unable to sleep. Her stomach hurt, but it was anger that kept her awake. She glanced at the clock. Eleven-thirty, and her mother still hadn't come to bed.

She crept downstairs and found Rose sitting at the kitchen table. Before her were three cookies on a plate.

"Whatsa matter, *bella*? How come you still awake?"

"I couldn't sleep." Lucy sat. "Can I have a cookie?"

Her mother handed her one.

"What happened to the rest?"

"I had a couple. I make you some more tomorrow. Here." She handed Lucy another cookie and took the last for herself. "We eat the last two. Don't tell your sister." She smiled, showing her gold tooth.

Lucy held the cookie, shaped like a witch. *Like Joyce,* she thought, but she knew better than to say so. Her mother wouldn't stand for it.

"Your sister, she just trying to help," her mother said, as though she'd read Lucy's mind. "It's okay for you. You still growing. Me, I'm an old lady. I got to watch what I eat."

Lucy swallowed hard. She had noticed it already. Other mothers wore Bermuda shorts and lipstick. Their voices were girlish. They did not have gray hair. The girls at school had noticed, too. Once, when her mother had walked her to school wearing a scarf over her head, Connie Kukla had laughed at her. "Your mom looks like a *stata baba,*" she teased. Lucy hated Connie

Kukla. It was the worst thing anyone had ever said to her in her life.

"Whatsa matter, *bella*? Come here."

Lucy settled into her mother's lap, the broad bosom dusted with cookie crumbs. She inhaled and wiped her running nose. "You're not old."

Her mother handed her the last cookie.

"You're a good girl," she said.

"I see what you've been doing."

Joyce looked up from her machine. The deep voice had startled her. The other girls had already filed down to the lunchroom. Alvin Blick stood before her, his hands in his pockets.

"I beg your pardon?"

"Helping that Purdy girl." He smiled, showing bad teeth. His fat face was flushed; pink blotches stood out on his neck. *Why, he's nervous,* Joyce thought.

"She was headed for trouble before you showed up," said Blick. "She slowed down the whole line. I was thinking about letting her go." He eyed the pile of finished collars in her bin. "Where'd we find you? Just out of school?"

"I was in the service."

"A WAC?" His eyebrows shot up. "I thought they got rid of those after the war."

"They did. But there are regular women's units now in the air force." Joyce sat back in her chair, feeling small. Her eyes were level with his belt.

"No kidding." He leaned one large hand on the edge of her table. Its legs squeaked in protest. "I was in the army, myself. Bastogne. That's where I got this." He patted a beefy thigh. "Two bullets. One of them's still in there. Leave it, I said. They just about killed me taking the first one out. It was worse than getting shot."

Joyce smiled stiffly. Every man she met seemed to have a similar story. Those who hadn't been wounded described their buddies' wounds. A few had offered to show their scars.

"I have to get to lunch," she said, rising.

"Okay, then." Blick stepped away from her machine. "Dismissed." He chuckled, giving her a clownish salute.

"Yes, sir," said Joyce, her voice cold. "Thank you, sir."

*   *   *

It was a joke to him. To all of them: the recruiter who'd signed her up, the enlisted
men who'd approached her at dances and
mixers—back at Lackland, when she was
green and foolish and still believed such
events were worth attending. She'd been
impressed with their uniforms and careful
manners, believed them different from the
crude miners who swore and chewed tobacco, the men who now laughed at her
uniform in the street. She'd learned differently her third week of basic training, when
a young private from South Dakota had
walked her back to her barrack after a
dance. Reeking of alcohol, he had bent to
kiss her; when she pulled away he grabbed
at her clothes and called her a name she'd
never heard before. There was the officer
who, examining a report she'd typed, laid
his hand on her shoulder and slid a fat finger under her bra strap. When she flinched,
he'd asked her if it was her time of the
month.

There was Sergeant Theodore Fry, who'd
overseen the recruitment office in Durham,
North Carolina, where she'd been stationed

her last ten months. He was married with
four children; a stiff, reserved man who reminded her of her father. For six years he
had run the office alone, until the air force
decided a woman would have better success attracting recruits. He had compli-
mented her efficiency, her quick grasp of office procedures. Yet in the end he failed her,
too, a night when they both stayed late at
the office. It was early December; by late afternoon the office was nearly dark. Together
they sifted through boxes of recruits' school
records and half-completed forms, looking
for a particular document Fry had neglected
to file. Joyce was so horrified by the chaos,
the laziness and indifference they repre-
sented, that she barely noticed him standing behind her, until the moment he grasped
her hip and pressed himself firmly against
her buttocks.

"For heaven's sake!" she cried. "What are
you doing?"

He apologized immediately, his face red.
He talked about his wife, how he had not
touched her in years; how he hadn't thought
about a woman in ages and might never
have again, if the air force hadn't sent him
Joyce.

The air force sent me to sign up recruits, she thought. *They did not send me to be your mistress.*

"I appreciate that, sir," she said stiffly. "But I'm not interested."

He stared at her a moment, his fat face disbelieving. "Not interested," he repeated. "Well, if you don't mind my asking, Joyce, what did you sign up for, then?"

And in that terrible moment it had all made sense. Until then she'd tolerated the groping hands, the rude comments. The soldiers she'd once idolized had disappointed her sorely, but she'd been able to forgive them. They were, after all, just men. Some of them she'd even pitied: the eighteen-year-old private, away from home for the first time; the officer who hadn't seen his wife in months. *Brush it off,* she told herself each time. She'd been slow to understand that the real humiliation didn't come from these men, but from the air force itself, which had gone through the charade of creating women's units for the simple purpose of keeping its real soldiers satisfied. She thought of the recruitment posters that decorated her office in Durham. SERVE WITH HONOR, they promised. The truth, she'd learned, was somewhat different. *Serve in silence,* she thought. *Service the men who serve your country.*

Quietly she served out her term in Durham. In July she notified the air force of her intent to separate. Two months later she was back in Bakerton.

Joyce arrived at the high school just after the final bell. The corridors were clogged with students: girls in socks and saddle shoes, awkward boys in plaid shirts. She ducked her head as she passed a group of laughing girls; she burned for an instant, an old feeling of loneliness and shame. They did not notice her; it took her a moment to realize why. In her hat and gloves she was invisible, as irrelevant as any other adult. The thought amused her, then filled her with relief.

She continued down the familiar hall, the linoleum with its alternating squares of green and gray. At the end of the hall was the principal's office. She tapped lightly at the door.

A secretary, obviously pregnant, showed

her to an inner office. Above the desk was a framed photo of President Eisenhower. Joyce studied his delicate features, his lovely eyes. To her he looked more like a handsome actor than a general.

"Sorry to keep you waiting," said a voice behind her.

She turned. She'd expected a stooped, wizened man named Milton Campbell, who'd been the principal as long as there'd been a high school. This man was tall, with sloping shoulders. His sleeves and trousers were an inch too short. His fair hair had thinned at the temples, but his face was surprisingly young.

"Mrs. Novak. I'm Ed Hauser, the vice principal." His hand was large and moist.

"Miss," she corrected. The letter had been addressed to Rose, but she was too nervous to come. "My mother couldn't make it. I'm Sandy's sister."

"Sorry about the letter," said Hauser. "It says here that you don't have a telephone."

"How strange," said Joyce. "I can't imagine why."

"I wrote to your mother once before, but she didn't respond."

"She's been ill," said Joyce.

"I'm sorry. I didn't know."

His voice was gentle, which confused her. She had expected a different kind of meeting. She was not prepared for kindness.

"Thank you," she said briskly, keeping the tremor out of her voice. "Of course she's concerned. We both are. Your letter took us by surprise. What exactly is the trouble with Sandy?"

"Did he tell you a truant officer picked him up last Monday?"

It took her a moment to respond. She was aware of his eyes on her. "No, sir," she said automatically.

"Apparently he and another boy jumped on board the train as it was leaving the station. A man spotted them and called the police."

"He could have been killed," she said, feeling sick to her stomach. The coal trains were slow, but still.

"He's a bright boy," said Hauser. "All his teachers say so. But he doesn't apply himself, and lately he's absent as often as he's present. If he continues like this, he's liable to be left back again. Or worse."

She frowned. There were worse things than failing a grade—being thrown from a coal train, for example—but just then she couldn't think of many.

"According to his records he turns sixteen next month," said Hauser. "I wouldn't be surprised if he dropped out of school."

Joyce thought of the evenings she'd spent at the kitchen table, poring over homework. Occasionally her father had looked up from his newspaper and given her a wink. He never would have let Sandy drop out of high school.

"This is terrible, Mr. Hauser. My father"— she took a deep breath—"was the disciplinarian in the family. He made sure we took our studies seriously. Sandy was just a little boy when he died." She cleared her throat, sat back in her chair. If she kept talking, she knew that she would cry.

"What about your mother?"

"Sandy doesn't listen to her." Joyce thought of the green Plymouth idling in the street on a school night, the girl waiting in the front seat. "He does whatever he pleases."

Hauser said nothing. He seemed to be watching her.

"I'm concerned about his future," she said. "He'll never find a good job if he doesn't graduate. I'd never forgive myself if that happened."

"Maybe you should tell him that."

"I will." Joyce's mind raced. Sandy was rarely home in the afternoon; in the evening he appeared briefly at dinner. He got irritated when she asked about his day at school. *Nothing happened,* he'd say. *Nothing ever happens.*

"Mr. Campbell has spoken with him already," said Hauser. "I can have a talk with him, too, if you'd like."

"I'd appreciate that. I've been away for several years. I had no idea things had gotten so bad."

Hauser smiled. "Were you away at college?"

"No." She hesitated. "I was in the air force."

"Where were you stationed?"

It was a reasonable question, one she herself might ask a fellow soldier. She waited for the joke.

"Durham, North Carolina," she said warily. "Before that, Bellevue, Washington." She waited for more—where and under whom he'd served, the bullet he'd taken, the medal he'd won.

"The Pacific Northwest. I hear it's a beautiful part of the country. I'd like to see it one day." He closed the folder on his desk. "Miss Novak, it was a pleasure to meet you. Have a talk with Sandy, and I'll do the same. He needs to know we're watching him. Sometimes that's enough to straighten them out." He stood. "Could I have your telephone number?"

Joyce felt her face warm.

"We should have it for the school records," he explained.

"Of course," she said, embarrassed. She recited the digits slowly, hoping she'd remembered them right.

Viola recognized her from the other end of the hall. A tiny thing, plainly dressed, with excellent posture. Her movements were quick and precise.

"Joyce," she called, surprising herself. In thirty years she hadn't raised her voice inside the school. "Joyce Novak!"

Joyce turned. "Miss Peale?"

They met halfway down the corridor.

"What a surprise to see you," said Viola. "Are you home on holiday?"

"I separated in September. I live here now."

Viola smiled uncertainly, unsure whether this was good news or bad. "What brings you to school?"

"I had a meeting with Mr. Hauser." Joyce colored, as though she herself were in trouble. "About my brother, Sandy."

"Oh dear." Viola paused delicately. "Nothing serious, I hope." She had taught Sandy a few years before. A poor student, she recalled, but pleasant and polite.

"Oh, no," said Joyce. "I'm sure everything will be fine." She glanced at her watch. "Miss Peale, I hate to run, but I'm due back at the factory. I'm on my lunch hour."

"Of course, dear." She took the hand Joyce offered and impulsively kissed her cheek.

"It was lovely to see you," she said. "Good luck to you, Joyce."

Back in her classroom Viola ate lunch alone. She remembered the girl as she'd once been, her blond head bent over a textbook. Joyce was interested in everything: world events, biology and chemistry, the strange diet consumed in the Philippines. It was this quality, Viola later realized, that had distinguished her from all the others. From Viola herself.

I want to see the whole world, she'd said, trying to explain why she'd joined the air force. Had she seen anything at all? Viola wondered. Or had she perhaps seen too much?

She had tried back then, timidly and ineffectually. *You're an excellent student, Joyce. Have you considered some kind of school instead?*

Joyce had looked at her as if she were senile, a foolish old woman. *My mother is a widow,* she said simply. Those few words had ended the discussion. Mortified, Viola had wished her luck; they had never again spoken of her future. All these years later, the memory still shamed her; the arrogance of her suggestion, as though a college education were something a coal miner's child might realistically afford. For years she had blamed herself for doing nothing. For failing the most promising student she had ever known.

In the distance the factory whistle sounded. Viola paid no attention. She heard it every day but had never wondered what it meant.

Across town, Joyce Novak hurried to her sewing machine and went back to work.

Hauser spotted him from across the street. He stood in the school parking lot next to a green Plymouth. With him were two girls, a brunette and a blonde. They were all smoking cigarettes.

"Novak!" he called.

The girls dropped their cigarettes and furtively stamped them out. Sandy Novak met Hauser's gaze.

All right, pretty boy, Hauser thought. *Drop the damned cigarette.*

Sandy took a leisurely drag, a long exhale. Then slowly, deliberately, he ground out the butt with his heel.

"No smoking on school property," said Hauser, approaching them.

"I put it out," said Sandy.

"Girls, would you excuse us?"

They glanced uncertainly at Sandy.

"It's okay," he said. "I'll walk home."

The girls got into the car. Sandy stared expectantly at Hauser.

"Your sister was here this afternoon."

Sandy didn't speak, just raised his eyebrows.

"We've been sending letters to your mother, but I understand she is ill."

Still the boy said nothing.

"Your sister gave us your phone number. You said you didn't have a telephone."

"We didn't," he said at last.

"The point is, I told her about the stunt you pulled at the train station. Scared her half to death."

"You told her that?"

"She had a right to know. As far as she knew, you were coming to school every day like a model citizen. She couldn't believe how many days you've missed."

Sandy avoided his eyes.

"The thing is," said Hauser, "we don't want any surprises. When you flunk the tenth grade, at least your family will know it's coming."

Sandy kicked at the ground with his shoe.

"I turn sixteen next month. I can quit then, if I want. You can't do anything about it." A smile tugged at his mouth. For a moment he looked like a little boy.

"That's true," said Hauser. "But the mines won't take you until you're eighteen. That's the law now. And you can't join the air force like your sister did. You need a high school diploma."

His smile faded. "You do?"

"That is correct." Hauser wasn't sure about this, but it sounded right. "Look, I don't care if you quit. I've got five hundred other kids to worry about. But your sister wants you to graduate. You could do it easily, if you cut out the funny business. All you have to do is show up."

Sandy waited.

"Can you do that much, Novak? Come to school every day and get yourself to class on time. You do that, and I'll make sure you pass." He paused. "Do we have a deal?"

Sandy shrugged lazily. Then grinned, a million-dollar smile.

"Sure," he said. "It's a deal."

They sent Sandy to the butcher's uptown, and he came back with a twelve-pound turkey. Rose stationed Joyce at the sink to peel potatoes. Dorothy, home from Washington for the holiday, sat at the table chopping onions for stuffing.

"That's some mighty wasteful peeling," Sandy teased, looking over Joyce's shoulder. "You're throwing away half the potato."

"Let's see you do any better."

"Don't look at me. I've done my part." He thumped his chest, caveman-style. "That bird's heavier than it looks."

He was in unusual spirits. Joyce couldn't remember the last time she'd seen him smile, let alone clown around in the kitchen. She had tried talking to him about his problems at school; he'd cut her off with a rare apology. *I'm sorry, Joyce. I'll straighten up. I promise.* Since then he'd been pleasant, even affectionate, the way he'd been as a boy.

"Is this enough?" Dorothy asked. She had accumulated a pile of chopped onions.

Rose clomped over to inspect them, in the new house slippers Joyce had bought her. "Try to get them all the same size," she advised.

Sandy frowned. "Mrs. Novak, these females have no business in the kitchen. No wonder they can't find husbands."

"Who says we're looking?" said Joyce.

"Well, what are you waiting for? That's what I'd like to know. Neither one of you is getting any younger. I'll bet Lucy beats you both to the altar. There will be two of you dancing in the trough."

"Eeee, the trough!" Rose clapped a hand over her mouth. "When your aunt got married I couldn't believe it. Her sister in the trough like a pig."

"Not an ordinary pig," said Sandy. "A *dancing* pig."

"She must have been humiliated," said Joyce. "To think her own family put her through that, just because her sister got married first."

"Them Polish, they crazy people," said Rose.

"I think it's a splendid tradition. I'm already looking forward to Lucy's wedding. Dorothy and Joyce will bring down the house." Sandy rose and performed a little jig, daintily lifting an imaginary skirt.

"Stop!" said Dorothy. She was flushed from laughing. "You're a terrible boy."

"I'm never getting married," said Lucy.

Sandy raised an eyebrow at Joyce. "You see the example you're setting?"

"Oh, honey," said Dorothy. "Why not?"

"I don't want to go away. I want to stay here."

There was a moment of silence.

"Do you ever hear from Georgie?" Dorothy asked.

"Once in a blue moon," said Joyce.

"He's not much for writing," said Dorothy. "Maybe I should get a telephone."

"He don't like the phone neither," Rose observed. "He call maybe once a month."

"He must be very busy," said Dorothy. "The baby and all."

They had never seen the child, Arthur

Quigley Novak, but several times a year George sent photos. The first few had been dutifully framed and placed on a bureau in the living room. More recent shots were tucked into a drawer. In Bakerton Arthur remained an infant. In actual fact he was nearly four years old.

Rose's face darkened. "It's that girl he marry. She don't like it here. She get a headache that time they come." After that first visit, Georgie had always come to Bakerton alone. The family hadn't seen Marion in years.

Silence fell over the kitchen. Joyce glanced at Dorothy. Her eyes were moist.

"What's the matter?" said Joyce.

"Onions." Dorothy rose, dabbing at her eyes with her wrist. "I should wash my hands."

Joyce watched her head upstairs. Dorothy had always loved Georgie too much. Every year she was devastated when he didn't come for Christmas, though by now no one else expected him to show. She didn't understand that Georgie had left Bakerton completely, as Sandy soon would; that neither love nor obligation nor concern for their mother would be enough to keep the Novak boys in Bakerton. It seemed to Joyce that men were made differently, that love and guilt didn't work on them in the same way. She didn't blame her brothers for this. She envied them. She herself had tried to leave. She probably would have succeeded, if she had been born a boy.

After dinner Joyce and Dorothy stacked the dishes beside the sink.

"Blick," said Joyce. "A heavyset fellow, with a red face."

"That's the one. I still have nightmares about him." Dorothy swiped at a plate. "Joyce, how can you stand it? I know what that place is like."

"It's not so bad."

"Did you ever think of coming to Washington? Mag Spangler is a supervisor now. She's the one who got me in at Interior, after all those wartime jobs were eliminated. Maybe she could find you something." She stacked a roasting pan in the drainer. "I wouldn't mind the company. It gets lonely down there."

Joyce studied her. Dorothy's face had

aged. The skin beneath her eyes looked thin and bluish, as though she slept poorly. "Maybe you should find a roommate. Didn't you have one once?"

"I did, years ago." After the deaf school-teacher retired and moved back to Georgia, Dorothy had taken over her tiny single room. "Never again. Let me tell you, living with a stranger isn't all it's cracked up to be." Dorothy hung her towel on the rack. "We could get ourselves a little apartment. It would be a treat to get out of the boarding-house."

Joyce had visited Dorothy the summer before, on a brief furlough from North Carolina. Dorothy's cramped little room had struck her as grimmer than the barracks. It seemed impossible that she had lived there almost ten years.

"I know you hate to leave Mama," said Dorothy. "But she's got Lucy and Sandy. It's not as if she's alone."

Joyce smiled, thinking of Sandy's dance in the kitchen. He was no help, but at least he was company. Meanwhile Rose had become more vigilant about her diet. Most days she wore her slippers without prompting. After dinner she'd refused a slice of pie.

"Maybe," said Joyce. "We'll see what the doctor has to say."

Joyce and rose left early the next morning with a lunch Dorothy had packed, sandwiches of stuffing and leftover turkey. Afterward Dorothy sat alone in the kitchen. She heard movement overhead. Lucy appeared on the stairs in her nightgown.

"Where's Mama?" she asked.

"She just left," said Dorothy. "Joyce took her to the doctor."

"Is she sick?"

"No, honey." Dorothy rose and poured her a glass of milk. "She went to get her eyes checked."

"Does she need glasses?"

"Maybe so," said Dorothy.

"I don't think she does." For as long as Lucy could remember, her mother had been perfectly healthy. She had eaten whatever she wanted. There had never been anything wrong with her eyes. All these problems had begun when Joyce came.

"Mama's getting older, honey. These things happen when people get older."

Lucy didn't respond.

"Come on," said Dorothy. "Let me make you some breakfast."

In the waiting room, Joyce flipped through a two-year-old magazine: Reds Sign Pact with China. Rose glanced nervously around the room, her pupils dilated from the eyedrops the nurse had given her. In one corner, a boy sat next to his mother, his eyes covered in bandages. An old man walked awkwardly with a white-tipped cane.

Finally the nurse called Rose's name. She clutched Joyce's arm as they walked down a long corridor.

The doctor, a wizened old man named Lucas, shined a flashlight in Rose's eyes, then turned off the lamp and had her read a backlit chart on the wall. He made her look into a large machine and asked her what she saw.

"How long have you been diabetic?" he asked.

"We found out last month," said Joyce.

"Are you controlling your blood sugar?"

"She's working on it," said Joyce.

He turned on the light. "You are suffering from a condition called diabetic retinopathy. Your blood sugar has been high probably for years and in that time an important nerve has been damaged, the nerve that connects the eyes to the brain." He paused. "When did you first notice a change in your vision?"

Rose hesitated. "Maybe last year," she said. Then considered. "Maybe two years."

Mama! Joyce wanted to cry. *Why didn't you say anything?* She thought of the broken windows at the house, the rotten floorboards on the porch. It was just like Rose to ignore the problem, and nobody else had been around to notice. Joyce gone. Dorothy and Georgie gone. Left to her own devices, Rose had simply pretended. That nothing had changed. That she wasn't going blind.

"This is a degenerative condition. Once it has begun, its tendency is to progress. How quickly, we do not know." The doctor paused. "Mrs. Novak, how old are you?"

"Fifty-three," said Rose.

His mouth tightened. "It's hard for me to judge. I can't see precisely what you're seeing. But it appears that your condition is quite advanced for a woman of your age. Do you live alone?"

"No," said Joyce. "I live with her."

"Good," said Lucas. "She'll need your help."

The treatments, called radioactive retinography, would be fourteen in all. Lucas scheduled them two weeks apart, which meant seven months of trips to Pittsburgh. The morning after the doctor's visit, Joyce sat at the kitchen table with pencil and paper, calculating the cost of bus tickets. A single round-trip ticket was ten dollars. But Rose's vision had deteriorated dramatically; she could not travel alone.

There was no way around it. Joyce would have to buy a car.

She walked to the dealership that Friday night, with fifty dollars in cash withdrawn from her savings account. The same salesman was on duty, the pimple-faced boy in the ill-fitting suit. "I'd like that car," she said, pointing. Her voice held a certainty she did not feel. "That Rambler."

The boy's eyes widened, stunned by the ease of the sale. He hadn't even said hello. "Don't you want to take it for a test drive?"

"No, thank you," she said. "May I use your telephone?"

Sandy answered. She knew he would; he always raced for the phone on Friday nights.

"It's Joyce," she said. "I need your help."

He taught her in six lessons. She drove hesitantly, with much grinding of the gears, but well enough to pass the licensing exam the second time out. The first failure, a mercifully brief humiliation at the hands of an avuncular state policeman, she did not allow herself to register. Brush it off, she repeated each time the engine stalled. She had never failed a test of any kind.

The officer wouldn't let her drive home afterward. Sandy took the wheel instead. When Joyce returned from failing her test, he was leaning against the registration counter joking with the clerk, a stout, matronly woman who'd held up the line to bring him a cream-filled doughnut.

"Weren't you nervous?" she asked him later. "She could have asked to see your license."

"Nah. I'm a good driver. I don't need a stinking license."

She watched him weave expertly through the Saturday traffic. *He's probably right,* she thought. Her brother seemed to have an instinctive gift for steering around obstacles. Because of his charm or his looks, or simply because he expected them to, people liked him. And if military life had taught her anything, it was this: if the right people liked you, the rules often did not apply. The realization had stunned her—its unfairness, its cruelty. Joyce had never charmed anyone in her life. It had never occurred to her to try.

Sandy hit the gas and raced through a yellow light. If he weren't her brother, if she'd met him somewhere out in the world—at school or in the service—she'd have disliked him on sight: his slouching posture, the palpable male confidence that hummed around him like an electrical field. His laziness would have infuriated her; his contempt for authority would have seemed a personal affront. But he was not a stranger. Lazy or not, cocky or not, Sandy was hers. Even his charm was forgivable. In some way it, too, belonged to her.

* * *

License in hand, Joyce faced other hurdles. The drive itself, for one, a nerve-shattering experience that left both her and Rose sweating and irritable. They were an hour late for Rose's first appointment. Joyce had stopped twice to ask directions; she had taken a series of wrong turns and nearly collided with another car when she drove through a stoplight. The parking garage mystified her; she had parked illegally on the street and would almost certainly get a ticket. Still, they had made it. We're here, she thought.

The treatments themselves were not painful. Rose sat for forty minutes in a tiny room, in what looked like a dentist's chair, her lap draped in a lead apron. A nurse instructed her to keep her eyes closed as the room was bombarded with brilliant light. Afterward she had a slight headache, but felt much like herself. The misery came the following day, a violent nausea that left her trembling and soaked with perspiration, so weak she could barely stand. This lasted for several days. When the nausea left her, she was extraordinarily tired. By the time she felt better, it was time for another treatment. Joyce helped her into the car, which they had both come to view as an instrument of torture. Rose had lost much of her sight. She complained that everything looked fuzzy, even her hand in front of her face. She had lost weight and was sick with dread of what lay ahead of her. *What am I doing?* Joyce thought. *What am I doing to my mother?*

The appointments were mostly on Saturday afternoons, but twice Joyce had to miss a day of work. This attracted some attention at the factory. Finally she explained the situation to Alvin Blick.

"Well, now," he said, scratching his head. "They *are* called sick days, but the idea is that you're the one who's sick. You can't go taking them when other people are sick." He smiled, showing his bad teeth. "Can't your mother get to the hospital by herself?"

"No," said Joyce. "She's—" She had never said it aloud before. It seemed a terrible betrayal. "Going blind," she finished.

Blick nodded, as though this were to be expected. "Mine's hard of hearing. Old age is no picnic." He rose. "I don't know what to

tell you, Joyce. You're one of my best girls.
I'd hate to lose you."

She watched him go, thinking how she
was already lost.

Salvation came in a phone call.

"Miss Novak?" said a deep male voice.
"It's Ed Hauser, at the high school."

In the next room, Rose and Lucy were
eating dinner. They'd set a place for Sandy,
but he hadn't come home from school.
Joyce had no idea where he could be. She
prepared herself for the worst.

"Is everything all right?" she asked, her
voice small.

"Oh, yes. In fact, I'm hoping you'll consider this good news. I have a proposition
for you."

It took her a moment to absorb what he
was saying. The school secretary was in the
hospital—her baby had arrived sooner than
expected—and he needed a replacement
immediately. He was offering her the job.

"Why me?" said Joyce.

"You come highly recommended. Viola
Peale was in my office today singing your

praises. She can't say enough about you, which is fairly remarkable considering she hasn't spoken a word to me in five years." He paused. "I'm hoping you can start Monday. Are you interested?"

"Yes," she said simply. "But don't I have to have an interview, or something?"

Hauser laughed. "The school day begins at seven-thirty. Interview at seven-fifteen."

And on Monday morning, Joyce Novak went back to school.

FIVE

The Bakerton Volunteer Fire Company sat at the corner of Main Street and Susquehanna Avenue, the busiest corner in town. Across the street was Keener's Diner, a bowling alley and a pool hall. Weekend evenings, after dances or football games, these places were crowded with teenagers. On warm nights the firemen set up folding chairs on the sidewalk and watched the girls go by, calling to the pretty ones who walked in pairs or threes down Main Street. Long shadows in the summer evening, a shimmery trail of female laughter.

The firemen were mostly single, mostly young. During the late forties and fifties they were all veterans, as if having once presented themselves for danger, they now did so routinely, without ceremony, as a matter of course. By day or night they worked in the mines; in their off-hours they congregated at the fire hall (*far hole*), playing pool or Ping-Pong, drinking coffee or Coca-Cola, sober always, just in case. They came from Little Italy, Polish Hill, the outlying farm country; from nearby towns like Kinport or Coalport, too small to support companies of their own. Even a volunteer company had expenses: clothing, equipment, upkeep on the trucks. To raise money they held Saturday-night dances in the hall. Two weekends a month, the floor was cleared. A band set up in the corner. Teenagers waited in line at the door.

For several months in 1941 and '42, George Novak's band had played the fire-hall dances, until the drummer and the trumpeter and finally the whole combo was drafted. For a few years Bakerton made do with phonograph records. It seemed that every musician in the county had been taken away.

At eight o'clock the dancing began. First the steady couples. Then pairs of girls—giggling, spunky girls who refused to stand by and wait. For a long time the boys did not dance, just walked in a slow circle around the dance floor—boys like Sandy Novak, slouching a little, a plastic comb peeking out the back pocket of his dungarees. Week after week they walked the Bakerton Circle, eyeing the girls on the dance floor. The circle moved counterclockwise, an orderly parade, as though someone had planned it that way. In nearby towns people laughed at the Bakerton boys: could you beat it, paying a quarter to walk in circles all evening? Nobody knew how the custom had started. Some things would always be.

In the second week of August, Bakerton hosted the Firemen's Festival—to the men, Holy Week in a year of Ordinary Time. For three days the firemen came, volunteer companies from across Saxon County, to drink and game at the booths set up along Baker Street. Friday night was the Battle of the Barrel. Men from two companies squared off, tug-of-war style. Above their heads was a rope tied between two telephone poles; hanging from the rope was a barrel filled with water. Each man was given a long wooden pole, to swat the barrel toward the other side, dousing his opponents with cold water. By the time the contest was over, both sides were soaked. The men wore their wet clothes proudly. For the rest of the evening they were regarded as celebrities—greeted with laughter and slaps on the back, treated to cups of yellow beer at the booths all over town.

Saturday afternoon was the firemen's parade. Up front, in a shining convertible, sat the Fire Queen: the prettiest girl from Bakerton High, handpicked by the firemen themselves. Next the pumpers came. Bleary, liquor-sick, wearing full equipment in the August heat, the men waved to the spectators from atop their trucks, hundreds of them, standing three deep along the parade route. Each truck stopped briefly at the judging stand, a platform of wooden risers stacked before the fire hall. Two or three men dropped down from the truck and opened all its doors. A voice over the loudspeaker gave its weight and dimensions and pumping capacity. For each engine, polite applause—for the fortieth truck, the fiftieth; to the untrained eye indistinguishable from the ones that came before. Shouts and whoops were reserved for the local boys, and in one unforgettable year, a standing ovation for Bakerton's brand-new Mack ladder truck, a slick red monster with bulging wheel wells and gleaming chrome. The truck cost $2,500, what a miner earned in a year. A sum raised through five years of fire-hall dances, ten thousand teenage nights walking the Bakerton Circle.

In the spring of 1954, defying all predictions, Sandy Novak graduated high school. A photo was taken at his commencement: Sandy in cap and gown, his mortarboard slightly askew; Sandy surrounded, as always, by women. Joyce in a summer suit and pearls, her lips pursed; Rose stout and white-haired, clutching her pocketbook. Lucy round-faced, suntanned, her black hair in braids. Dorothy's eyes closed, her hat askew. Only Sandy is smiling, showing beautiful teeth; the Hollywood version of a high school graduate.

The photo, like all photos, raises a question: Who took the picture? Who, in those days, even owned a camera? Georgie, Dorothy would later claim. Joyce disagreed: he hadn't even attended the ceremony.

Lucy suspected one of Sandy's girlfriends. No one remembered that the photographer was Ed Hauser, the high school principal; that he and Joyce had started dating that spring. He was the sort of man whose actions are forgotten, a mild but capable man whose sins and virtues alike go unnoticed.

After graduation Sandy moved to Cleveland with his buddy Dick Devlin, whose brother was a foreman at Fisher Body and got them jobs on the line, building chassis for Pontiacs and Chevies. For the first time since Dorothy was born, the house on Polish Hill had an empty bedroom. Joyce spent a Saturday painting the walls lavender, Lucy's favorite color. She bought a matching rug and a flowered spread for the bed, and at the age of eleven, nearly twelve, Lucy moved into her own room. Her parochial school jumpers were hung in the closet. Under the bed she stacked her board games—Monopoly, Parcheesi and Candy Land, which she had outgrown but secretly played when she was alone. She went to bed every night at nine-thirty and lay awake for hours, waiting for the house to quiet. Then, when her sister was asleep, she tiptoed across the hall and climbed into bed with her mother.

In later years, a number of people would ask Dorothy why she'd left Washington. If she responded at all, she would answer vaguely, airily—I can't remember, exactly. With a wave of the hand, an absent smile. Still a young woman, she had acquired a spinster-ish charm.

Her mother and sister asked; her brother Georgie; a woman sitting beside her on the train back to Pennsylvania. Mag Spangler's mother—in the late fifties, when Dorothy went into the shop to buy a hat for Rose's funeral. Doctors, again and again, old men in dark suits, in white coats; men who wore spectacles or whiskers or vests and shirt-sleeves. To all of them, but to the men especially, she would find the truth unspeakable: that she had left because of the bleeding.

If only it had come on schedule, the same time every month. Her sister's cycle was as brisk and efficient as Joyce herself. Her periods had begun when Dorothy was in high school, and for a brief time, as if by magic, Dorothy's bleeding became regular, too. The same thing happened while she lived with Patsy Sturgis. On its own, her body seemed uncertain what to do; she needed another girl close by to show her the way. She needed someone to follow. It was a sensation she had felt all her life.

She had learned to sense it coming: pain in her breasts, a certain taste in her mouth. Agitated, perspiring, she lay awake waiting. A day, two days would pass. Then something inside her would uncoil, and out of her a deep peace would flow.

Her last winter in Washington she could not bleed. Months passed. A strange anxiety gnawed her stomach. She imagined a mass growing inside her, a soft cancer filled with blood.

It came furiously, as in her nightmares, a hot lick of blood trailing down her leg. It was a Monday afternoon in February, a crisp rain turning to sleet. She'd returned from lunch and was sitting at her desk. When she rose she felt wetness between her legs. She looked down and saw a dark pool on her chair. She sat down quickly, her mind racing, her face hot and full of blood.

Around her the office ticked away: thundering typewriters, a ringing telephone, a chirping voice answering *hello.* Finally she rose, taking her coat from the rack near her desk. She put it on quickly and hurried to the washroom.

She closed herself in a stall and sat there bleeding. Winter light grayed the frosted windowpanes. Women came in and out, and she thought about the stain on her chair. Someone would see it, perhaps already had. There was nothing she could do.

She listened to the hiss of the boiler, phones ringing in the office beyond. At last chairs scraped the linoleum; a hundred pairs of shoes shuffled down the hall. Behind the wall the elevators groaned. She counted the trips up and down, up and down: the office emptying out, the workers carried to the street below. At last the building quieted.

She cleaned herself with rough paper towels from the dispenser on the wall, then buttoned her coat as though she were simply leaving for the day. As though she would soon return.

Years later she would try to remember, to identify the precise moment she decided she would never go back. The next morning the alarm clock woke her as usual. She shut it off, rolled over, and went back to sleep. She slept for most of the day. In the evening she went downstairs to dinner.

She was surprised by how easy it was, simply to stop. The struggles of twelve years, the daily gauntlet of loneliness and anxiety—deciding what to wear each day, knowing from long experience that whatever she chose would be wrong; waiting for the bus in the rain; the elevator full of strangers' smells; stilted conversations with the new hires, impossibly young, who chattered in the powder room about dates and weekend plans. All that she had endured in those years, thinking she had no choice. Then one day she stopped, and no one even noticed.

She stopped setting the alarm. In the morning she heard noises overhead: footsteps on the stairs, the other boarders setting out into the world, to live another day in the city. She drifted back to sleep. She had surrendered everything. Her sleep was deep and peaceful as a child's.

For the first week she went downstairs each night to dinner. *I'm on vacation,* she said when Miss Straub inquired. Soon she was no longer hungry. She left her room only to use the toilet, to take a bath.

She bathed during the day when the house was empty, lying in the tub while the water slowly cooled. Afterward she crept downstairs to the kitchen and foraged through the cupboards, taking what she could find: crackers, bread, a piece of fruit.

Two weeks passed, then three. After that she lost count. Toward the end she heard knocking at the door. Once, Miss Straub's voice; later, Mag Spangler's. Finally her sister came. *For God's sake, what happened?* Joyce demanded, looking around the room. If she'd said something else, Dorothy might have responded; but that one unanswerable question had paralyzed her. And so began her time of quiet.

Joyce was astounded by how long her sister could sleep. She hadn't noticed at first; she had been preoccupied with details: getting Dorothy from boardinghouse to taxicab to train station, from train to automobile to her mother's house in Bakerton. Simple enough. But Dorothy was so weak she could barely stand; so confused or addled, so something, that she couldn't follow the simplest instructions. And now that the crisis was past, she would not stay awake. Joyce did the cleaning and shopping and laundry, paid the bills and helped Lucy with her homework. Now that Sandy was gone, she raked leaves and shoveled snow and cut the grass with the old reel mower. Every night, bone-tired, she banked the coal furnace and fired it again at dawn. All this in addition to her actual job at the high school. What reason Dorothy had to be tired, she could not imagine.

"Dorothy." Joyce gave her a gentle shake. "Dorothy, wake up."

Dorothy sighed. A moment later her eyes opened. They had put her in the lavender bedroom, which Lucy had surrendered without complaint. Facing north, the room stayed dark all morning. Unless someone woke her, she'd stay in bed until suppertime.

Joyce sat on the edge of the bed, willing herself to be patient. "Dorothy, I have to leave now. Ed's brother is getting married. We're going to the wedding."

Dorothy sat up, dazed.

"I need you to put on some clothes and get Lucy her breakfast. Can you do that?" Joyce made an effort to keep the edge out of her voice. "I have to run. Ed is waiting in the car."

Dorothy blinked. "When will you be back?" she asked softly. Her speech had returned, but her mouth was clumsy, as though she'd forgotten how to form the words.

"Suppertime. Maybe sooner." Joyce rose

and took a dress from the closet. "Here. Put this on."

Dorothy raised her arms like an obedient child.

"Lucy's in the kitchen," said Joyce. "Have some breakfast with her. Then you can take a bath."

She hurried downstairs and out the front door. Ed Hauser was waiting in the car.

"Sorry I'm late," said Joyce, a little breathless. "I had to wake Dorothy."

"That's okay." Ed kissed the cheek she offered. "We've got to get that girl an alarm clock."

When exactly it started—when her sister lost her footing—Joyce never knew. By the time the family was notified, it was too late. Dorothy had already begun to slide.

That year, like every year, she had visited at Christmas. Later Joyce would remember that she'd seemed distracted, her attention elsewhere, as though she were listening for sounds in the next room. "Too skinny," Rose added, as though that clinched it. To her, thinness was always a sign of trouble.

Later, after the thing happened, Joyce would blame herself for not noticing. She'd been preoccupied that Christmas. Baker Brothers had put its company houses—Rose's included—up for sale. Joyce couldn't afford the down payment. If another buyer came along, the family would lose the house. Rose was seeing a new doctor, a diabetes specialist several towns away. The laser treatments had failed to save her eyesight, but there was her heart to worry about, her kidneys, a sore on her foot that refused to heal. More, and still more, that she might lose.

The call came late on a Friday evening, after Lucy had gone to bed. In the parlor, Rose sat dozing in her chair. Joyce stood at the kitchen sink, drying the last of the supper dishes. The ringing startled her. Since Sandy had left, the phone seldom rang. Georgie had already made his monthly call.

"Joyce?" A female voice. "I don't know if you remember me. This is Mag Spangler."

It took her a moment to recognize the name. They'd met years before, when Joyce spent a weekend visiting Dorothy in Washington. They had toured nearly every monument and museum in the capital. Mag had led them around town like a drill sergeant.

"I hate to call so late," said Mag, "but this is an emergency. Something is terribly wrong with Dorothy."

"Is she sick?"

"Not exactly. I got a call this afternoon from the landlady at the boardinghouse. She said Dorothy hasn't come out of her room in weeks."

Joyce thought of the tiny room, cramped and dark, its one window facing an alley lined with trash cans.

"When I went over there, she wouldn't open the door. The landlady had to let me in with her key." Mag hesitated. "Joyce, I don't know what to say. I think she's had some kind of nervous breakdown. Someone really should come and get her."

Joyce took the train the following day. At the boardinghouse she was greeted by Miss Straub, who'd inherited the place from her mother.

"Your sister's room is a disgrace," she said. "This is a respectable establishment. I can't allow this sort of thing." She was a pale, fleshy woman, tightly corseted. Her hair was teased in the elaborate style of ten years before.

"How long has she been in her room?"

"Honey, *I* don't know. A few weeks, maybe. I've got a dozen people living here. I don't keep tabs." She knocked briskly at the door. "Miss Novak. Your sister is here."

They waited. Miss Straub knocked again, then opened the door with her key. The room was dark, the shades drawn. It smelled dankly of mildew, an odor sweet and dark, like rotting fruit. Stiff towels covered the radiators. The mattress was bare. Dorothy lay curled on her side, facing the wall.

"Dorothy?" Joyce stepped around the piles on the floor—sheets, towels, dirty clothes.

"I tried talking to her. She acts like she doesn't hear." Miss Straub sounded annoyed.

Joyce sat on the bare mattress. Dorothy's forehead was cool to the touch.

"Has she seen a doctor?" she asked.

"How would I know?"

Joyce took a deep breath. "Well, could you call one, please?"

Miss Straub crossed her arms. "First things first. She hasn't paid rent in three weeks."

"Oh, for heaven's sake." Joyce reached for her pocketbook. "I'll pay whatever she owes, but she has to see a doctor."

Miss Straub took the money.

"Has she been eating?" Joyce asked.

The landlady shrugged elaborately.

"Well, I just paid you room and board," said Joyce. "So could you please bring her something to eat?"

Miss Straub's heels clicked away down the hall. Joyce took Dorothy's hand. It felt cool and very light, as though it were filled with air.

"Come on," she said softly. "We need to get you out of bed."

Dorothy frowned slightly, as though she had forgotten something. Her skin had a greasy shine.

Joyce rose. "Let's get some light in here."

She raised the shades. The disorder of the room astonished her. Clothes were piled on the floor. The wastebasket overflowed: blackened banana peels, an apple core astir

with ants. Everywhere were piles of old
magazines. *Silver Screen. Backstage Gossip. Screen Stars.*

Dorothy mumbled something, a single
syllable. She covered her head with a pillow.

"Ready?" said Joyce. "We're going to get
you cleaned up."

She slipped an arm around Dorothy's
waist. Dorothy moaned softly but didn't re-
sist. She wore an old cotton slip, decorated
with stains. Through the thin fabric Joyce
could feel her ribs. She picked a ratty plaid
bathrobe off the floor and draped it over
Dorothy's shoulders.

Slowly they made their way down the hall,
Dorothy leaning heavily on Joyce's shoulder. The corridor was empty; so was the
washroom. Joyce ran a bath and eased
Dorothy into the tub. Her neck was ringed
with grime. Her oily hair clung to her head
like a cap.

"Sit and soak a while," she said. "I'll be
right back." She closed the door behind her
and hurried down the hall. *Straight ahead,*
she thought. It was a phrase she'd picked
up in boot camp and repeated in her head
while she marched: in the mornings, half
asleep; in the afternoons, in the heat.

She found a clean dress in Dorothy's closet, a comb and toothbrush in the bureau drawer. She laid them on the bed, then attacked the room with the broom and dust cloths Miss Straub had provided. She filled a trash bag with magazines, then a second. The clothing on the floor had a fungal smell, as though it had been dropped there soaking wet. The stiff towels smelled strongly of soap.

The doctor arrived an hour later. Dorothy sat waiting for him on the bed, bathed and dressed, her hair curling damply at her shoulders. He took a stethoscope from a leather bag and listened to her heartbeat. He took her blood pressure, then examined her ears and eyes and throat.

"She's a little weak," he told Joyce. "Underweight. Her blood pressure is low; she may be dehydrated. But she isn't running a temperature. Physically, there doesn't seem to be anything wrong with her."

"But why won't she talk?"

He closed his bag. "Has she experienced some kind of emotional trauma? Trouble with a boyfriend, that kind of thing?"

"I don't think so."

"Problems at work?"

"I don't know," said Joyce. Dorothy rarely phoned; lately her letters had been erratic. They hadn't heard from her in more than a month.

In the end they went home to Bakerton; there was nowhere else to go. They made it to the station in time for the last train—thanks to Mag Spangler, who'd promised to send the rest of Dorothy's things. Dorothy still hadn't spoken, but she ate the sandwich Miss Straub had packed and slept peacefully the whole way home.

Back in Bakerton, Joyce told her mother as little as possible. "Dorothy was sick," she said simply. "She needed to come home and rest."

Lucy waited in the kitchen. She was twelve and would have preferred to make her own breakfast—bacon and eggs, fried toast with syrup—but there were rules about what she could eat. Each morning she made the best of it, doctoring her oatmeal with butter and brown sugar. Still it went down slowly, the flavors bland and gray.

The pot of oatmeal simmered on the

stove. Joyce had told her to wait for Dorothy, but there was no telling when she would get out of bed. Lucy would have been perfectly happy if she stayed there all day. Dorothy made her nervous. Once, at night, she'd come downstairs for a drink of water and found Dorothy sitting on the porch swing, humming softly to herself. She looked up, but didn't speak, when Lucy said hello.

She glanced at the clock. *Space Patrol* would begin at nine, followed by *Captain Midnight* and *Sheena, Queen of the Jungle.* She carried the Saturday-morning schedule in her head; it was the best television of the week. Having Joyce gone on a Saturday morning was a rare gift. She disapproved of television watching during the day. If she caught Lucy at it, she'd come up with a list of chores that needed doing immediately: sweeping, dusting, ironing a stack of pillow-cases; though why a pillowcase had to be ironed, Lucy couldn't imagine. Her mother was more tolerant, although she sometimes told Lucy to go out and play. Lucy didn't know how to explain that girls of twelve did not play, that even if she'd wanted to, there was nobody to play *with.* The boys spent

Saturday mornings at baseball practice; they'd all joined the town league that spring. What the girls did Saturday mornings, Lucy didn't know. The nicer ones simply ignored her. The mean ones called her Jumbo—almost, but not quite, behind her back.

She rose and scooped her own oatmeal from the pot. The last bite was the sweetest, caramel-flavored and slick with butter. In the parlor she turned on the television. The set was a gift from her brother Georgie; each Christmas he sent a wonderful present from Philadelphia. The television had arrived two years ago. It hadn't worked at first, until Sandy fiddled with the antenna and wrapped its branches in tinfoil. Then they watched television every evening, Lucy and Joyce and even Sandy, when he had nothing better to do. Her mother stayed in the kitchen, where the old radio now sat. She preferred it to television. Lucy suspected that for her there wasn't much difference.

She waited for the set to warm up, then adjusted the antenna. Her mother's eyesight was something they never talked about; it was hard to know what she could see and what she couldn't. She could still bake bread—every Friday she made four loaves. She moved from room to room with relative ease, but she seldom left the house. A few times Lucy had used this to her advantage, claiming the weather was bad when her mother sent her outside to play. Afterward shame overcame her. She vowed never to do it again.

It terrified her to think that her mother couldn't see her, a dreadful foretaste of the day she would leave them forever. Yet in one way—a horribly selfish way—it was a relief. Lucy's fatness was on display to the rest of the world, but her mother would never see her that way. She'd remember Lucy small and perfect, as she'd been at her First Communion, the prettiest one in her dress and veil. And as long as her mother didn't know, Lucy could pretend it wasn't happening: the rapid fleshing of her thighs, the rolls at her middle, the new clothes that fit for a month or two and then never again.

She didn't eat all that much. An average amount, in her estimation. An average person would eat more than Joyce, who took tiny helpings and then pecked at her food like a bird. Lucy ate only oatmeal for breakfast, though she sometimes stopped at

Bellavia's on the way to school. (Mrs. Bellavia baked bread every morning. With the leftover dough she made a special, tiny loaf for Lucy.) She ate lunch in the school cafeteria; the cook, an old Polish lady who liked her, gave her extra helpings of her favorites: mashed potatoes with gravy, thick noodles with buttered bread crumbs and cheese. After school she walked to McClanahan's for a bag of penny candy. Joyce kept a jar of change in the kitchen cupboard. Lucy had learned to fish out the coins without making a sound.

More, but not much more. It didn't seem fair.

The water pump chugged in the basement. Dorothy was running a bath. Lucy went into the kitchen and returned with a slice of buttered bread. Joyce had a strict rule about not eating in the parlor, but Joyce wasn't home. Lucy sat back and ate it, luxuriously, on the couch.

"Well, she looks all right," said George.

He and Joyce sat at the kitchen table drinking black coffee. Brown, really: he could almost discern the flowered pattern at the bottom of his cup. The family brew was famously weak, hot water faintly flavored with coffee. In truth he preferred it to Marion's espresso, to date the only thing she'd ever concocted in their kitchen.

"She's a little better," Joyce agreed. "A month ago she couldn't get out of bed on her own. Really, Georgie. She scared me half to death."

"What I can't figure out is why she won't talk." When he arrived from Philadelphia the night before, Dorothy had greeted him warmly, clinging and a little weepy; but that was nothing unusual. He'd tried talking to her at dinner, but she had simply smiled. When she did speak, her answers didn't make sense. *How nice,* she said when he asked how she was feeling.

"She's been alone a long time," he said. "Maybe she just got out of the habit."

"Don't be silly. There's more to it than that." Joyce rose and washed her cup at the sink.

"You're looking good." It was, he thought, different from *good-looking.* Joyce's hair was carefully set, her blouse tucked neatly at her waist. The kitchen, too, was immaculate. His sister ran a tight ship.

"I'm tired." She said it matter-of-factly, as though it were just a piece of information. "Mama had a doctor's appointment yesterday, and Lucy has parent-teacher conferences on Monday. It's always something."

"You need a vacation," he said automatically. Marion's friends went to France or Italy every summer, Palm Beach or Bermuda in the winter. The moment he said it, he realized it was a ridiculous suggestion. In Bakerton nobody took vacations.

"The front porch is starting to settle," said Joyce. "Would you mind taking a look?"

He shifted uncomfortably in his chair.

"What about Baker? They're the landlords,
after all. They're supposed to maintain the
place."

"I've talked to them already. Daddy built
the porch. They say it's not their problem."

"I forgot."

"Oh, Georgie."

His sister didn't waste words, George reflected; her tone said everything. Her weari-
ness and disappointment, the countless
ways he had failed the family, the deep sadness his selfishness would have caused
their father, if only he had lived to see it.

He drained his cup. "I'll go take a look."

He went out to the porch. Joyce was
right: the floor listed to one side. A few
boards had been replaced recently, but
most of the wood was original, the planks
his father had cut nearly thirty years ago. A
boy then, George had watched him cut the
wood with a handsaw. His father had been
proud of the porch, the first on Polish Hill. It
had set their house apart: a company
house, yes, but different from the others. He
had painted the boards forest green, a
handsome color. The paint was blistered
now, peeling in strips.

Gingerly he tested the floorboards. A few

gave slightly with his weight. He imagined driving across town to the lumberyard, buying nails and two-by-fours. There his vision faltered. No way could he fit the lumber into his Cadillac. He could bang a nail as well as the next guy, but the finer points of leveling and cornering were beyond him. He was as helpless a carpenter as Marion was a cook.

He glanced across the street. A truck had pulled up to the Stusicks' house, and two portly, balding men—Gene's older brothers, he realized—were struggling with a brown plaid sofa. The house had been empty since Gene's mother died. Now, apparently, someone was moving in.

"Hey there," he called. "Need a hand?" He jogged easily across the street, grabbed a corner of the sofa and helped heft it up the front steps. "Who's the new tenant?"

"No tenant." The taller brother—Fred—wedged his end through the front door. "You didn't know? Baker's has the whole hill up for sale."

"No kidding." George glanced over his shoulder, wondering who would buy a company house on Polish Hill. Cheap little cracker boxes, even when they were new; and the houses hadn't aged well. His mother's windows leaked cold air. One day soon the roof would have to be replaced.

"Gene bought it," Fred said, as if answering his question. "He's rolling in the dough now. He's a boss over at the Twelve."

They wedged the sofa through the front door. The house was as familiar to George as any he'd ever known; his whole childhood he'd traipsed through its rooms. Most of the old furniture had remained: the braided rug, the worn armchair where Mr. Stusick had read his Polish paper, the telephone table draped with a crocheted doily. On the wall, the same photographs found in every house on the Hill: Pope Pius and John L. Lewis, the legendary president of the Mineworkers, a face as familiar as family. Apparently Ev would inherit these items. George supposed she would keep them; how else would you furnish a house on Polish Hill? Marion's abstract art would look ridiculous here, as utterly misplaced as Marion herself.

They set down the sofa.

"Think that's where she wants it?" Fred asked.

The other brother shrugged. "That's Gene's problem."

"True enough." Fred wiped his hand on his trousers, then offered it to George. "Thanks for the hand, George. Stop over tomorrow, if you're around. Ev and Gene's girl is making her First Communion. They'd be glad to see you."

"I will," said George.

Again he crossed the street. His mother was sitting on the front porch. "Georgie?" she said as he climbed the stairs. A question in her voice. The realization hit him like a sucker punch: she couldn't see. At least, not well enough to recognize him.

"Hi, *bella.*" He called her this rarely, hadn't done so in years. He'd known her eyes were bad, but still.

"Where you been, Georgie?"

"Across the street. Looks like you've got some new neighbors. Gene and Ev bought the old homestead."

"Eee!" She clapped her hands. "I always love that Evelyn. That's a nice girl."

George waited.

"Georgie," she said. "How come you never marry her?"

He laughed uneasily. "That's ancient history, Ma."

"How come?" she persisted.

"It was Ev's decision. I was overseas, and somewhere along the line she decided she liked Gene better. Good choice, if you ask me."

"But how come? If he was here, I could understand. But he was in the war, too. How come she like him better?"

"Maybe he wrote better letters." Across the street Gene's brothers were moving a kitchen table. George lowered his voice, hoping his mother would take the hint.

"I guess it was my fault," he admitted. "I stopped writing."

"You *stop*?" She clapped a hand over her mouth, as outraged by his behavior as if it had happened yesterday. "Eee, how come?"

He shrugged. "Ev was all hot to get married. I had my doubts, but she couldn't wait. I had a furlough coming up, and without telling me, she went and talked to the priest. That burned me up." He paused. "Remember that time I was supposed to come home?"

"That furlough!" she cried. "And then they don't let you come."

"That's right," he said. "And you know what? I was *relieved*—that's how bad I didn't want to get married. After that I never wrote to her again. I guess she got the message, because the next time I came home, she and Gene were engaged."

His mother eyed him for a long moment. A flush crept over his cheeks. *What does she see when she looks at me?* he wondered.

"I'm not proud of it," he said. "It's just about the most cowardly thing I've ever done. But there you have it."

Still his mother said nothing.

"It worked out for the best, though. For both of us." He forced a cheerful tone. "Gene's a good man. And I've got Marion now."

Across the street Gene's brothers got into the truck.

"Georgie," she said, "are you happy?"

"Sure. Sure I'm happy." He rose, feeling his heart. "You don't know Marion; you haven't had the chance. But trust me, Mama." He bent and kissed her. "She's a wonderful girl."

They'd been married seven years. Compared with other periods in his life—adoles-

cence, the navy—his marriage seemed
much longer, though in fact little had happened. The first year passed in a haze of
sex and alcohol. He was working for
Marion's father, at the flagship Quigley's
store downtown. The old man had put him
on the sales floor. *To learn the engine,* he'd
explained to George. *If you want to know
how a machine runs, you've got to watch
the gears grind.* Quigley's own son was
spared this indoctrination: Kip, when he
showed up at all, spent his days behind
a desk. Meanwhile George hawked furniture and appliances, menswear and ladies'
shoes. No one told him so, but he understood that he would have to prove himself.
A son-in-law was not a son.

He started in Men's Furnishings. Long
days on his feet, a tape measure around his
neck, fitting trousers to grumpy old codgers
with balding legs and gin-blossom noses.
The customers resembled his father-in-law;
George had an unwelcome mental picture
of how Arthur Quigley must look in his
shorts. Yet he didn't mind the old coots;
he'd have enjoyed their company, if not for
the misery of his daily hangovers. Every
evening, Marion waited for him with a

pitcher of martinis. They drank for an hour or two, then tumbled into bed. Afterward they drank some more. Often they fought bitterly; though the reasons for the disputes, or how they resolved themselves, he rarely remembered in the morning. Sick, red-eyed, he struggled out of bed. Even in top form, he was not a natural salesman; with dry heaves and a splitting headache, even less so. Marion slept late and looked fresh and lovely when he returned in the evening; but George wondered how long he could sustain the pace. His marriage stretched eternally before him, fifty years of nausea and crippling migraines. Something would have to give.

Something did. Marion became pregnant. She blamed George—silently at first; later with streams of invective, acrimonious and profane. She spoke of traveling to Switzerland, "to have it taken care of"—a procedure she'd apparently undergone before. Then her father suffered a stroke, and for reasons George didn't wholly understand, Marion changed her mind. The baby was born a month premature, so small George might have held him in one hand, if he'd dared. They named him Arthur, for Marion's father.

The birth changed her. Once an insomniac, she now spent whole days in bed. She wept easily, an astonishing development: in all the time he'd known her, George had never seen her cry. At night he came home to the house they'd bought—a large colonial in Newtown Square, a few miles from his in-laws'—and mixed himself a drink. Upstairs his wife and baby cried, indifferent to each other and to any ministrations he might offer. He had hired a temporary nanny. Arthur was small and terrifyingly fragile. Until Marion was ready to look after him, George reasoned, his care was best left to a professional.

How to care for Marion, he had no idea. With increasing frequency, doctors came. Once she overdosed on sleeping pills—accidentally, she later claimed; though George had his doubts. Her obstetrician was no help, and neither was the Quigleys' family doctor. Marion dismissed them as idiots, and refused to see a psychiatrist. Then George found Ezra Gold.

Gold was an internist with offices on Park Avenue. George paid him extra to come to

Philadelphia; later, when Marion was well enough, she took the train into New York for her checkups. She returned from each visit with a new prescription: for anxiety, insomnia, an underactive thyroid. Amber plastic bottles lined her bathroom shelf. She swallowed pills with breakfast, at bedtime. And in the space of just a few weeks, she got better.

The transformation was astounding. For the first time George could remember, she slept through the night. She rose when he did, dressed and smiled at him across the breakfast table. She did not paint—she'd stopped during her pregnancy when the turpentine nauseated her, and had no desire to resume. She didn't read, or play with Arthur, but her demeanor was sane and pleasant. In the afternoons she shopped or had lunch with old schoolmates from Miss Porter's and Bryn Mawr. That, too, was new: she'd never shown the slightest interest in girlfriends. Her oils and canvases gathered dust in the attic. The temporary nanny moved into a spare bedroom upstairs.

At first he was filled with relief. Only later, when the crisis was past, did he understand what he had lost. At night, with the new,

changed Marion sleeping peacefully beside
him, he remembered the mysterious, vora-
cious woman he'd married, her unpredictable passions, the shocking detour his
life had taken when they met. He wondered
where she had gone.

He didn't miss her; not at first. The old
Marion had fascinated him; but he couldn't
remember being happy in her presence. His
memories were tinted like an old photograph: yellow with anxiety, red with anger,
green with drunkenness, blue with lust.
But at least he had *known* her. The new
Marion—a polite, remote woman, carefully
coiffed, who stared absently at the television while he read the newspaper, who
clutched his arm as they crossed the street,
who poured herself a single drink at bedtime and fell dead asleep on the couch—
was a stranger to him. A different woman
had led him into this Philadelphia life with its
invisible codes of behavior; a place where
he would forever remain a stranger. She'd
regarded Main Line society as an elaborate
maze constructed for her amusement, and
she'd enjoyed leading George through it,
laughing at its provincialism and pretense.

Shortly after they'd bought the Newtown

house, new neighbors moved in across the street, a pleasant young couple named Peter and Libby Hill. Peter was an attorney with a year-round suntan; he played golf every Saturday and had once asked George to come along. Though George didn't golf, he'd have liked to learn. But he had refused the invitation, because while Marion found Libby merely tedious, she *despised* Peter Hill. He was perfectly vacuous, she said; smug, venal and nearly illiterate—though how she'd gleaned all this from the occasional pleasantries they exchanged, George had no idea. The invitation had never been repeated; like the rest of his well-heeled neighbors, Peter Hill remained a stranger. Now, without Marion's ironic commentary, these people no longer struck George as ridiculous. He found them exotic and utterly intimidating, and felt himself completely alone.

He had loved to make her laugh. He was an excellent mimic, a fine physical comic. Working at Quigley's had provided him an abundance of material. At the end of the day, with a few drinks in him, he'd entertained her by impersonating the boozy customer who couldn't fasten his suspenders, the stout woman in the shoe department who refused to step on the fluoroscope because she thought it revealed her weight.

"It's an X-ray machine," George had explained. "It shows us the bones in your feet, so we can fit your shoes properly."

"Don't tell me, young man," the woman huffed. "I know ex*actly* what it shows."

Tipsy herself, Marion had shrieked with laughter; and somehow—who knew how these things happened—it had become a private joke. In bed, or at her parents' dinner table, or at First Presbyterian as Kip exchanged rings with a very pregnant bride, George had only to whisper the words into Marion's ear to send her into peals of laughter. *Don't tell me, young man. I know exactly what it shows.*

A few years later, toward the end of Marion's illness, they had attended an exhibition of abstract art at the Metropolitan. She had begun seeing Dr. Gold; for the first time since Arthur was born, she and George were spending an evening out in public. At one time she would have spent hours at such an event, but the new Marion moved quickly from canvas to canvas, clutching George's arm. Ahead of them, a scraggly bohemian type critiqued each painting, in exhaustive detail, to a suntanned old woman in a pink Chanel suit. Without thinking, George leaned close to Marion.

"Don't tell me, young man," he whispered. "I know ex*actly* what it shows."

She stared at him blankly.

"Remember, honey? The lady in the shoe department?" Thinking *Jesus, she's lost her memory, too.*

"Oh, yes," Marion said vaguely. "I remember. But I don't understand, George. What does it *mean*?"

By midmorning, the road was lined with cars, parked at odd angles on both sides of Polish Hill. The Stusicks' porch was crowded with neighbors and relatives. In the living room, card tables were loaded down with food: the usual Polish favorites, plus a hodgepodge of casseroles. A ceramic basket held ornate psanky—hand-painted Ukrainian Easter eggs. Children picked through a mountain of cookies—some store-bought, some homemade. There were cupcakes and Bundt cakes, a rhubarb pie, green and yellow gelatin salads studded with fruit.

"Beep beep," said Ev's sister Helen. George stepped aside, and she set down a plate of deviled eggs dusted with paprika. "Georgie. We didn't see you in church."

"Hi, Helen." George didn't know her married name; she lived at the top of the hill and was a notorious gossip. "We went to the first mass. Joyce is an early riser."

"How's your other sister? I heard she came back from Washington a little under the weather."

"Who told you that?"

"Ida Spangler, at the hat shop." Helen lowered her voice. "Nothing serious, I hope."

Goddamned small town, George thought. "Bronchitis," he said. "Turned into pneumonia. She's still recuperating." He spied Gene heading out the back door. "Excuse me. I want to say hi to Gene."

He wove his way through the crowded kitchen to the back porch. Gene stood at the kettle grill digging at the charcoals, a bottle of Iron City in his hand. He was still in his Sunday clothes, suit trousers and a short-sleeved shirt.

"Eugenius," George called.

"Georgie." He had thickened around the middle, but otherwise looked much as he had in childhood: fair hair standing up in a cowlick, glasses repaired at the temple with electrical tape. "Glad you could come."

They sat in folding chairs overlooking the small yard, which had been taken over by children playing a noisy game of tag. "So you're a homeowner now," said George. "Congratulations."

"Can you believe it?" Gene handed him a bottle from the cooler. "I wish my dad had lived to see it. He hated living in a company house. It about killed him, having that money taken out of his pay every month."

George nodded. *You pay rent, you never have nothing:* his own father had said it a thousand times.

"They're solid houses, Georgie. Nothing wrong with them a little elbow grease won't fix. It's hard to believe Baker's letting them go." Gene took a pull on his beer. "What about your mom? Any chance she'll buy her place?"

"She hasn't said anything. To tell you the truth, I didn't know it was for sale."

The screen door opened and Evelyn appeared, carrying a plate of snacks: celery stuffed with cream cheese, more deviled eggs. "Well, look who's here."

"How are you, Ev?" He embraced her quickly, avoiding Gene's eyes. The three of them had spent their adolescence at

Keener's Diner: George and Ev on one side
of the booth, hip to hip; Gene on the other
side, alone. Ev had felt sorry for him,
George remembered. A few times she'd offered to set him up with one of her girlfriends, but Gene wasn't interested. Always
it had been the three of them.

Ev sat, smoothing her skirt. "How's life in
the big city, Georgie?"

"Not bad. Good to be back here, though.
There's no place like home."

"It must be hard, being so far away. You
must worry about your mother."

"Joyce takes good care of her," said
George. "But yeah, I do."

"If you're interested," said Gene, "we're
hiring over at the Twelve."

"Oh, Georgie's not looking for a job." Ev
pulled up a chair. "Aren't you about finished
with medical school?"

"Oh, I gave up on that a long time ago."
George took the beer Gene offered. "I work
in retail. Marion's father has a department
store."

"He sell Caddies at that store?" Gene
asked, a twinkle in his eye.

George grinned. "Oh, *that*. My brother-in-
law has a dealership." After a series of ac-

counting missteps that would have landed anyone else—George included—in prison, old man Quigley had given up on teaching his son the family business. He'd bought Kip a Cadillac dealership, a business so foolproof that even a proven fool couldn't run it into the ground.

"Told you," Gene said to Ev. He grinned. "My wife here was ogling your Eldorado."

Ev blushed to the roots of her hair. "It's beautiful, Georgie. And so *clean.*"

"What do those go for new?" Gene asked. "Four grand?"

More like six, George thought but didn't say.

Ev gasped. "Four thousand *dollars*? For a *car*? That's more than we paid for this house!"

George shifted uncomfortably. He'd felt guilty about spending the money—his wife's money—on such a luxury; but on some level he felt entitled. The car made him happy. Except for his son—a clever, hyperactive five year old, sweet-natured and affectionate—it was the only thing in his life that did.

"Georgie's no fool," Gene said, laughing. "I told her you must have got it at cost."

"Gene!" Ev protested, her cheeks flushing. "Ignore him, Georgie. He's got no manners. Never has."

George watched her. Later—days, months,
years later—he would replay the moment in
his mind, the flush creeping up from her
throat. He had always loved her skin, its ut-
ter transparency. She'd never been able to
keep a secret; her feelings were written on
her face, all over her body. There was no
mystery to a redhead. A redhead was inca-
pable of deceit.

"Sure," he lied. "I got a nice discount." He
turned to Gene. "I hear you're doing well for
yourself, Mr. Crew Boss."

Gene beamed. "It's a hell of an operation,
Georgie. Right now we're bringing up eight
thousand tons a day. That's enough to heat
eight hundred homes for an entire winter."

He adjusted his glasses, which had
slipped down his nose—a gesture George
had seen him perform a thousand times.
Despite his swagger, Gene hadn't changed
at all. Underneath was still the same boy
who had rattled off the list of presidents,
who could multiply and divide in his head.

"Eugenius," George said, raising his glass.
"It's good to be home."

*   *   *

Afternoon stretched into evening. Cold bottles of Iron City appeared from the cooler; empty bottles were whisked away. George watched the children chase one another across the yard: red-haired Lipnics, blond-haired Stusicks, a few girls still in Communion dresses, like tiny brides. Adults crowded the living room—young couples, old women. Past a certain age the men seemed to disappear. The lucky ones, like Gene's uncles, hobbled around on canes, crippled by Miner's Knee, Miner's Hip, Miner's Back. The rest were at home breathing bottled oxygen, their lungs ruined from years of inhaling coal dust. You'd have to call them moderately lucky, George reflected. The unluckiest were like his own father, keeled over in his own basement. Dead at fifty-four.

He watched Gene flip hamburgers at the grill. *Smarter than me,* George thought, *and what is he doing? What is this life he's signed on for?* In his boozy state, his old buddy seemed to him a kind of bookmark, holding his place in a life he himself had started but decided not to finish. The company house, the redheaded children, the woman George could have (and maybe should have—probably, definitely should have) married. Eugenius would be the one who finished that book. Eugenius would let him know how it all turned out.

He watched Ev carry plates back and forth to the kitchen. She wore a yellow dress cinched at the middle. He was aware of breasts and arms, a round behind. She had been his first, and he'd been hers. One time only, the night before he left, but enough to qualify for the title. *I love you. In my heart we're already married.* At the time he'd meant it—at least he thought he did. And she had taken him at his word.

She pulled up a chair next to him. "Whew. I'm beat."

"Are they all yours, Ev?" George asked, pointing.

"Gosh, no. Leonard's in fourth grade." She pointed to a boy in striped trousers. George would have recognized him anywhere: his father's thick glasses, his mother's red curls. "You met him when he was a baby. Then the two girls. Gene wants to try for another boy, but I'm ready to retire." She laughed. "How old's your boy, Georgie? I don't even know his name."

"Arthur. He'll be six in July."

"Just the one, Georgie?" She smiled; again the hint of a blush. "You're not planning on more?"

"Marion's awfully busy. I'm not sure what she'd do with another one."

"Is she—a career girl?" She used the phrase hesitantly, as though she weren't sure it applied. *I could kiss her,* George thought.

"I guess," he said. And then, because an explanation seemed necessary: "She's a painter."

"A housepainter?"

"Oh, no. She's, you know, an artist."

Ev blushed a deep red. Again he felt his heart quicken. His own cheeks heated, as if warmed by hers. *I'm drunk,* he thought.

"Well, she sounds fascinating. I'd love to meet her someday."

He let himself imagine this: Marion in Ev's living room on Polish Hill, eating deviled eggs, swapping recipes for gelatin salad. Marion's recap afterward: *My picnic with Evelyn Picnic. Her progeny screaming in the next room. Her milkmaid's arms as big as my thighs.* The old Marion: skewering Ev with a few turns of her vast vocabulary, in the bored, flat tone that let you know how little she cared.

"Oh, sure," he said miserably. "You two would hit it off." He rose, a bit unsteady, and began clearing plates from the table.

"Georgie, sit! You don't have to do that."

"It's the least I can do."

She gave him an odd look: he'd said it with more feeling than was appropriate. He couldn't help himself. Picturing Ev at Marion's mercy unsettled him deeply. As though he himself were sadistic and cruel, as though he'd imagined her violent death.

The street was dark by the time the party broke up. George crossed the street, feeling guilty. He'd spent the whole day—a third of his visit—at Gene and Ev's. Now his mother's windows were dark.

He climbed the porch stairs on tiptoe. The old floorboards creaked beneath his weight. *The porch,* he remembered: he had promised to help Joyce with the porch. But he was due at the store Monday afternoon. He would have to leave first thing in the morning.

He glanced over his shoulder at the Cadillac gleaming beneath the street lamp. He'd stopped along the highway and paid a dollar to have it washed. Now the small extravagance shamed him. He'd always been vain about his cars.

He closed the screen door quietly behind him; feeling along the wall, he climbed the stairs to his room. His suitcase sat at the foot of the bed; he hadn't even bothered to unpack it. Shame prickled his skin. Had his mother noticed? Did she know he was in such a hurry to leave?

He clicked open the suitcase. In the pocket of his trousers he found his checkbook. *Why not?* he thought. *For God's sake, what is money for?*

His hand shaking, he wrote a check for $5,814, the exact sticker price of a '55 Eldorado ragtop, payable to Joyce Novak. On the memo line he wrote, in wavy letters: *You pay rent, you never have nothing.*

He left the check on top of the bureau. By the time she found it, he would be halfway to Philadelphia.

Every year, in the third week of July, Mount Carmel Church held its annual festival and spaghetti dinner. Tents were raised on the church lawn. In the street, a bandstand and rides for the children: chair swings, a miniature carousel. Susquehanna Avenue was closed off with sawhorses, causing a tangle of traffic on the street below. Every year the local merchants grumbled. Might as well shut down for the weekend. No one does business on Dago Day. A few wrote letters to the mayor. But John Mastrantonio chaired the town council. Every year the requisite permits were issued, and Dago Day was celebrated as planned.

Every Italian in town worked at the festival. When Rose Novak was a girl, her aunts fried sausages and rolled meatballs in the church basement. Before he went away to war, her brother had helped build the gaming booths—darts, ringtoss, chuck-o-luck—and hammered the posts into the parish lawn. Her uncle Vincent had built the wooden platform used in the procession, to carry Our Lady of Mount Carmel through the streets of the town. Each year the platform was decorated with fresh-cut roses, the statue draped in a long cloak of sky blue velvet. Carried, always, by six young men, and followed by the Legion of Mary, the Knights of Columbus and the church choir. The procession wound its way through Little Italy, a slow-moving beast sluggish in the afternoon heat, easily caught by the small dark-eyed children who pursued it, carrying dollar bills punctured with safety pins. The bills were pinned to Our Lady's cloak. The sign of the cross was made.

The festival ended with a pyrotechnics display; for many years, Rose's father had driven his wagon to Punxsutawney to buy the firecrackers. All of Bakerton watched the fireworks, but the Italians had the best view, from the steep hill behind the church.

As a girl of eleven, Rose cleared tables at the spaghetti dinner. She had just come over with her mother. Starting fifth grade at the grammar school, she had learned, cruelly, that her English was poor; but at Mount Carmel that didn't matter. The patrons spoke to her in Italian. The women in the kitchen called her *bella,* gave her anisette cookies and exclaimed over her long hair. As a teenager, she helped decorate Our Lady's platform. During the procession she sang in the choir.

After her marriage, Rose stopped working at the festival. Her children were baptized at St. Casimir's, and she acquired a collection of dowdy hats, which the Polish women favored over mantillas. Her life was in all ways Polish except for one day each summer: on the third Saturday in July, Stanley stayed home alone; Rose and the children trekked across town to the festival. There, Georgie and Dorothy chased around the churchyard with their Scarponi cousins. Rose sat under an awning with her aunts, playing bingo and drinking Sambuca, speaking Italian and breaking out periodically in cawing laughter. Years later, her children would remember that Rose laughed more on Dago Day than on all the other days of the year combined.

* * *

The third saturday in July was the hottest
day of the year. At eleven in the morning the
temperature reached a hundred degrees.
"It's not so bad," Rose told the girls, in defi-
ance of all evidence. She could still distin-
guish light from dark, could recognize certain shapes; but her feet were swollen, a
sign her heart was failing. Still she would
not miss the festival.

Joyce drove them into town and dropped
them off at the church—the nearest parking
space was blocks away. Dorothy led Rose
to a chair under the canopy, where her
aunts were playing bingo.

The aunts—in their seventies now—
greeted them with hugs and shrieks. "You
looking good, honey," said Aunt Marcella,
kissing Dorothy loudly. "You hang in there,
you be good as new."

Dorothy guided Rose to a folding chair.
She *did* feel well. She had regained a little
weight; her daily walks had improved her
appetite. Little by little, her speech had returned. She'd set her hair and wore a new
dress. Joyce had taken her shopping for her
thirtieth birthday that spring.

"Dorothy," said Aunt Bruna. "Come here, *bella*. I got a job for you." The kitchen was shorthanded, she explained; the second seating had begun, and there weren't enough waitresses. "We need some girls to pour coffee. Pretty girls," she said, winking. "Keep the men occupied while they wait."

In this way Dorothy found herself in the church basement, an apron wrapped around her waist. Long tables stretched from wall to wall, set with folding chairs. Families sat close together: grandparents, young couples, children in Sunday clothes. There was no telling where one family ended and the next began. The same features repeated up and down every table: brown eyes, black hair, sharp noses, square chins. The overflow crowd waited in line at the door. The room seemed to Dorothy very full—perfume, cigar smoke, laughter, all tightly contained by the cinder-block walls.

There was no room for shyness, no time. She hurried from table to table pouring coffee; the simplicity of the task reassured her, the impossibility of making conversation in the loud room. Men laughed and called to her. *Hey, coffee girl. Another refill here. Good thing you so skinny, get between*

them tables like that. Old men, strongly per-
fumed, in pink shirts and pastel slacks.
Some bald, with oiled scalps; others with
low hairlines, graying pompadours beginning just above the eyebrows. Dorothy
smiled back; it was impossible not to. She
filled their cups and returned to the kitchen
for a fresh pot.

For an hour or more she raced and
poured. Packed full of bodies, the room
grew close. The heat of the kitchen astonished her, the enormous pots of boiling
macaroni, the steaming vats of tomato
sauce. She wiped her brow. Around her the
room began to spin.

"Whatsa matter?" someone called. The
voice seemed very far away.

"She gonna pass out," said another.

"I got her." Someone took the coffeepot
from her hands; she felt herself lifted, briefly,
off the floor. A man's arms beneath her. *I'm
swimming,* she thought.

"Hey, you okay? Lights still on in there?"
He was her age, perhaps older. He looked
like the others: the eyes, the hair.

"Poor girl, she need some air," a woman
crowed. "Angie, be a good boy and take her
outside."

*   *   *

They sat on the back steps of the rectory, shaded at that hour by a gnarled cherry tree.

"That was a close call," he said. "You almost hit the deck."

"I don't know what happened."

"Hotter than hell in there." He fumbled in his pocket for a cigarette.

"I've been ill. I'm still getting my strength back." She leaned against the brick wall, slightly cooler than her skin. "Thank you for helping me. I'm sorry to take you away from your dinner."

"That's all right." He loosened his tie. His neck looked thick and powerful; his white shirt was damp under the arms. "I'd rather sit here with you."

"I should get back," she said, rising.

"Easy." He laid a hand on her leg. A large, handsome hand, the wrist covered with black hair. "Sit a minute. I'll get you some water."

He returned with a paper cup and a piece of garlic toast. "Here. Eat this."

She took the bread, warm and buttery. It

left an oily film on her fingers. She realized she hadn't eaten all day.

"My mother says you're too skinny. I said I like you the way you are." He said it simply, as though it meant nothing.

"She asked me your name," he said.

"Dorothy Novak."

"Angelo Bernardi. They call me Angie."

"Angelo," she repeated. It was a beautiful name.

"Bernardi," said Joyce. "The undertakers?"

The sisters were sitting on the front porch, drinking glasses of lemonade. Up and down Polish Hill the neighbors were doing the same. The fireworks had finished; the children had been put to bed. It was too hot to sleep.

"There were three of them that I remember," said Joyce, ticking them off on her fingers. "Jerry was two years ahead of me. Plus there were two older boys, twins. They were all in the service."

"Victor and Sal," said Dorothy, who had graduated with them. "I remember Victor and Sal."

It was an exercise performed in small towns everywhere: the tracing back through generations, the connecting of in-laws and distant cousins, names familiar from church or school. Rose and her sisters were masters of the art; Joyce and Dorothy had grown up listening to their aunts exchange information over coffee and cake. It could not accurately be called gossip; there was nothing malicious in the talk. It was simply the female way of ordering the world, a universe where everyone was important and all activities worthy of notice.

"Angelo?" Joyce frowned. "There was another cousin, older, but he got married a few years ago. A Scalia girl. Her sister was at the factory with me."

"I know he said Bernardi." An exotic name, lovely in her mouth. Already she had said it a dozen times. He had asked for her phone number but hadn't written it down. *Right here,* he said, tapping his temple. *I got it right here.*

"Wasn't one of the Bernardis a ballplayer?" Joyce asked. "Do you remember this? He played for Baker, and then got drafted by one of the professional teams."

Dorothy frowned. "You're thinking of Ernie Tedesco. That was a long time ago."

"Could be," said Joyce. "I don't know why I thought Bernardi. Why don't you just ask Mama? She's an expert on the Italians."

Dorothy nodded. It would have been logical to ask Rose first, but something had stopped her.

"Don't say anything just yet," she said. "He might not even call."

He didn't call.

Weeks passed. In the afternoons she walked through Little Italy, glancing at parked cars, peering into shop windows. Above every store were two floors of apartments, their windows covered in lace. He might live anywhere. She might walk past his window every day. She would never know.

(On those long walks she did not think of her mother, the summer Rose spent looking for Stanley Novak, before he wandered into the seamstress's shop to order his wedding suit. The way she had hunted him, the nakedness of her need. Stanley himself had never known. Rose would carry the secret to her grave.)

One afternoon Dorothy bought a pastry at Bellavia's and sat there a long time eating it, at a tiny table facing the window. An old woman passed, dressed in black. At the end of the block the parochial school had let out for recess: shouts and squeals, the singsong voices of girls jumping rope. Across the street, cars idled in front of the funeral parlor; at the head of the line, an old-fashioned black hearse, chrome gleaming in the sun. Mourners filed out of the building, stopping to shake hands with the old man who stood at the door. The man was thin and very stooped. He looked a hundred years old.

The mourners got into their cars. One by one the doors slammed shut. The old man picked his way, roosterlike, across the sidewalk, and got into the passenger side of the hearse. The car rolled forward, its lights flashing. Dorothy squinted into the sun. A moment later she caught her breath.

The driver was Angelo Bernardi.

"Where are they going?" she asked Mrs. Bellavia.

"St. Brigid's," the old lady explained. "A McDonald died."

After that Dorothy passed the funeral home every day. Each morning she checked the obituaries; in the afternoon she walked the Catholic cemeteries: St. Brigid's, St. Casimir's, Our Mother of Sorrows, Mount Carmel. When she spotted the hearse, her heart quickened; but always the wrong cousin was driving. Most days the driver was Jerry; a few times, Victor or Sal.

She did not give up. And on a windy afternoon in early October, she saw Angelo Bernardi.

An Italian child was to be buried: a boy, Nicholas Annacone, crushed by a car as he chased a ball into the street. Dorothy set out at noon under a clear sky, the vibrant blue of early autumn. An hour later she climbed the hill to Mount Carmel. The service had ended; the mourners were returning to their cars. A canopy had been erected at the grave site. Two men in overalls struggled to refold it, the canvas flapping loudly in the wind. Cars cruised toward the cemetery gates. At the grave site a man stood leaning against the hearse.

For once she did not hesitate. She had

missed too many chances already: Walter
Parish, a young clerk at Treasury who'd spoken to her at the watercooler; men who'd
tipped their hats or smiled at her on the bus.
Chick Rowsey in the pool at Glen Echo: his
arms around her on the train platform, his
mouth on hers. Each disappointment had
weakened her; losing hope was like losing
blood. She could not survive another failure.
Already she was hemorrhaging from regret.

She walked toward him. The wind blew
petals and loose dirt. A car horn blared.
Later she realized she hadn't even looked;
she could have been run over like Nicholas
Annacone. She had forgotten everything:
her fears, her self-respect, what her sister
called common sense. All she could remember was a name, Angelo Bernardi.

He reached into his pocket for a cigarette
and lit it. Then he saw her.

"Hey," he said, tossing away the match. "I
know you."

"Dorothy Novak," she said quickly, before
he could ask.

"From the festival. What, you think I forgot? I'm kidding," he said, flashing her a
smile. "What are you doing here?"

"Just walking."

"In the graveyard?"

"My grandmother is buried here. I put flowers on her grave." *I'm lying,* she reflected calmly. Just then it didn't seem to matter. She watched his hands.

"What a beautiful day. Makes you glad to be alive." A stream of smoke shot out his nostrils. "Did you hear about this kid?" He nodded toward the fresh grave. "Eight years old. Those parents, my God. You shoulda seen it. Out of their minds with grief."

"It's horrible."

"Makes you think. Beautiful day like this: How many of them are you gonna get? I haven't seen the sun in a week." He noticed her frown. "I work at the Twelve. It's my day off. I'm helping out my uncle for the day."

"That's nice of you."

"Tell me about it." He inhaled deeply. "Nah. Tell him. I'm tired of hearing how I never lift a finger. I been hearing that song my whole life."

He flicked a cigarette ash from his lapel.

"I'm sorry. I got no manners, running at the mouth like this. But I don't mind telling you, I got frustrations." He tossed away his cigarette. "I got the car all day. You feel like taking a ride?"

* * *

They took the back way out of town, a winding road that cut through cool acres of forest, connecting Bakerton to the neighboring towns: Coalport, Fallentree, Moss Creek, towns too small for even a post office. A hand-lettered sign—U.S. MAIL—hung above a walk-up window on somebody's front porch. Dorothy had seen these towns from a train window, the slow local. She'd imagined them much farther away.

He drove fast and expertly. Wind rushed through the open windows, ruffled the silky curtains, and Dorothy remembered she was riding in a hearse. At first the speed delighted her. Then her stomach churned. Closing her eyes made matters worse. She clutched helplessly at the seat.

"Whatsa matter? You carsick?"

"A little dizzy," she admitted. "Can we stop for a minute?"

He signaled and pulled off the road. "You okay? You look a little green." He leaned across her to roll down the window. For a moment his head was level with her breasts. His black hair looked dense as moss.

"My fault," he said. "I drive too fast. The

old man is always on me about it. Good for the engine, though. Cleans out all the shit. Excuse my French." He looked at her closely. "You don't talk much, do you?"

Dorothy flushed.

"That's unusual in a girl. I got four sisters, they never shut up." He reached for her hand. "I thought about calling you. I could kick myself. Things got complicated. I don't know what to say."

His hand was broad and heavy in her lap, his skin warm to the touch.

"Kiss me," she said.

He dropped her off at the bottom of Polish Hill. "Bunch of busybodies in this town," he explained. "You can't take a crap without somebody knowing about it." She knew he was right. She'd be curious, too, if she saw one of her neighbors step out of a hearse.

At home her mother and sisters were sitting down to supper.

"Where have you been?" said Joyce. "We were starting to worry."

"I took a walk. I lost track of time." Dorothy tore into a hunk of Rose's bread.

She was suddenly ravenous. "It was a beautiful day."

Joyce peered at her. "Looks like you got some sun."

Dorothy ate in silence. She often ate in silence, but that day it weighed on her. For the first time in months she was dying to speak. Instead she shoveled in chicken, potatoes, her mother's fried eggplant. It was the only way she could keep quiet, until she could be alone with the memory of him.

Her boldness had surprised him. *You're something, aren't you?* Then he pulled her close, wrapping her in his smell—cigarettes, garlic, cologne.

They had kissed a long time. His cheeks were rough as sandpaper. Later, in her bedroom mirror, she saw that Joyce was right: her mouth and cheeks looked sunburned; her neck, her ears, her throat. Even her chest was flushed, down to the top button of her blouse. She had stopped him there.

I should go, she said. *I have to be home for supper.*

His mouth had felt warm and alive. Eyes closed, she had imagined herself swimming. Now she wondered what would have happened if she hadn't stopped him. She wondered if she would be red all over.

"I ran into someone when I was walking," she blurted out. "That fellow from Mount Carmel Day. Angelo Bernardi."

Joyce set down her fork. "Wasn't he supposed to call you?"

"He lost my number," Dorothy lied.

"Bernardi?" said Rose. "Eeee, I know him! That one that got divorced."

"Divorced?" Dorothy repeated. "Oh, Mama. You must be thinking of someone else."

"No, it's him! He marry that Scalia girl. She living at her mother's now, with them kids."

"Children?" Dorothy's voice quavered; for a moment she thought she might cry. "Oh, that's impossible. It simply can't be."

"He don't tell you?" Rose's face darkened. "Bad enough he get divorced, but how come he lie about it?"

Dorothy rose, clearing the plates. She was unable to sit still.

"Mama, I'm sure you're mistaken," she said evenly. "He has so many cousins. You must be thinking of one of them."

*   *   *

The thing was, it didn't matter.

They met four days a week in the municipal park on Indian Hill. The park was deserted in the fall; the swimming pool drained, the chain swings taken down from their frames. Late afternoon, the sky a deep blue; they walked a slow circle around the park as Angelo told her about his day. A new boss the men despised, jokes he'd heard—the clean ones only—from a fellow on his crew. She smiled and waited. She sensed he was waiting, too. Finally he led her to his car, parked discreetly behind the pool house. He smelled of soap and hair oil, his after-work shower. His shirts were freshly laundered, his hands clean as a priest's. Once, thinking of her father, she asked how he got his nails so white.

"Gloves," he said bashfully. "The guys have a good laugh over it, but goddamn if I'm going to go through life with black fingernails."

His mouth covered more of her. One day he led her to the backseat of his car. "More room back here," he said softly. He eased her backward onto the seat and stretched

out on top of her. For a moment she panicked, but his weight reassured her. The
world seemed very small, no wider than the
confines of his car. For once it seemed a
manageable size.

Afterward he dropped her at the bottom
of Polish Hill. She noticed curtains moving
in the windows—her neighbors wondering
where the Novak girl was coming from. *Let
them wonder,* Dorothy thought.

They didn't go out on dates. Her mother
wouldn't have stood for it. Other girls might
have minded, but Dorothy felt secret relief.
She couldn't imagine sitting across from
him in a restaurant, making conversation;
or navigating the crowded dance floor at
the Vets, surrounded by strangers. A date
would mean wearing stockings, fixing her
hair, inviting him inside to chat with her family. Joyce did these things every week, when
she went to the movies with Ed Hauser; but
to Dorothy they seemed impossible. She
came to Angelo in her natural state. She
wore no lipstick; she spoke only when she
felt like it.

It seemed too good to be true.

The three girls crossed the railroad tracks and started up Polish Hill. Clare Ann Baran and Connie Kukla, with their look-alike pageboy haircuts, their skinny legs in navy blue kneesocks. Behind them, a head taller, was Lucy Novak. The girls had stayed after school to practice their presentations for the science fair. Clare Ann and Connie had done a project together, a complicated experiment involving bacteria and petri dishes. Lucy had worked alone, observing different types of cloud formations and sketching them in a journal. All scientific research, Sister had explained, began with a hypothesis. The hypothesis was tested by conducting experiments. The class had written out their hypotheses on index cards and handed them to Sister. Lucy's hypothesis was, *Different cloud formations predict the weather.* She had determined that her hypothesis was correct.

"He didn't do it himself," Clare Ann was saying. "I know for a fact that his dad made it for him." They were discussing a fifth grader, Leonard Stusick, who'd built a papier-mâché volcano. No one had been impressed until it exploded with foamy lava, a chemical reaction of vinegar and baking soda.

"I knew it!" Connie cried. "He never could have figured that out by himself. He's only in fifth grade."

"It isn't fair," said Clare Ann. "He isn't even supposed to compete until sixth. Those are the *rules.*"

Lucy said nothing. Leonard Stusick had moved into the house across the street from her, and the two sometimes played together, even though Lucy was two grades ahead. She would have been ashamed to admit this to Clare Ann and Connie, who weren't really her friends. They were the only other Science Club girls who lived on Polish Hill, and every Monday after practice they allowed her to walk home with them.

This, too, was embarrassing, but not nearly so humiliating as walking alone.

The girls climbed the hill, their poster boards rattling in the wind. The sky had darkened. *Cumulus,* Lucy thought, eyeing the horizon. *Cumulus and nimbus.* Headlights flashed behind her: a hearse was climbing the hill. It passed the girls, then idled a moment. The driver stepped out. He was tall and handsome, with curly hair like Rock Hudson; he moved with an athlete's grace. He went around to open the passenger door. Out stepped Lucy's sister Dorothy.

Clare Ann and Connie seemed not to notice.

"He ought to be disqualified," said Clare Ann. "That's what happens when you break the rules."

Later, at supper, Lucy watched her sister closely. Dorothy was her odd, distracted self, speaking little, staring vacantly out the window. After supper she skittered around the kitchen clearing plates, wiping counters, scraping leftovers into Tupperware containers. She did whatever Joyce told her to do, even though Joyce was five years younger. This struck Lucy as horribly wrong, a clear violation of the family hierarchy.

Now she studied her sister in a scientific way. Dorothy was round-shouldered and flat-chested, plain and dreary in her pilling sweaters and baggy skirts. She had a pretty face, though. Her eyes were beautiful, deep brown flecked with gold. Rock Hudson might have noticed her eyes. Maybe pretty eyes were enough.

Maybe so; what did Lucy know? She'd been raised by women, and her teachers were nuns. Her whole life her brothers had ignored her, and she had no memory of her father. Leonard Stusick didn't count; he was only ten, a little boy. The man Lucy knew best was Ed Hauser, who showed up every Friday night to take Joyce to the movies. Ed was tall and ungainly, nearly bald; his trousers an inch too short, as if a flood were coming. After supper Joyce would monopolize the bathroom for an hour. She'd emerge in one of her schoolmarmish dresses looking no different than before, except for the dash of red lipstick at her mouth. *For cripe's sake,* Lucy wanted to say. *It took you an hour to do that?*

When the doorbell rang, Joyce answered it in a sugary voice. She made a big show of inviting Ed into the kitchen, where he shook hands with Dorothy and Lucy, like the Fuller Brush salesman. Then Joyce took him into the parlor to say hello to Rose. For reasons Lucy didn't understand, her mother was crazy about Ed. He sat beside her on the couch and tried speaking to her in Italian, which he had learned in college. His Italian was so bad that it made Rose laugh. This, Lucy supposed, was Ed's best quality. As pitiful as he was, as awkward and unattractive, he could make her mother laugh.

When Joyce and Ed came back from the movies, Lucy was always awake. Lying in bed, she heard their footsteps on the porch, Ed's clumsy shuffle, the quick tick of Joyce's pumps. There was a pause before the door opened, and Lucy knew they were kissing good night. The very thought of it turned her stomach.

Now she watched Dorothy stack the plates in the sink. Her boyfriend was handsome. Lucy liked his dark hair, his big shoulders, the elegant way he'd opened the car door. She could imagine them dancing, even kissing. She didn't mind the thought of

Dorothy being kissed. Dorothy wasn't mean like Joyce; she simply lacked a backbone. Now Lucy wondered if it were all an act, a way of deflecting attention so that she could do as she pleased.

After supper Lucy took her marbles across the street and knocked at the Stusicks' back door. The supper dishes were stacked in the drainer. Leonard sat at the table hunched over his homework, his glasses sliding down his nose.

"Whatcha doing?" Lucy asked.

He looked up from his book. For a second you could see how happy he was to see her. Then he rearranged his face into a more reasonable expression.

"How'd you like the volcano?" he asked.

Lucy wondered, for a moment, if he'd heard what Connie and Clare Ann had said. She'd been aware of him some distance behind them—walking alone, carrying his volcano in a shoe box. She hadn't dared to say hello.

"I liked the explosion," she said. "Wanna shoot some marbles?"

"Sure," said Leonard. "But you have all of mine from last time."

"That's okay. I'll let you win them back."

Leonard rose. "We could play on the front porch. The light is better out there."

Lucy thought about the picture they would make, sitting on the porch steps: the little boy with glasses, the fat girl twice his size.

"Nah," she said. "Let's go out back."

They went out the back door and crouched over the sidewalk. It hadn't rained all week; faint chalk lines were still visible from the last time they'd played. Carefully she redrew the lines.

"Was that your sister?" he asked.

Lucy nodded.

"Did somebody die?"

"Nope."

"Then why was she getting out of a hearse?"

She let him shoot first. "I don't know. I think he's her boyfriend."

"She has a boyfriend?" He looked dumbfounded, as though she'd told him Dorothy could fly.

Lucy gave him a dirty look. "Why shouldn't she?"

"How should I know?" He took another shot. He had small, careful hands, like a mouse's paws. "I just wouldn't have thought so, is all."

"Me neither," she admitted. "Anyway, I'm not even sure it's true. It's"—she captured one of Leonard's marbles—"a hypothesis."

She tested her hypothesis over the next few weeks. Dorothy came home from her walks in a shapeless wool coat, a plaid muffler wound around her throat. One night after supper, Lucy examined the coat pockets (empty); she sniffed the muffler for perfume (none). She studied Dorothy at breakfast, lumping out bowls of oatmeal; in church, her lips moving silently as she fingered her rosary. She waited for a knowing look, some hint of secrecy. None came.

In November, All Saints' Day fell on a Wednesday—a free day for the parochial students, although the public school was open. Joyce went to work as usual; Lucy spent the morning in front of the television. In the afternoon Dorothy left for her walk. Lucy waited a few minutes, then followed behind.

They walked through the center of town, past the fire hall and St. Brigid's, to where the road climbed Indian Hill. Dorothy moved briskly; Lucy, breathing heavily, could scarcely keep up. At the base of the hill were the coal-company offices; at the top, a custard stand and the municipal swimming pool, both closed for the season. The hill was steep; there was no sidewalk. Still they climbed.

At the top of the hill Dorothy stopped. She smoothed her hair and unbuttoned her coat. Lucy had fallen far behind; she was sure Dorothy hadn't seen her. Still she stepped back from the road, behind a clump of teaberry bushes. She heard deep rumbling in the distance, a car's engine. A moment later, a shiny Pontiac climbed the hill. Lucy blinked, confused. She had expected the hearse.

Dorothy turned at the car's approach. She smiled and gave the driver a wave. Lucy ducked lower, grateful for her hiding place. Her legs trembled weakly, exhausted from the climb, but now she didn't care. Things were getting interesting.

The car disappeared behind the pool house, shuttered for the season. A moment later the engine died. Lucy heard a car door open and close. Then Rock Hudson appeared. He wore dark trousers and an Eisenhower jacket. He ran a hand through his curly hair.

He said something in a low voice. "Oh, I think so!" Dorothy answered brightly. She fell into step beside him; they strolled the path that snaked through the park. They did not touch. *They're walking,* Lucy thought. *Big deal.*

She looked up at the sky. Cumulus clouds, gray underneath; rain was coming, or maybe snow. Her left foot hurt across the instep, blistered by the strap of her Mary Janes. She wished she had worn her tennis shoes. Who knew Dorothy would walk so far?

She breathed on her hands to warm them. The two figures strolled the perimeter of the park—the man talking, Dorothy nodding agreement. Finally he took her hand, and they disappeared behind the pool house.

Lucy rose from behind the bushes, her legs stiff from crouching. The grass was marshy. Her feet were silent as an Indian's.

She peered around the building, as she'd seen the Hardy Boys do on television. She watched Dorothy step daintily into the backseat of the Pontiac. The man followed, closing the door behind him.

Lucy squinted. The sky had darkened; she could barely see inside the car. Dorothy's head disappeared from sight. Then the man's. *They're lying down,* Lucy thought.

A raindrop struck her cheek. She stood in the rain, watching.

SIX

Fall froze into winter. The Monday after Thanksgiving, men donned their orange vests. The firemen held a 5 a.m. pancake breakfast. At the high school, Viola Peale taught Latin grammar as usual, despite the empty desks. All the boys, and a few girls, were absent on Opening Day. Some teachers gave up and held study hall. A few called in sick and went hunting themselves.

Deer appeared in the beds of pickups, trussed and hanging upside down from trees. Vic Bernardi bagged a ten-point buck; he was shown holding its antlers on the front page of the *Herald*. Leonard Stusick shot his first deer, a respectable six-pointer. Excitement gave way to boredom, his sisters' complaints: endless meals of deer sausage and venison stew. Taxider-

mists worked overtime the month of December, to mount all the heads in time for
Christmas.

That winter, without fanfare, Baker Brothers
closed its company store. A small notice
appeared on the back page of the Herald;
when Joyce read it aloud, Rose was astonished. She hadn't been inside the store—
any store—in years, but Baker's remained
clear in her memory: the green tiled floor,
the window displays of pots and china, the
fabric samples hanging from hooks on the
wall. The dark wooden counter lined with
spice jars and medicines, earthenware vats
of pickled cucumbers and peppers and
cabbage and beets. From childhood on, the
store had seemed to her a complete universe, containing everything a person could
want, however fanciful her tastes or exotic
her interests. Baker's stocked the everyday
things Rose needed—flour and soap powder, cooking oil and salt—plus other, more
glamorous items—beef roasts, a trestle
sewing machine, sugar cubes decorated
with tiny rosettes—she coveted but couldn't

afford. That left plenty—musical instruments, a typewriter, crystal figurines shaped like animals—she couldn't imagine finding a use for, even if she had a hundred dollars to spend.

Years before, the Pennsylvania Railroad had built a siding to Baker's back door, to accommodate shoppers arriving on the local. Now a few widows went to Baker's out of habit, but the miners' families hadn't shopped there in years. The union had done away with company scrip, and big grocery chains—Acme, Quaker, A&P—had moved into town. Joyce shopped at the A&P every Saturday; the new store was cool in summer, brightly lit. You could take your time browsing, she told Rose, and fill your cart with what you wanted. There were no officious McNeelys behind the counter, reminding you when you'd charged too much.

That year, the Novaks got rid of their coal burner. The new electric furnace was a Christmas gift from Georgie. Since Sandy had left for Cleveland, the sisters had taken turns stoking the fire and hauling in the coal, chores nobody would miss. A few months later, Joyce replaced the coal cookstove. An electric one would heat faster, she explained. Dinner would be ready in half the time.

The old stove was hauled away. Sitting on the porch, Rose watched it go. Stanley had bought it from Friedman and Sons, the Jewish furniture dealers in town. Izzy Friedman had given him a special price and delivered the stove in the middle of the night. Rose had lain awake with a pounding heart, furious with Stanley for taking such a risk. Miners who lived in company houses had been told to buy their furnishings from Baker's. Shopping elsewhere was a firing offense.

The new electric model sat in the corner of the kitchen. Leaning close, squinting, Rose could make out letters on the dials: MED LO, MED HI. The words meant nothing to her. For the first time in her life she burned the polenta. Black bits of onion floated in her tomato sauce. Her meatballs came out of the oven raw in the middle. Bread rose too high; the slices resembled Swiss cheese, shot through with holes. It was as if she had forgotten everything she had ever known.

By springtime there were no more treats for Lucy: no popcorn balls stiff with molasses, no homemade macaroons. Her lunch bag contained apples and Fig Newtons, sandwiches made from store-bought bread.

The electric stove required no stoking, no nightly polishing with paraffin wax. Rose's life had been filled with work; now, absurdly, there was nothing to do. Her daughters took over the cooking, slipshod meals of casseroles, vegetables thawed from the freezer. She began to believe the doctors. For years she had ignored them; now she felt old and sickly.

She cursed the stove and waited to die.

The funeral was held at St. Casimir's, where Rose and Stanley had been married. If anyone had asked her, Rose would have chosen Mount Carmel, the church of her girlhood: its ceiling painted salmon pink, like a tropical sunrise; its profusion of Madonnas like a collection of dolls. Years ago, the parish had maintained a funerary band; when Rose's mother died, a uniformed trumpeter and drummer and accordionist had followed the hearse to the cemetery, serenading the casket with hymns. No one knew where the custom had originated. "In the old country," they all assumed. Rose had found the music comforting, a joyous wave of sound to carry her mother away.

It was George who remembered this, standing at his mother's grave. He was the

only Novak old enough to remember his
Nona, and the aged Italians who'd played
music at her funeral. He wished he'd
brought his clarinet along; he hadn't played
in years but was sure he could muster up
something. It would have seemed an ab-
surd gesture to everyone but Rose. Rose,
he knew, would have been delighted.

Afterward, walking back to his car, he
watched his three sisters make a beeline for
the hearse. They all seemed determined to
ride in the front seat. The driver had graduated high school a few years ahead of
George. A loudmouth, not too bright, the
oldest of the Bernardi boys.

"What's that all about?" he asked Sandy,
who was riding shotgun in the Cadillac. He
was glad to have a passenger. Marion had
declined to come, and there hadn't been
time to fetch Arthur from his school in Connecticut. "I've got plenty of room, and they
have to ride in the hearse?"

"Beats me," said Sandy. He'd come in
from Cleveland on the Greyhound bus; he
was between jobs and didn't have a car.
He'd gotten rid of his teenage pompadour,
and his suit cost more than George's. He
looked like a million bucks.

That fall Lucy started at St. Joseph's, the parochial high school, a long walk from the center of town. Walking to school, she sometimes spoke to herself in her mother's voice: *Lucy, it getting cold out. Bella Lucy, you got to wear your gloves.* She supposed this was how it began, how crazy people first went crazy. She didn't care. Going crazy was better than forgetting. She would not forget her mother's voice.

St. Joe's was larger than her grammar school, larger even than Bakerton High. Parochial students were bused there from all over the county. Lucy had been the oldest in her eighth-grade class, but at St. Joe's she felt like a child. The upperclassmen seemed to inhabit another world entirely. The girls wore lipstick; some, engage-

ment rings. The senior boys drove cars to
school.

In the crowded hallways she felt invisible.
Strange faces everywhere, girls from Kinport, Coalport, Fallentree. They paid her no
attention, a nameless fat girl. Lucy didn't
mind; in fact, she preferred them to the Bakerton girls—Clare Ann Baran, Connie Kukla,
the prissy blondes who'd tormented her
childhood. They watched her now with
silent pity, as though they knew everything
about her: the fat girl whose mother had
died.

The house felt empty when she came
home from school: no Rosemary Clooney
on the radio, no heavy footsteps on the
stairs. Sometimes Dorothy was home, but
to Lucy it made no difference. Dorothy seldom spoke; her presence was insubstantial.
Her footfalls barely made a sound.

After the final bell, Lucy sat on the back
steps of the school, bare-legged in her uniform, shivering in the cold. She looked often
at her watch: three o'clock, three-thirty. At
four o'clock Joyce would come home from
work; Lucy would sit in the kitchen and
watch her prepare supper. She still disliked
Joyce intensely; that had not changed,

would not change. The unchangingness comforted her; that, at least, could be counted on. Sturdy, unlikable Joyce could be counted on.

For the first time in her life, she slept alone. She understood that this was normal, that everybody else—her classmates, her sisters—had slept alone their whole lives. Still her sleep was shallow and anxious. She dreamed often of being lost. Always in these dreams she was looking for her mother.

The days were quiet and sad. Only Fridays were different. When Lucy came home from school, Angelo Bernardi would be sitting at the kitchen table. Knowing this, she did not linger on the school steps. She walked briskly, resisting the urge to run.

He sat at the table across from Dorothy, a glass of beer at one elbow, an ashtray at the other. He wore a black shirt, open at the throat, showing dark hair. The house filled with his generous laugh, the smoky buzz of his voice.

"Hey, Miss America," he'd call when she came in. "Staying out of trouble there at St. Joe's?"

His attention made her shy, a sensation

she'd rarely felt. Seldom could she think of anything to say, but it didn't seem to matter. It was enough to be in the room with him. Like Dorothy she was dumbstruck, a silent moon in his orbit.

Only one thing could break the spell. Joyce came home on Fridays with a great commotion. "Hello, all," she'd call, plunking down a bag of groceries in the middle of the table, blocking their view of one another. She turned on the overhead light and made a big, noisy show of starting dinner: chopping celery, opening soup cans, putting water on to boil. After a few minutes of this Angelo rose and excused himself. Dorothy walked him to the door.

"What's the hurry?" Lucy asked Joyce once, after Angelo had left. "You're running around like a chicken with its head cut off."

"Ed's picking me up at six. We're seeing the early show."

This ended the conversation. Joyce must have known it would. Nobody, Lucy reflected, wanted to hear about stupid Ed.

Ed Hauser was waiting for Joyce in the car. As they did every Friday, they would see the early show at the Rivoli. Joyce liked to be in bed by ten. On Saturday morning she had an eight o'clock class at the Penn State branch campus, an hour's drive away. Ed had urged her to complete the paperwork, and to her surprise, he was right: her military service entitled her to the same educational allowance as any other veteran, a hundred and ten dollars a month. After Rose's death, she had enrolled in summer school. She hoped to become a teacher. She was six semesters away from a bachelor's degree.

"Dorothy has company," she fumed, slamming the car door. "He was sitting there when I got home."

"He must have Fridays off."

"Ed, that's not the *point.*"

He shrugged. "I saw Dorothy uptown the other day. She seemed relaxed and, well, normal. Maybe it's good for her. You know, having someone."

"Good for her?" Joyce stared at him. "He's a married man."

"Divorced."

"That's even worse."

"You sound like your mother," he joked.

Joyce didn't laugh.

Ed started the car. It wasn't like her to be so narrow-minded. Then again, he tended to underestimate the Catholic craziness on the subject of divorce. Though he attended St. Casimir's each Sunday with Joyce, he'd been raised a Methodist. Divorce struck him as unfortunate and disheartening—not evil or tragic, and certainly not sinful. It was, he thought, an odd wrinkle in Joyce's character: for all her intelligence, she was as Catholic as they came, susceptible to the same superstitions and ancient prejudices as the rest of her tribe.

"Let me get this straight," he said. "If Bernardi were married and cheating on his

wife, that would be better than being divorced?"

"He's got four children."

She hadn't answered his question. He
was tempted to point this out, but he understood they weren't having a rational discussion. On most days, and nearly all subjects,
Joyce was as logical as a man; but when
it came to Bernardi she couldn't think
straight. He thought of her behavior at
Rose's funeral, piling into the hearse with
Bernardi and Dorothy and Lucy as though
she'd temporarily lost her mind. Ed knew
Joyce as he knew himself; he'd understood,
then, that she was making a point. It would
have been inappropriate for Dorothy to ride
alone with Bernardi. He was merely the
driver, paid by the mortuary. Joyce wanted
everyone—Dorothy especially—to remember that.

Bernardi. The mention of his name
brought an edge to her voice. She referred
to him alternately as a womanizer, an ignorant lout and once, memorably, a jackass.
Memorably because Joyce never cursed;
her speech was prim as a Sunday school
teacher's. Ed found the transformation as-

tonishing. And, he had to admit, rather attractive.

"My mother had his number," Joyce said. "If she were alive, Dorothy wouldn't be carrying on like this. I hate to think of her looking down from heaven, watching him hold court in her kitchen like some kind of sultan. Drinking and smoking in her own house."

Ed sighed. This was another problem with Catholics: nobody ever *died.* Joyce often spoke of her parents looking down from heaven—sometimes with pride or amusement, but usually with disapproval or downright horror. This struck Ed as a terrible burden, this sense of being watched by all your dead relatives, by numberless saints who'd been dead a thousand years but still kept a hand in things, interceding for the sick, finding lost objects, looking out for coal miners and whoever else had a dangerous job. Ed believed in God, but he also believed in death. He'd been fond of Rose Novak and saddened by her passing, but the poor woman, God love her, was dead. And that was the end of that.

"Look," he said, "you don't like Bernardi, and your mom wasn't crazy about him either. But Dorothy is a grown woman. If she wants to date a divorced guy, that's her decision. There's nothing you can do about it."

"But what about Lucy? What kind of example is this setting? She looks up to him, heaven knows why."

"He pays attention to her," Ed said. "Girls her age are starved for that." It was a phenomenon he witnessed daily at school. Once or twice each term, a particular girl would hang around his office for no good reason, and the secretaries would tease him about it: *She has a crush on you.* Always he denied it, in equal parts flattered and uncomfortable.

Joyce stared at him. "She's a child," she said, clearly appalled.

Ed didn't respond. Lucy was fifteen, a young woman. She certainly didn't *look* like a child.

"Anyway," said Joyce, "it bothers me that he and Dorothy are alone in the house all afternoon. Who knows what she might walk in on."

Aha, Hauser thought. *Here's the real issue.* Joyce didn't really care that Bernardi was divorced—or if she did, it was a secondary concern.

"Why?" he said slyly. "What do you think they're doing?"

"Never mind," said Joyce, her cheeks scarlet.

He'd never known a woman so easily embarrassed.

They had dated for years—steadily, eventlessly, with few arguments and none of the petty squabbles he'd suffered with other girls. Early on they'd even worked together, a potentially awkward situation that Joyce, being Joyce, had handled with professional grace. After Helen Bligh returned from maternity leave, Joyce had taken a clerical job at the junior high. Now Ed saw her mainly on weekends, years of movies and dinners and dances at the Vets. He looked forward to these evenings, the hours spent in her company; he'd never felt so comfortable with a woman, so accepted and understood. He admired her strength and intelligence, the fierce way she tended her family. She was in every respect the woman he wanted to spend his life with. In every way, perhaps, but one.

He wondered if they'd simply waited too long. In the beginning he'd been cautious, tentative. She was a resolute creature, with firm views on everything; he feared there would be no second chances, that one false move would alienate her forever. She'd had bad experiences with men in the air force. She didn't elaborate, and Ed didn't press, but the knowledge made him even more careful. When he kissed her, she didn't pull away; but neither did she warm to him. Her response was oddly neutral. She did not object to his touch; she might possibly have found it pleasant. Sometimes she smiled at him in a friendly way. Her attitude—he hated even to think it—was *cordial.*

For her thirtieth birthday he'd given her a ring, but Ed was in no hurry. He wanted to wait and see.

After the movie he suggested a drive. The night was clear, the moon full. He drove westward out of town, the Towers glowing in the distance.

At the top of Saxon Mountain he rolled down his window. A few snowflakes had begun to fly. There was a rich, leafy smell, dark and fecund. He parked the car and flicked on the radio.

"It's cold," said Joyce, hugging her arms.

"Come here." He loved the smallness of her, the tiny bones of her shoulders and neck. She nearly disappeared in his embrace, but he could feel her, birdlike, a delicate warmth against his heart.

He kissed her, softly at first. Her eyes closed; he felt her relax in his arms. Deeper then, pressing her to him. Fingers splayed, his hand was nearly as wide as her back.

At one time or another he had touched her everywhere, always outside her clothes. She had not touched him at all. Lately he'd felt keenly the inequity of this, but it had been their unspoken agreement, as far as they would let themselves go.

Still kissing, he took her hand and placed it on his groin. She stiffened in his arms.

"Shh," he said, pressing her hand to him.

"Ed!" She pulled her hand away as though something had burned it. "What's the matter with you?"

"Joyce, come on. We're not schoolkids."

She retreated to her corner of the seat. "Can you take me home, please?"

"Fine," he said, hating himself. He wasn't sorry, not for a minute. He thought of Bernardi and Dorothy, who spent Friday afternoons alone in the house, doing things Lucy might walk in on. Angelo Bernardi would not have taken her home. He'd have thrown her over his shoulder and carried her into the woods.

"Let's not argue. You know how I feel about this," Joyce said, fumbling with the buttons of her coat.

"I know." He started the car. "Don't tell me again. I think we've covered it."

At her doorstep they said a stiff good-bye. Later he regretted being cross with her. She would spend all Saturday in class; in the evening he'd call and apologize, take her to dinner as though nothing had happened. More and more, their weekends followed this pattern. They had reached an impasse. Nothing would free them, it seemed, but marriage; and that posed its own set of dangers. He feared marrying a cold woman, as his brother had. The term, *frigid,* Ed knew from his reading. Apparently there was no telling beforehand. His sister-in-law was an attractive girl, charming and vivacious. There was simply no way to know.

He had dated loose girls, but not often and not for long. For love he had chosen a girl of admirable character; he hadn't wanted any other kind. Now, with marriage looming, he wished for a change—no, nothing so drastic; just a slight moderation of her temperament. Joyce had proven her virtue. Now he wanted her to relax, to metamorphose into the passionate creature she would be in their married life.

But Joyce didn't relax. She didn't change in the slightest. Engagement wasn't the same as marriage, she insisted. Certain things would have to wait.

He'd tried reasoning with her. "You see the problem, don't you? It's like buying a car without a test drive."

"I did that," she said, without a trace of irony. "My Rambler. It runs fine."

"But, honey. How are we supposed to know if we're compatible?"

"Of course we're compatible. If we had any more in common we'd be the same person."

This was true. They were both churchgoers, Democrats; on bank holidays they flew the flag. They believed in education and personal responsibility, fair trade and equality for Negroes. Senator McCarthy, they felt, had taken leave of his senses. On books and movies they had lively discussions, but their deepest values were utterly the same.

"I mean sexually compatible."

Joyce blushed violently. "Oh, Ed. I don't know what you're talking about."

She meant it sincerely; he could see that she did. She was a thirty-year-old virgin, her sexual experience limited to kissing in his front seat. The rest—things they would do at some vague time in the future when the ban had been lifted, the danger removed—had been set apart in her organized mind. For now it was a murky abstraction, impossible to think about. That the act could unfold smoothly or awkwardly, rapturously or disastrously, hadn't occurred to her. She was like a dispatcher of trains whose entire attention is directed toward scheduling arrivals and departures. The actual driving of the locomotives she had never even pondered.

In the spring Lucy began to disappear.

She was still a big girl, but no longer a fat one. Food tasted wrong now, or didn't taste at all: Dorothy's oatmeal, the cafeteria slop, Joyce's bland casseroles. The daily trek to St. Joe's was a brisk half hour each way. Lucy walked in all weather, in rainstorms, in snow. It was better than riding with Joyce.

The weather warmed, and she returned to her spot on the school steps, joined, now, by a junior named Marcia Dickey, a freckled girl who smoked menthol cigarettes. Marcia talked, and the two girls smoked.

Marcia was a farm girl. Her father raised dairy cows on a tract west of Moss Creek. Lucy had seen the name stamped on neat aluminum boxes on porches all over town—DICKEY'S DAIRY—and felt as though she were meeting a celebrity. The Dickeys' farm was so remote the school bus didn't come near it, so every morning Marcia rode into town on one of the milk trucks. For two hours she sat in the cafeteria with the other farm kids, waiting for the classrooms to open. After school she rode home with her boyfriend Davis, in his father's car. Davis played on teams: baseball in the spring, football in the fall. While the teams practiced, Marcia waited on the steps.

Lucy had seen Davis around school, a lanky boy with hair like an Irish setter. He was as quiet as Marcia was talkative; they looked so alike they appeared to be related. Once he'd walked by the steps when the girls were smoking, and Marcia had introduced him to Lucy. It was as close as she had come all year to talking with a boy. At St. Joe's the classes were segregated by gender. Boys and girls saw one another only in the halls. They were permitted to sit together in the cafeteria, though only the steady couples did. Couples like Connie Kukla and Steven Fleck, a senior with comically large shoulders. Connie wore his class ring on her engagement finger, heavy as a penance on her tiny hand.

The cafeteria was as large as a train station. Girls filled the tables at the front of the room, while the boys gravitated toward the back. Lucy liked the noise of it, the bustling anonymity. She and Marcia Dickey sat with their backs to the wall, watching. One by one the students filed through the line, holding their trays, looking for a place to sit. In that moment, they all wore a panicked, baffled expression. In that moment they were all the same.

Sometimes boys stared at Lucy. She had not noticed this herself; Marcia had pointed it out one day in the cafeteria line. The school uniform, a plaid jumper, was designed for petite girls like Connie Kukla. The snug fit, the busy pattern, made Lucy's chest look enormous.

"It's not my fault," Lucy said, her cheeks reddening.

"Who said fault?" Marcia smiled. "I'd kill for a figure like yours." For a moment Lucy heard her mother's voice. *Lucy is beautiful. She'll always be beautiful.*

"This lunch is disgusting," she said, covering her meat loaf with a napkin. She busied herself with not eating, afraid she was about to cry.

* * *

They were sitting on the steps when Davis pulled up in his car. Music on the radio, a song Lucy recognized.

"Ready?" Davis called out the window.

Marcia looked up at the sky. "It looks like rain. Can we give Lucy a ride?"

"Oh, don't worry about me," she said quickly. Two boys were already sitting in the backseat. "I don't want to take you out of your way."

"You won't," said Davis. "I'm already taking these jokers into town. Hop in."

The back passenger door opened and a tall boy stepped out, wearing gym shorts and a damp white T-shirt. Lucy recognized his broad shoulders, his shiny black hair. He was Connie Kukla's boyfriend, Steven Fleck.

He nodded toward the car, and Lucy slid over to the middle of the seat, next to a small, blond boy she didn't know. Marcia got into the front seat, leaned in close to Davis, and kissed him on the mouth.

They peeled away from the curb, and Davis turned up the radio. Frankie Avalon backed by hushed female voices, a song

Lucy heard everywhere that spring: *Venus, make her fair/A lovely girl with sunlight in her hair.*

Oh, brother, Lucy thought. Even Frankie Avalon was in love with Connie Kukla.

"Whew. It stinks in here." Marcia rolled down her window. "Carful of sweaty guys. Ew."

Steven Fleck laughed, so Lucy did, too. His face and neck and arms looked moist and flushed, as though he had been running hard. In the gym shorts his legs looked thick and muscular. She was relieved to see that his thighs were wider than hers.

Davis drove fast and carelessly, like her brother Sandy. The first time he made a left turn, Lucy lurched to the right, directly into Steven Fleck's lap.

"Sorry," she said.

"That's okay," he said, laughing.

It was amazing what you could learn about a person without talking, just by sitting close. His hands were large, the nails bitten low. (She bit her nails, too.) His legs were dirty, the skin scraped raw and bleeding a little at the knees. You had to take a game seriously to slide that hard at practice. Lucy had played the same way: kickball, dodgeball, she had always wanted to win. Baby games, she knew; that was a long time ago. She hadn't played anything in years.

Davis stopped at a traffic light. "Where to, Lucy?"

"Polish Hill," she said.

The blond boy piped up. "Fleck's girl-friend lives up there."

Lucy had forgotten he was there; she looked at him now with intense dislike. She often felt this way toward small, blond peo-ple: Connie Kukla, her sister Joyce. Steven Fleck was big and dark—like her mother, like Angelo Bernardi, like Lucy herself.

Davis looked over his shoulder. "Fleck, you want me to let you off at Connie's?"

"Nah, that's okay." He glanced sideways at Lucy. "I just saw her at school. That's enough for one day."

In the front seat Marcia burst out laugh-ing. Lucy, too, started to laugh. They were still laughing when Davis pulled in front of her house. Steven Fleck stepped out of the car and Lucy slid out, holding down her skirt with her hand. The seat was warm where he had sat. The vinyl stuck to her bare thighs.

"See you in school," said Steven Fleck.

"Sure," said Lucy. "See you."

She stood in front of her house a moment, watching the car drive away. Then
Leonard Stusick rode up on his bike, his
book bag and lunch box tied to the rear
fender. He wore his navy blue pants and
sweater, the grammar school uniform. He
was twelve but looked ten. "Who was that?"
he asked.

"You wouldn't know them."

"How do you know?" Leonard squinted,
shielding his eyes from the sun peeking
through the clouds. "The big one is Steven
Fleck. He plays in the Pony League, for
Reilly Trucking."

"He does?"

"Watch this." Leonard spun a fast circle in
the road, wheeling up on his back tire.

Lucy ignored him. "How'd you know
that?"

"You didn't even watch." Leonard stopped
suddenly, spraying gravel. "What? Is he
your boyfriend now?"

"Don't be stupid."

"That guy's an idiot," said Leonard.
"Don't say I didn't warn you."

"What do you mean?"

"Trust me." Leonard popped a wheelie

and pedaled into his driveway. "I know what I'm talking about."

In the kitchen Joyce stood at the sink, rinsing lettuce for salad. "You beat the storm," she said. "I was about to come and get you."

"I got a ride home."

"I see that." Joyce shut off the water. "Who are your friends? I didn't recognize the car."

Lucy's cheeks heated. "Nobody. Just some kids from school."

"Well, I figured that much."

Joyce waited.

"Marcia Dickey," Lucy said finally.

"What about all those boys?"

"You were *watching*?"

"I heard a car come up the hill." Joyce dried her hands on a towel. "The radio was playing full blast. I'm sure the whole neighborhood heard it."

"It wasn't that loud."

"Lucy, who were the boys?"

Am I under arrest? Lucy thought. She wished she had the nerve to say it.

"Davis somebody," she said instead. "He's Marcia's boyfriend. And Steven Fleck. The other boy I didn't know."

"You don't *know* him?" Joyce crossed her arms. "Lucy, do you think that's wise? Getting into a car with a boy you don't know?"

It was just like Joyce: asking questions when she didn't really want to hear the answers. *Obviously,* Lucy thought. *Obviously I think it's wise.*

"I know the others," she said. Her face felt hot.

"David *somebody*?"

"Davis. He's Marcia's *boyfriend*," Lucy said, exasperated. "She's my *best friend*."

"Well, excuse me, Lucy, but I've never met this Marcia, or heard a word about her, as far as I can remember. And I'll thank you not to take that tone with me."

Lucy dropped her books loudly on the table. Without another word, she went upstairs to her room.

Joyce listened to her go, her tread heavy on the stairs. *If I'd stomped around that way when I was fifteen,* she thought, *Daddy would have had my head.* She often had such thoughts about her sister, who balked at even the gentlest sort of correction. The older Novaks—Georgie, Dorothy, and Joyce—had been scolded, lectured and worse; Georgie in particular had been slapped and swatted and, on one memorable occasion, chased around the backyard with their father's belt. Lucy had never had so much as a spanking, as far as Joyce knew. She'd never been sent to pick scrap coal at the Number One tipple, never slipped a coat over her nightgown on a winter night and trudged through the snow to the outhouse. It was as if she and Sandy had been raised in another family entirely.

Joyce dried the lettuce and shredded it for salad. Her questions, she knew, had been perfectly reasonable. She tried to picture herself at fifteen, riding home from school in a car full of boys. It was hard to imagine. Few families had had cars back then, and those who did would never have entrusted them to teenagers. Even at school she had seldom spoken to a boy. Her nervousness had made her timid—a problem Lucy seemed not to have.

She stood over the sink peeling a cucum-

ber, thinking of a Saturday afternoon a few
weeks ago, when she'd taken Lucy shopping for an Easter dress. Since her weight
loss, none of her old clothes fit properly;
twice her school uniform had been taken in
at the waist. The day had been unseason-
ably warm, a blast of summer in late March.
They'd left their coats in the car and walked
a few blocks to the store, the sun warm on
their bare arms. Joyce wore a crisp white
blouse, Lucy a cotton sweater borrowed
from Dorothy; later Joyce noticed that it fit
her snugly across the chest. As they walked
past a building under construction, a chorus
of wolf whistles followed them down the
block. The realization had hit Joyce like a
physical blow: the men were whistling at her
little sister.

"Ignore them," she said, her cheeks flam-
ing.

Lucy said nothing, but a tiny smile pulled
at her lips. Later, as she waited outside the
changing room, Joyce remembered that
smile. Lucy wasn't embarrassed by the
crude attention. She had actually enjoyed it.

That summer, men campaigned for president. Joyce and Ed scrambled to register voters. They canvassed Polish Hill and Little Italy, the new developments of West Branch and East Branch, nearby Coalport and Fallentree. From house to house, Ed expressed his enthusiasm for Kennedy's Peace Corps. Joyce's approach had more success: Elect the first Catholic president.

Another presidency was also at stake: Bakerton Local 1450, United Mineworkers of America. For twelve years the incumbent, Regis Devlin, had run unopposed. Regis was silver-haired and silver-tongued, ready with a joke, trusted by the Bakers and well liked by the men. On his watch the union had demanded little of management. His few requests were promptly granted:

bonuses at Christmas, hot coffee at the tipple, an on-site shower room at the Twelve. The men felt appreciated; their jobs were secure. For the first time in their working lives, they went home clean.

Everyone was surprised when Gene Stusick declared himself a candidate—sheepishly at first, with apologies to Regis; then with increasing confidence. Gene was a poor politician; he lacked Regis's quick wit, his Irish charm. What he did have were numbers.

He outlined his position in a mimeographed letter, as blunt and unappealing, as thorough and informative, as Gene himself. The miners' contract was up for renewal that spring. Except for an annual cost-of-living adjustment, the men hadn't had a raise in six years. In the same period, profits had grown 40 percent. The Twelve was the largest bituminous mine in the state, and the company still hadn't touched the ten thousand acres to its north. If, as planned, the reserves were tapped the following year, Baker would make money hand over fist. Meanwhile the miners would be locked into another meager contract, the same sweetheart deal Regis Devlin had given Baker Brothers for years.

Neither of these elections interested Lucy. All summer she brooded over another race, the contest for Fire Queen.

She hadn't entered, herself; she was too aware of the potential for humiliation. Years of name-calling, of Joyce taking her shopping in the Chubbette Department, had taught her that much.

Dozens of girls competed for Fire Queen. The contest happened behind closed doors; the firemen themselves judged. From a window booth at Keener's Diner, Lucy and Marcia Dickey watched the girls arrive at the hall. Clare Ann Baran and Connie Kukla in pale pink gowns, their blond hair teased into identical flips. Girls in strapless shifts, in satin, in tulle.

"Look at that one," said Marcia Dickey. Two streams of smoke shot out her nostrils. "The strapless. A padded bra would have been a good idea."

Lucy giggled. "Her dress is going to fall down."

"That's the only way she's going to win."

It helped to have someone to watch with. Marcia was as unlikely to be Fire Queen as Lucy was. Both treated the whole thing as ridiculous, but Lucy wondered if Marcia secretly felt the same way she did. She would have done anything to be Fire Queen. Anything in the world.

The girls said good-bye on the sidewalk. Davis's car idled at the curb; he was taking Marcia to see *Please Don't Eat the Daisies*. "Have a good time," said Lucy, with something like longing, knowing that no boy would ever ask her to the drive-in.

A moment later, crossing the street, she heard a voice behind her—"Hey, Miss America! Wait up." She turned to see Angelo Bernardi coming out of the hall.

"I thought that was you." He fell into step beside her, a little out of breath. "We had the contest tonight. Where were you? I was saving my vote for you."

Lucy flushed with pleasure. "Me? Oh, I don't think so."

"What, you don't think you're pretty enough? Trust me. That girl we gave it to, she couldn't hold a candle next to you."

Lucy smiled. It was enough that he'd said so. It didn't need to be true.

"Who won?" she asked.

"Connie something. Pretty little blonde. Said she knows you from school."

Two calamities competed for her attention: Connie Kukla winning Fire Queen. Angelo and Connie talking behind her back.

"You *talked* about me?"

"She said she went to St. Joe's. I said I knew you."

Lucy's stomach lurched. She thought of Connie Kukla leading the parade in her pink dress, waving to the crowd with her saccharine smile. *No,* she thought. *It isn't possible.*

"But she's only a junior," she said. "They always pick a senior."

Angelo shrugged. "She's cute. The guys liked her. She looks like Sandra Dee."

Lucy couldn't speak. Hate bubbled up inside her, the grilled cheese she'd eaten at Keener's turning sour and liquid in her stomach. Connie Kukla with her skinny legs, her perfect flip, her saddle shoes as tiny as a doll's. She was as different from Lucy as any girl could possibly be. If Angelo thought she was cute, then he must find Lucy

hideously ugly. She must be an absolute
monster.

"Whatsa matter?" said Angelo. "You don't
look so good."

It was the last thing she needed to hear.

"I have to go," she said.

She ran through the town, past the pool hall
and the five-and-ten. On Baker Street, she
heard hammering noises: men were building the concessions booths. In the lot behind the Quaker, carnival trucks were
parked. A crew was assembling the Ferris
wheel. Normally Lucy would have stopped
to watch. Now anything to do with the festival—Connie's festival—was repulsive to her.

She crossed the railroad tracks. The sun
had set along the river; the windows of the
dress factory glowed orange pink. Drums in
the distance, the high school marching band
practicing for the parade. Connie would be
everywhere this week—inescapable, infec-
tious, like a sneeze during flu season, spraying deadly germs. Her picture in the paper;
then the street dance, the parade on
Saturday night. By then Lucy would be dead

from envy. It seemed impossible that she could survive that long.

She ran over the footbridge. Water bubbled deep beneath it, a hollow sound. A few cars were parked at the ball field. An occasional *thwack* in the distance, the brittle crack of bat and ball. The late summer evening hummed with bugs.

Lucy slowed. Her side ached; she had not run in a long time. She bent at the waist, gulping air. At the ball field a small crowd had gathered. Boys stood behind home plate drinking from cans. The other team was spread across the outfield, socks and sneakers glowing in the twilight. The white letters on their T-shirts spelled REILLY TRUCK-ING.

Dusk was falling; in half an hour the sky would be dark. Lucy shooed a mosquito away from her ear. She thought of her silent house: Dorothy holed up in her room. Joyce at the movies with Ed. The empty chair where her mother used to sit.

She climbed the bleachers and sat on the top row. She had never played at this park; girls' games like dodgeball were not allowed. The ball field was reserved for the municipal leagues: Little League, Ponies, all boys.

"What are you doing here?"

She looked up. Steven Fleck stood on the bottom bleacher, a can of Iron City in his hand.

"Nothing. Just sitting." For a moment she remembered what she was wearing: Bermuda shorts, a sleeveless blouse stained gray under the arms. She fumbled with a stray bra strap.

"We won tonight," he said. "We beat Nicastro's Tavern. I had three hits."

"Congratulations."

"There was a guy in the stands. I think he was a recruiter for Baker."

"Really?" said Lucy. "How could you tell?"

He shrugged mysteriously. "Well, he could have been. There are three seniors on the team." His older brother had been recruited right out of high school, he explained. He played third base and worked at the Number Eight tipple.

He sat down beside her. "Were you over at the fire hall?"

"Yeah," she said. "Connie won."

"Good for her. It's a big deal, right?"

"Sure," Lucy said miserably. She swatted at a mosquito. A giant welt was rising on her thigh, between her kneesock and the hem of her shorts.

"I figured. She's been talking about it for months. Between you and me, I'm glad it's finally over." A soft hiss as he opened his beer. "What about you? You didn't enter?"

She shook her head.

"Why not?"

"I wasn't interested."

The words just sat there. She sounded like a bad actress on television.

"That's not why," she said. "I knew I wouldn't win."

"Why not? You're pretty."

He said it so easily, the thing he would say a thousand times in her memory. Each time Lucy would ask herself the same question: *Was he stupid, that Steven Fleck? Or was he just so sweet?*

"Not like Connie," she said, smiling a little.

"Well, no. You're a different type."

She waited for him to elaborate.

"Some girls aren't pretty at all, and that's too bad," he mused. "But the rest are. Connie, and Clare Ann, and you, and so on. So in a way, from a boy's perspective, one girl is just as good as another."

He chewed thoughtfully at a thumbnail.

"That's where it gets complicated. That's where other things start to matter."

"Like how nice a girl is?"

"Sure," said Steven Fleck. "And—other things."

Lucy nodded. These were questions she had long pondered, questions she would have asked years ago if she actually knew any boys. She understood that something remarkable was happening: Steven Fleck talking to her like this, the two of them sitting on the bleachers, night falling softly around them. An hour ago, eating sandwiches at Keener's with Marcia Dickey, she never would have imagined it possible.

He had moved closer to her; their thighs were touching. When she looked up she saw the other boys were gone.

"It's late," she said. "I should go home."

Steven Fleck stood and offered his hand. "I'll walk with you."

They didn't walk far. Under the bleachers, grassy and damp, a place that hadn't seen the sun. Trash around them: pop bottles, newspaper. A phone number was carved into the wood of the bleachers. The last two numbers were the same as hers.

"You're tall," he said when he kissed her. She didn't ask if that was good or bad. She felt the raised letters on his back: REILLY TRUCKING. His mouth was wet and beery, somehow familiar. He tasted the way Angelo smelled.

Her hair was loose; she had lost her barrette. She held her breath when he unbuttoned her shirt. His mouth pulled gently at her breasts. Did he do this with Connie Kukla? She looked down at his bent head, his shiny hair, and thought, *Mine.*

He put her hand on him, taught her the motion. It was like petting an exotic animal: she was scared, then delighted, then a little bored. After a while his eyes closed. She wished he would kiss her some more.

Hand in hand they walked through the town. Her other hand was sticky, as though she'd been eating candy. He walked her to the bottom of Polish Hill, then stopped. He lived across town, he explained, and it was almost midnight. She walked the rest of the way alone.

That week the *Herald* was full of news. The lead story on page one: TOWN HOSTS FIREMEN'S FESTIVAL. In smaller type, below the fold: New Fire Queen Is Crowned. On the social page: *Hauser, Miss Novak Announce Engagement.* A winter ceremony was planned.

It would be a small wedding, Joyce explained at the breakfast table. After five years, Ed was suddenly in a hurry. Fine by her: weddings were a waste of money, and she didn't like a fuss. Still, she couldn't imagine what had gotten into him.

She eyed the front page. There was a large photo of the Fire Queen and her court. The girl wore a satin sash and a rhinestone tiara. Joyce sighed.

"Fire Queen! That poor child. It's disgraceful, making those young girls parade themselves in front of the whole town. And those cavemen gawking and cheering. They're grown men, for heaven's sake. It ought to be illegal."

Dorothy rose and poured more coffee. She saw no point in defending the cavemen. It was a Friday morning. In a few hours Angelo would arrive.

"I suppose the girls don't know any better, but what are their parents thinking?" Joyce folded the paper and tossed it into the trash. "Someone should put a stop to it."

For once Lucy might have agreed with her, but she wasn't listening. She stared out the window, lost in thought. Beneath her elbow was the sports page. Reilly Trucking had won its final game, the top-ranked team in the Pony League. Lucy wondered if Connie Kukla had cheered from the bleachers. She wondered if Steven Fleck had scored.

In November, elections were held. Joyce and Ed's efforts paid off: a record number of voters came to the polls. Nationally, it was a close race; in Saxon County, a landslide. Levers were pulled at the VFW, at Bakerton High School, at the Grange hall in Fallentree. Down Susquehanna Avenue and halfway around the block, voters waited in line to elect the first Catholic president.

A week later, Gene Stusick was voted president of the local. He'd spent election day at the Legion with his son Leonard, handing out hundreds of mimeographs.

At the Baker offices on Indian Hill, the company lawyers prepared for a fight.

* * *

Just after Christmas, in the middle of a snowstorm, Joyce and Ed Hauser were married. The altar at St. Casimir's was laden with poinsettias. Georgie drove in alone from Philadelphia to give the bride away. Sandy had promised to come, but begged off with a late phone call, claiming his flight was grounded. He was living in Los Angeles, a fact the family had learned secondhand, from Dick Devlin's brother. His Cleveland number, when they tried it, had been disconnected. They hadn't heard from him in months.

A reception was held in the church hall. Most of Polish Hill attended, plus the bride's Italian cousins, the groom's few relatives and his colleagues from the high school. Without Sandy to insist upon it, nobody danced in a trough. His absence from the reception was remarked upon.

"North Hollywood, California," Joyce said when anyone asked.

"My goodness," said Evelyn Stusick.

Ted Poblocki grinned broadly. "That figures, don't it?"

Joyce never lied, but it was her wedding day; she permitted herself this one dance with the truth. Her whole life she had been convinced of Sandy's specialness, the unique promise that he, growing older, had failed to demonstrate in any tangible way. She'd worried for years what would become of him, watched with dismay as he wandered from job to job: salesman, bartender, taxicab driver. She only wanted the neighbors to think well of him, and now they did.

California.

She never claimed he was a movie actor. Nobody could say she'd lied on purpose. She had simply told them where he lived.

SEVEN

Just before Christmastime, Gene Stusick presented a new contract to Baker. Free eyeglasses for miners and their families. New washhouses at the Three and the Nine. A modest cost-of-living raise for all.

Baker Brothers communicated its displeasure. As Gene had predicted, the company had tapped its reserve lands north of the Twelve. New hires, new equipment: Baker had overextended itself. The new agreement was the best they could do.

The old contract ran out on December 31. Late that afternoon Gene called an emergency meeting of the local. The men sat at long tables at the American Legion. The room was already decorated for the evening's festivities. A plastic banner hung across one wall: RING IN 1963 WITH IRON

CITY BEER. Gene stood before it, hair still wet from his after-work shower. His glasses were mended with electrical tape. On the table beside him was an old-fashioned dinner bucket.

"The same old contract," said Gene.

A murmur of assent, nods of agreement.

"Baker's got money for everything else," he pointed out, raising his voice over the din. Just recently the company had bought a new longwall machine and shipped it over from England, at the outrageous price of a hundred thousand dollars. It was as if management thought they could mine the coal themselves.

He opened the dinner bucket. "Let's show them how well that longwall works with no one down there to run it."

He withdrew a thermos bottle, unscrewed its cap, and poured its contents onto the floor.

It worked, he told Ev later that night. She'd discouraged him from dumping the bucket—he wasn't going to make any friends over at the Legion, dirtying their floor

on New Year's Eve. Gene had decided otherwise. Dumping the bucket was as old as
the union itself, the way a miner of his
father's generation would have started a
walkout. The act wasn't just symbolic: a
man underground without a supply of drinking water was taking his life in his hands.
Dumping Coca-Cola on the floor of the Legion was pure showmanship, Gene knew;
but the gesture had served its purpose.

Local 1450 voted to strike.

They lay in the lavender room, the radiators hissing, the early dark gathering around them. It was late January; outside, the snow radiated blue twilight. Slowly, almost imperceptibly, the days were getting longer.

Angie lit a cigarette. His body was still magnificent. Naked, he was sleek and heavy as a lion. A few silver hairs sprouted among the black thicket on his chest.

"Cut them out," he told Dorothy, laughing.

Kneeling beside him, her tiny nail scissors poised, she did. His laughter caused a spastic rumbling deep in his chest. He was forty-six that August, and his lungs were bad.

Angie examined one of the white hairs she'd clipped. "Old grayback," he marveled. "How the hell did that happen?" He reached for her. "What's a nice girl like you doing with an old bastard like me?"

"I missed you," she said. That morning Lucy had taken the bus back to Pittsburgh; for three weeks she'd been home from college on Christmas break. At first Dorothy had been happy to see her, but three weeks was a long time without Angie. Over the years they had settled into a routine. Every Friday she had lunch waiting for him—pots of minestrone and tomato sauce, the dishes her mother had cooked. They spent a long time eating, talking and listening to the radio. Afterward they retired to the lavender room.

"Lucy has another vacation coming up in March," said Dorothy. "Maybe she can stay with Joyce and Ed."

"Sure," said Angie. "Have a talk with your sister." Joyce was a married woman, he pointed out. She would understand about these things.

"I will," Dorothy said, knowing she wouldn't. Married or not, Joyce was still Joyce. The morning after the wedding, Dorothy had studied her for some sign of transformation, some evidence that Joyce and Ed had done the things she and Angie did. She'd watched her sister carrying arm-loads of wedding gifts out to the car—a toaster, a stockpot, stacks of dish towels and bed linens and embroidered dresser scarves. *Did you?* she wanted to ask. *Were you? Truly, Joyce, wasn't it?* But the words had not come.

Angie rose and stepped into his trousers. Beneath him the bed creaked.

"I won't see you tomorrow. The rehearsal dinner, remember?" His oldest daughter, Shirley, was getting married that weekend.

"Isn't that in the evening?" Dorothy curled into the warm spot he'd left. She wasn't ready to move.

"Six o'clock. But I should stick around in case Shirl needs anything." He pulled on an undershirt.

Dorothy had never met Shirley, but she had her own opinions about the kind of girl who'd accept an expensive wedding from a father she barely spoke to, a father who hadn't drawn a paycheck in a month. The rehearsal dinner was a Friday, the wedding Saturday afternoon. Angie always ate Sun-day dinner with his ex-wife and the children, so Dorothy wouldn't see him until the fol-lowing week.

She sat up in bed and slipped on a
housecoat. "Let me go put on some coffee.
Warm you up before I send you outside."

Downstairs, she busied herself in the
kitchen, distracting herself from the knowledge that he would soon leave her—a
thought that, if she dwelled on it, could
make her physically ill. She understood that
leaving was normal, that husbands left their
wives every day to go to work. The difference, she knew, was that Angie left her in
secret. She could not, like her neighbor
Madge Yurkovich, spend the morning
washing his miners and hanging them out to
dry. Lately Angie kept a few things at her
house—a comb and toothbrush, an extra
shirt and trousers. She found their presence
reassuring; they were all she had. She
couldn't comfort herself with the sound of
his name, dropping it into casual conversation. She never mentioned him to her sisters, so that even in their company she felt
horribly alone.

"Whatsa matter?" Angie came up behind
her and wrapped her in his arms. "Did I say
something?"

"Oh, no." She leaned into him—a head
taller, his shoulders broad. She wanted to

disappear inside him. "I'll miss you this weekend. That's all. I'm being selfish."

"You? Never."

They stood there a long moment, his breath warm on her cheek.

"I never gave you a wedding," he said. "Here I am marrying off my kids, and you haven't had your turn yet. That doesn't seem right."

"I don't care about a wedding," she whispered, and that much was true. The thought of walking down the aisle in front of all her neighbors and relatives was enough to make her sweat.

"I'll stop by on Sunday morning," Angie said. "Bring you some bread from Bellavia's before church."

He'd been divorced for eight years, nearly as long as he'd been married. His ex-wife, Julia, lived with their four children in West Branch, in a house Dorothy had walked past many times. Angie had bought the house when they married, and he still made the payments every month. His two younger daughters were in high school, his son in seventh grade.

Once, at the beginning, she had asked: *Why did you get divorced?*

Oil and water, he explained. *Every stinking day there was something to butt heads about.* Julia had fought like a cat with his mother and sisters. She resented the time he spent playing baseball; in ten years of marriage she hadn't come to a single game. She complained bitterly about how his uncle ran the business, said Angie helped out too much and got nothing in return. *She's a person who thinks everyone is robbing her,* he said. *You give her the world, it's still less than she deserves.*

The rest of his family had witnessed these struggles. His own mother told him, in so many words, that his marriage had been a mistake. But all that changed the day he got divorced. Now Julia came to his mother's each year at Christmas. Wherever Bernardis gathered—at weddings, baptisms, First Communions—she was invited. She was treated like a saint in the family, while his own presence was merely tolerated. It had been that way for years.

Dorothy had never met his children, but

she had seen pictures. On Sunday afternoons she pictured them sitting around a
dinner table, eating the meal Julia had prepared. Every Sunday morning they attended
mass at Mount Carmel: Angie and Julia at
either end of the long pew, the four children
placed between them. Both continued to
take Communion; according to the priest it
was allowed. Divorce itself was no impedi-
ment to grace. As long as neither remarried,
there was no sin.

A month into the miners' strike, Sandy Novak came back to town. In recent years his appearances had been rare and brief, like a comet shooting across the sky. He hadn't been seen in Bakerton since Rose's funeral.

He arrived on a Sunday night in a lemon yellow convertible, causing a stir in Joyce and Ed's quiet subdivision. At Polish Hill he might not have been noticed, among all the crying babies, the barking of hunting dogs, the screen doors slamming late into the night. During the strike there was no need to whisper, no miner upstairs sleeping off his shift. East Branch was different: strike or no strike, its modest ranch houses contained their noises. Pets and children were kept indoors. On hot days, air conditioners hummed quietly in bedroom windows. In

summer, in winter, East Branch was quiet as
the grave.

Joyce answered the door in her housecoat. In the den, Ed was watching *The Ed
Sullivan Show.*

"I'm home," Sandy announced, lifting her
into his arms. His face was deeply tanned;
he wore a wrinkled linen suit. He had driven
for six days, nearly two thousand miles.

Across the street, the neighbor's porch
light came on.

"Well, aren't you something?" Joyce's
face was flushed with pleasure. "I'll bet
Dorothy had a bird."

He set her down. "I haven't been over
there yet."

She blinked, oddly touched: he had come
to see her first. "Then how'd you know
where to find me?"

"I asked some smart-aleck kid hanging
out at the Esso." He grinned. "Every juvenile
delinquent in town knows where the principal lives."

"You should have called to tell us you
were coming."

"I wanted to surprise you."

Bad idea, pal, thought Ed, joining them on
the porch. His wife hated surprises, a lesson

he'd learned repeatedly in their first year of marriage.

Joyce clapped delightedly. "Let me put on some clothes. We'll go surprise Dorothy. She'll have a *bird.*"

He took over Joyce's old room, pressed his own shirts on the ironing board she'd kept in the closet. The shirts were fine cotton, expensively monogrammed. Dorothy offered to launder them, but the old wringer washer made him nervous. Finally he took them to the dry cleaner in town.

In the evenings he ate the meals Dorothy prepared; afterward he washed their two plates. Lucy had gone away to college that fall. The house was emptier than it had ever been.

He rarely used the telephone. "If anyone calls for me, I'm not here," he told Dorothy. "Got it? You never heard of Sandy Novak. There's no one here by that name."

He was vague when Joyce asked how long he could stay. "A week or so. Maybe two."

"That's wonderful," she said, "but don't you have to get back to work?"

Where and when he worked was a subject that puzzled her. When he called (infrequently, at odd hours), he was usually between jobs. This time he was a fry cook in a diner. A few months ago, he'd been a valet parking attendant at the Biltmore Hotel.

You've always liked cars, she'd told him once. *Have you considered a trade school? You could study automotive repair.*

I don't care what's under the hood, he'd answered, laughing. *Just put me behind the wheel.*

"That's quite a ride you've got there," Ed said, pointing out the obvious: How did a fry cook afford a car like that?

Anyone else would have felt the need to explain, but Sandy only smiled.

"Thanks, Ed," he said.

Each morning he shaved and put on a suit. He wore no winter coat, despite the January freeze. Smartly dressed, he drove uptown. Ed saw him there several times a week: standing beside his car on Susquehanna

Avenue, shooting the breeze with the firemen; at Keener's Diner, reading the paper
over a plate of ham and eggs. Every evening
the convertible was parked outside the Legion or the Vets, though Sandy was no veteran. Asking around, Ed heard he'd been
drinking with the Bernardi boys.

"What's he doing for cash?" Ed asked
Joyce. "I don't know what kind of savings a
fry cook has, but he must have drunk it
away by now."

"I have no idea," Joyce said crisply. "I
haven't loaned him any more, if that's what
you're asking."

So far it had been the only argument in
their young marriage. Once, twice, he'd
caught Joyce writing checks to Sandy—fifty
dollars here, a hundred there. "It's a loan,"
she'd explained. "He's between jobs." The
money was never repaid, which didn't surprise Ed. The surprise was his thrifty wife—
she'd worn the same winter coat for six
years—buying sharp suits for the best-
dressed fry cook in Los Angeles.

"I saw him uptown this morning," Ed said.
"If he's got time on his hands, Dorothy
ought to put him to work. Her porch could
use a coat of paint." He spent his own sum-

mer vacations doing repairs on Polish Hill; he was the only one who gave the old place any attention. Left to Rose's sons, the house would have fallen to pieces long ago.

The strike dragged on. The union offered a month of strike pay, enough to buy a few groceries. Wives put in applications at the dress factory.

A bitter cold settled in the valley. Good news for the union, Gene Stusick said: heating coal was in demand. How much money was Baker willing to lose? It was just a matter of time.

Businesses shut down for the winter: the shoe store, Spangler's hat shop. No one was buying, and until the strike ended, nobody would. Friedman's Furniture closed its doors for good. Izzy Friedman, who'd delivered Stanley Novak's coal stove in the middle of the night, held a gigantic sidewalk sale. After that the store stood empty. In the dark window hung a hand-lettered sign: FOR SALE NOW.

A few businesses did prosper: the Vets and the Legion, the Sons of Italy and the

Slovak Club. On snowy afternoons, the tav-
erns were full. Men congregated at the fire
hall, the pool hall. The bowling alley opened
at eleven in the morning. They did a brisk
trade in games, sandwiches and beer.

In February, strike pay ran out. Still Baker
Brothers wouldn't budge.

Angie Bernardi grew tired of the fire hall.
More and more, he spent the afternoons on
Polish Hill. He didn't mind the presence of
Dorothy's brother. Sandy was good company; he laughed at Angie's jokes, and he
knew when to make himself scarce for an
hour or two. When he returned, he'd join
Angie for a beer while Dorothy cooked their
supper.

On one of these afternoons, Sandy suggested a game of cards.

"Sure," Angie said. His free time weighed
on him. His lungs kept him from hunting,
and he'd never been much for reading or
television. He could spend just so much
time in his apartment, two cramped rooms
above Travaglini's barbershop.

Fridays became their regular game. Angie
invited his brother Jerry; Sal, too, when his
wife would let him out of the house. Sandy
asked his old buddy Dick Devlin, who'd

moved back from Cleveland to marry and mine coal and who was now out of work like everyone else. It being Polish Hill, there were always some Poblockis knocking around. The kitchen filled with cigarette smoke, cursing and men.

Dorothy didn't seem to mind, though she told Angie, once, that she missed what they usually did on Fridays. He laughed and kissed her; he liked how she never complained. At the beginning she had watched them play, but it bothered Angie, her hearing that language. "Go over to your sister's," he suggested. And Dorothy did.

Money was lost, money was won. It was a friendly game. If Angie lost more than he won, he figured that was the price of entertainment: movies, show tickets, nothing was free. If he wanted to win back some of his losings, Sandy pointed out, they could always pick up the game later, at the Vets.

And they did.

Notices appeared on church bulletin boards: available for babysitting, for housecleaning, to paint or repair or plow snow. Women peddled Tupperware and Avon cosmetics. The cold snap continued, and coal prices soared. Most of Bakerton had kept its coal stoves. They bought their house coal from Baker—they had to—at triple the usual cost.

"The bastards are gouging us blind," Gene said, when Ev showed him the bill.

Ev kept her mouth shut. She was tired of hearing how the strike was almost over, how the cold weather would bring management to its knees. For two months she'd paid bills and bought groceries from Leonard's college fund. He had skipped the eleventh grade and was now a senior in high school. Even if Gene went back to work tomorrow, there wouldn't be time to recoup what she'd spent.

"Goddamn Baker," said Gene. "They screwed us coming and going."

No, Ev wanted to say. *You did that to yourself.*

At first Ed didn't notice. After a few weeks it dawned on him: Dorothy spent every weekend at their house.

"What's going on?" he asked Joyce. "What's your brother up to?" Sandy had been in town for more than a month. What had brought him to Bakerton, Ed couldn't imagine, but it certainly wasn't Dorothy's company.

Joyce hesitated. "They play cards," she said. "Poker, I guess. He and Angelo."

"Bernardi?" Ed howled. "Let me get this straight. Dorothy gets kicked out of her own house so the boys can play poker, and you haven't raised hell about it? That's not the Joyce I know. What gives?"

"It's Sandy's house, too," she said meekly.

That, at least, made sense. Bernardi couldn't take a breath without drawing Joyce's fire. Her devotion to Sandy was equally blind.

"Let me go over there," Ed said. "I'll drive Dorothy home. Find out what's going on."

He came home that night reeking of cigar smoke. "A friendly game," he explained. He was slightly drunk and had lost twenty dollars. He didn't tell Joyce.

In late March, Baker Brothers came through with a new contract. The hourly raise was exactly what the union had asked.

"We did it!" Gene Stusick exclaimed from the podium. "We hung in there, and we got them by the short hairs."

A vote was taken. Gene ordered a celebratory round of beers. But by now the men were sick of meeting, sick of drinking. They were sick to death of Gene Stusick.

The strike had lasted a hundred days, the longest in Bakerton's history. Now the bowling alley resumed its regular hours. Women quit their jobs at the Quaker. Easter came and went. This year nobody cared much for celebrating. Everyone went back to work.

The snow melted. Sandy Novak wandered the town in his summer suits. There was no more Friday poker. The Bernardis and Poblockis were back on day shift. Dick Devlin worked Hoot Owl. Once or twice he and Sandy played pool, after Dick had slept off his shift.

One night the telephone rang. Dozing in front of the television, Sandy heard Dorothy's soft "hello."

A brief pause as she listened.

"I'm sorry," she said. "There's no one here by that name."

When she woke the next morning, Sandy was gone.

EIGHT

Forever after, when the story is told—in newspapers and on the radio, by public figures in commemorative addresses, by aged grandparents years later, when the world seems a safer place—the telling begins, rightly, with the weather. So: that December was the warmest on record. On Polish Hill, Evelyn Stusick's crocuses bloomed. Hunters rushed their kills to basement freezers. Christmas trees cut too early lost their needles in the heat.

At the diamond behind the junior high, jackets and sweaters were piled on bleachers. Boys ran the bases in their undershirts. The Knights of Columbus held a car wash in the Quaker parking lot. Tinsel Santas looked garish in the bright sun.

"June is bustin' out all over," said the

weekend weatherman on KBKR. The baro-
metric pressure stood at thirty and a half
inches. It was a piece of information nobody
registered: thirty inches of what? A week
later, a generation of schoolchildren would
know what it meant.

The false summer lasted through the
weekend. Then, on Sunday night, a cold
wind blew down from Canada. Monday
morning the windows were crusted with ice.
Coats were dug out of closets; hats and
mufflers, boots and gloves. Winter came
overnight for everyone but the miners. For
them there was only one season. It was always fifty degrees underground.

They sat in their usual spots—Mrs. Hauser
at her desk, Susan Jevic at her smaller one
in the front row—eating the lunches they
had brought from home. Outside the snow
had begun to fall. Joyce was relieved at the
change in the weather: the balmy afternoons had made her pupils squirrelly. The
last hour of each day had seemed interminable. Only Susan seemed interested in

discussing *The Red Pony,* taking notes in her careful hand.

Joyce had taught eighth grade for just more than a year, taking over the classroom Viola Peale had surrendered when she retired. A few changes had been made since then: new desks, a filmstrip projector on a wheeled cart at the back of the room. Above the chalkboard hung a color portrait of the young president, which Joyce had placed there herself. For weeks, now, she had avoided looking at it: the handsome face, the unbearable hopefulness of his intent blue gaze. Soon another photo would arrive, a framed portrait of President Johnson. Joyce would hide it in the bottom drawer of her desk.

She'd been married three years, the exact length of Kennedy's presidency. Married life suited her: the quiet evenings alone with Ed, watching television or reading before the fire. Their small house was pleasant and orderly, a silent sanctuary after the noisy corridors of the high school. To her relief, the marriage had produced no children, though Ed reached for her every Saturday night without fail. She did not tell him that childlessness suited her, that after years of car-

ing for her mother, Sandy, Lucy and
Dorothy, she felt entitled to this freedom.
Her husband was a capable man, reasonable and self-sufficient. She had no one to
worry about but herself.

The truth was that she had raised a child
already. She had loved Lucy like her own
daughter, admired and disciplined and protected her, even sent her away to college—
a fact Joyce still found incredible. A good
student, Lucy had won a small scholarship
to the nursing program at the University of
Pittsburgh, enough to pay her living expenses. Joyce's savings—from her air-force
pay, then the dress factory, then her school
secretary's job—had covered the rest. It
was a moment she would never forget, writing the check to cover Lucy's first-semester
tuition: more memorable than her wedding,
her own college graduation. It was the best
thing she had ever done.

Susan finished her lunch, then rose to
wipe the chalkboards. Afterward she would
take the erasers outside to dust. She performed these tasks without being asked, a
child used to doing what needed to be
done. She was a serious, pretty girl, with a
long straight nose and somber brown eyes,

more at ease with adults than with children
her own age. Watching her, Joyce wondered if her stillness was innate or acquired,
a reaction to growing up in the chaos of the
Jevic household. She spoke often of her
brother and sister—the youngest Jevics,
now in high school. Joyce had taught each
of them in the eighth grade. Susan was as
different from the chatty, effervescent Mon-
ica, the boisterous, high-spirited Billy, as a
child could possibly be.

How's your sister doing? Joyce had
asked her once. *Still working at the factory?*

Susan seemed surprised. *You know
Irene?*

Of course, Joyce said. *We were in school
together. We were very good friends.*

I didn't know, Susan said. *She never mentioned it to me.*

The bus was nearly empty that evening. Two hours before, in Pittsburgh, Lucy had secured a seat up front. The bus had stopped a half-dozen times since then, in towns so small they had no stations: Temperance, Buckhorn, Salt Lick. Passengers debarked at churches and gas stations, at lunch counters with signs in their windows: BUS TICKETS SOLD HERE. By four-thirty night had fallen. The dark window reflected her face back at her.

She looked the same, or nearly so—a bit thinner, her hair cut shorter and teased into a flip. Her eyes were circled with black liner, a look Joyce detested. Lucy read the disapproval in her tight smile, but for reasons she didn't understand, Joyce did not criticize. Her sister had changed. Never affectionate, she now embraced Lucy each time she saw her. Instead of giving orders, she asked a million questions about classes and professors, and listened intently to the answers. To her own surprise, Lucy didn't mind the questions. She preferred Joyce's tidy house to Dorothy's messy one, her sincere interest to Dorothy's moody silence. Her first night back they would talk for hours at the kitchen table, long after Ed had gone to bed.

The bus climbed Saxon Mountain: lights in the valley, rooftops covered with snow. Lucy made the journey four times a year— Christmas and early summer, at midsemester breaks in spring and fall. Each time she rode into Bakerton one person—her confident adult self, fast moving and fast thinking—and rode out someone smaller and softer, crippled by tenderness. Her visits unfolded according to a pattern. Her first day in Bakerton she felt displaced and restless, preoccupied with the life she'd left behind: friends and classes, a boy who'd hurt or disappointed her, another who'd asked for her phone number, who seemed different from the rest. But in a few days the friends and classes, even the boys, would seem distant and imaginary. Exams and term papers, her job at the campus pub, walking back to her dorm at night, the dark, noisy streets—her entire college life would seem hopelessly beyond her, like something she'd dreamed. She'd begin to dread leaving Bakerton: the interminable good-byes, the long bus ride alone.

Leonard Stusick was waiting for her when she stepped off the bus.

"Hi there," she said, surprised. "What are you doing here?" She hadn't seen him since summertime: he'd started at Penn State that fall, and their midsemester breaks hadn't coincided. Occasionally—late at night, after her shift—she considered writing him a letter, but rejected the idea as corny.

"Waiting for you." He was taller than she remembered, his plaid hunting jacket too short in the sleeves. *He's still growing,* she thought, amazed. He had started college a year early; he was only seventeen.

"Ed's coming to pick me up," she said.

"No, he's not." Leonard grinned. "I saw him uptown this morning. I told him I'd come and get you." He took the suitcase from her hand. "Come on."

He led her to a pickup truck parked at the curb.

"Your dad has a new truck?"

"It's mine," he said proudly. "I got it secondhand, but it runs like new."

Lucy blinked. At school she traveled on foot, or took the trolley. She had never considered owning a car, herself. It struck her as very adult.

They drove to Keener's and ordered sandwiches. Lucy had eaten dozens of meals there—with Marcia Dickey, or Marcia and Davis—but never with Leonard. Cookies and milk at her house, or peanutbutter sandwiches made by his mother, that was more their speed. She watched him study the menu, the careful way he laid his napkin across his lap. She felt suddenly shy.

He talked about his classes—biology, organic chemistry, calculus and statistics— his part-time job at the student union, a second job he would start next term, working in a lab with his biology professor. They had taken a booth in the corner. Over his shoulder she stared out the plate-glass windows, watching the snow fall.

She'd spent many evenings like this, listening to a boy in a diner, her mind and eyes wandering. Boys she'd met on campus, at parties, in the pub; confident boys who joked and flirted, who smiled down at her as she served their drinks. Leonard did not joke. He was describing, now, the research being done by his professor, something to do with the Krebs cycle. A familiar feeling washed over her, an odd mix of irritation and tenderness. *Oh, Leonard,* she thought. So sweet and so hopeless. His sincerity was both touching and tedious.

"It sounds like you're very busy," she said politely. "What do you do for fun? You know—on the weekends."

"Well, I come home," he said, as though the answer were obvious. "That's why I bought the truck."

"You come back every weekend?"

"Sure." He looked puzzled. "Wouldn't you, if you had a car?"

Lucy considered this. She was happy at school, and happy at home; what pained her was the transition between the two. She could not imagine so much leaving: every Sunday, more good-byes.

"Maybe," she said. "I don't know."

He gave her a searching look. "Don't you miss anybody? Dorothy? Joyce?"

The waitress arrived with their sandwiches.

"Sure," Lucy said. "I miss them all."

They ate fast and silently. She was hun-
grier than she'd imagined. Outside, a boy
and girl crossed the street, their hands
joined. Someone had put money in the juke-
box: Brenda Lee singing "Break It to Me
Gently." Lucy ate half her hamburger, then lit
a cigarette.

"You're *smoking*?" Leonard said.

At that moment the door opened and the
young couple came in, stamping snow from
their shoes. In the distance the fire whistle
squealed, as though someone were in danger. Lucy's heart quickened. She would
have known them anywhere: Steven Fleck
and Connie Kukla.

"Oh, brother," she said in a low voice,
sliding down in her seat. "Don't look now."

He turned his head toward the door.

"Leonard!" she whispered. But it was too
late: Connie had already spotted them.

"Lucy?" she called in a high, clear voice.
"Is that you?" She wore fuzzy earmuffs. Her
blond hair was flocked with snow.

"Hi, Connie," she said miserably. The fire
whistle rose in pitch. She felt Steven Fleck's

eyes rest on her a moment. She smiled uncertainly, her cheeks heating. His eyes darted away.

"There's an open table in the back," he mumbled, his hand at Connie's waist. "Come on. Let's go."

"It's nice to see you," Connie called, giving Lucy a little finger wave. "Merry Christmas."

Lucy watched them go. Steven sat first, his back to Lucy. His broad shoulders were dusted with snow.

"What gives?" said Leonard. "Aren't they friends of yours?"

"Sort of." After the night under the bleachers, Steven had never spoken to her again. She'd passed him often in the school corridors, hand in hand with Connie. When the two girls exchanged hellos, he'd kept his eyes on the floor.

"Not really," she said. "It's hard to explain."

Later that evening, she would remember the fire whistle. At the time it had barely registered, so distracting was the noise of her heart.

The music on the radio had changed. It was the first difference George noticed that year, the Christmas he brought Arthur home to visit. Driving over Saxon Mountain, he dialed through the usual riot of AM stations: polkas, Christmas carols, a cowboy singer's crackling baritone. In the valley they faded into static. On the local station, the DJ played the most requested tune of the week, a sweet ballad called "My Blue Heaven." George hummed along softly—a strolling rhythm, the breathy moan of a tenor sax. He broke into a smile. Negro music in Bakerton! A town that had never seen a black face, now clamoring for Fats Domino.

He reached to turn up the volume, then stopped himself. Arthur was slumped down in the backseat, eyes closed, hands hidden in the sleeves of the winter jacket he hadn't quite grown into. His dungarees looked stiff and new; he would outgrow them before they could fade in the wash. He had little need for casual clothes. At the Wollaston School he wore white shirts and crested blazers, a maroon cardigan after hours in the dorms.

He was thirteen but small for his age. At Parents' Weekend, George had been stunned by the maturity of the other eighth graders: the broad shoulders, the deep voices. Next to them Arthur still looked like a child. Undersized, with Marion's long thin face, blue-veined at the temples; her intelligent gray eyes, alert, a little alarmed. He resembled George in invisible ways: the delicate constitution, the measles and ear infections, the periodic bouts with the flu. His sickness was nearly a year-round affair. In spring and fall, allergies aggravated his asthma. Every winter, from infancy on, he'd developed a stubborn chest cold and a resounding cough, a remarkable imitation of a coal miner's guttural hack. Night after night, his coughing shook the house awake. *For God's sake, can't we give him something?*

Marion had whispered to George in the dark—in those days, long ago, when they still shared a bed. She was a steadfast believer in *somethings.* But Arthur's colds were impervious to treatment. He coughed for weeks on end.

He was ten when Marion proposed sending him to Wollaston—her father's school, and Kip's; the *alma mater* of all the Quigley men. *Arthur's not a Quigley,* George had pointed out, but Marion had merely shrugged. Wollaston was the best of the best, she informed him; no local school could offer a comparable education. Arthur would come home for summers and holidays, and George could drive up to Connecticut to visit him. *Whenever you have time,* she said pointedly. He worked at the store six or seven days a week. Even when Arthur had lived at home, George had scarcely seen him at all.

The song ended and another began, a lively dance tune George recognized. Unconsciously his fingers found the notes, lightly pressing the steering wheel. He hadn't played in years, but the impulse had never left him; whenever he heard music, he hammered out the notes with his fingers.

Early in their courtship Marion had found this fascinating, him tapping on the small of her back as they danced. Now it drove her crazy. She had not danced with him in years.

He wondered if Ev and Gene still danced together. George thought of her often lately. Redheads reminded him, and pregnant women and the fall weather. Her birthday was in September; on her sixteenth they'd had their first date. Before that her father hadn't allowed it, so George had waited. He'd been patient then, sure in his devotion. A better man at sixteen than he'd been since.

The fire whistle squealed in the distance, a sound George hadn't heard in years. The noise sent a chill up his spine. In the backseat Arthur stirred.

"That's the fire whistle," said George. "We're almost there."

Arthur sat up. "What's that smell?"

"Over there." George pointed. "They're called the Towers. They're bony piles."

"Why do they smell like that?" His voice nasal, as though he were holding his breath.

"Sulfur gases. From the scrap coal."

Arthur considered this. "But why do they

leave it there? Why don't they throw it in the garbage?"

"They're landmarks." George peered through the windshield. "When the wind blows they turn sort of orange. It's something to see."

"They stink, though."

"I know," said George.

Abruptly the whistle stopped. Arthur settled back into his seat. Again his eyes closed. He'd spent the previous day on a train from Connecticut; now he seemed perfectly content to be driven into this town he'd never seen before, for reasons George had found difficult to articulate.

Marion, for her part, had been dumbfounded. *You're taking him to Bakerton? For heaven's sake, whatever for?*

Later, alone, George had pondered the question. Bakerton had been calling to him lately. Rose's death, he supposed, though it was his father's that haunted him—the funeral he'd missed nearly twenty years ago, a young soldier at sea.

I grew up there, he said simply. *I want my son to see it.*

In the end they compromised: he and Arthur would spend Christmas Eve in Bakerton, then drive back early the next morning. They would arrive in Haverford in time to eat Christmas dinner at the Quigleys'. At one time a battle would have ensued, but the years had drained the struggle out of his marriage. They had both stopped caring long ago.

The porch furniture was shrouded in plastic, the floor covered with artificial turf. A wooden sign hung above the door: THE STUSICKS, fancy script burned into a flat pine board. In the front yard stood a statue of the Virgin Mary, up to her knees in snow.

Ev's eyes widened when she came to the door. "Georgie! This is a surprise."

"Merry Christmas." He leaned in and kissed her cheek. "Ev, this is my son, Arthur."

"How do you do." Arthur stood up straight, removed his hat, and offered his hand. The Wollaston manners. For once they seemed worth the thousand dollars a year.

"What a gentleman," Ev said, beaming. "My son will be home in a little while. Can you teach him that?" She gave Arthur's shoulder a squeeze. "It's freezing out there. Come on in."

She led them through the living room. A new pope hung on the wall; beside him, a portrait of the dead president. In the center was still John L. Lewis. "My girls are down in the rec room," she told Arthur. "Go say hello, like you did just now. They won't believe it."

At the kitchen table she poured coffee. "Well, this is a first. Having you home at Christmas." She sat. "How's Dorothy?"

"I haven't seen her yet. She was upstairs taking a bath. You're our first stop."

She smiled. "Still no wife, Georgie? I'm starting to think you made her up."

"She's in New York for a few days." Lately Marion spent most of her time there, buying clothes or art, seeing Dr. Gold in one capacity or another. Occasionally George wondered if they were lovers. He didn't care enough to find out.

"I've always wanted to see New York," Ev said.

"You've never been?"

She laughed. "Oh, Georgie. I've never been anywhere."

"I'll take you someday. You and Gene," he added hastily.

"Oh, sure. Gene wouldn't be caught dead in New York. He won't even drive to Pittsburgh." She rose and stirred something in a pot on the stove.

"What's that? It smells familiar."

"*Pasta e fagioli.* Your mother showed me how to make it. It's not as good as hers, but the kids like it." Ev wiped her hands on a tea towel. "I still miss her, Georgie. It was nice having her across the street."

"I miss her, too." He thought of Rose sitting on the front porch the last time he'd visited, her blind eyes seeing right through him. *Georgie, are you happy?*

"She was crazy about you," he said. "She couldn't understand why we didn't get married. Sometimes I wonder about that myself." It was his memory of Rose that brought the words out in a rush. His loneliness, his regrets; the recurrent, haunting dreams of his mother. His life with Marion, the life he had chosen for himself.

Ev flushed a deep red, nearly purple. She sat a long time without speaking.

"Why did you stop writing?" she asked finally.

"I was a kid," said George. "I didn't know what was good for me. I got cold feet."

"You broke my heart." She said it calmly, as though the injury were not emotional but anatomical: a working part damaged, then successfully replaced. "You stopped loving me. I didn't know that was possible. I didn't know anything then."

"You knew more than I did. I was so anxious to get out of here, I couldn't think straight." He looked down into his cup. "I never stopped, Ev. I just—forgot."

"You forgot." She laughed, then stifled it, covering her mouth. For a moment he thought she might cry.

"Oh, this is silly," she said, recovering herself. "Why even talk about it? We're forty years old, Georgie. It's all water under the bridge."

"I guess so," he said.

Ev cocked her head to one side. "Georgie, are you happy?"

"I married the wrong woman," he said. "I made a terrible mistake."

Then the telephone rang.

* * *

They drove to the tipple in George's car. They had sent Arthur across the street to Dorothy's, Ev's daughters to their grandparents' up the hill. A heavy snow coated the roads. Beneath it, a slick of ice.

"When did it happen?" George asked.

"Around lunchtime." Ev stared straight ahead. "At least, that's when the power went out. They think it was an explosion." Her chin quivered violently. "Georgie, they've already been trapped down there half a day."

George tried to imagine it: the cold, the damp. He knew little about mine work; he tried to remember what his father had told him. How the mine walls weren't black but gray, from the crushed limestone the men spread there to keep the dust down. How he'd once seen a locust mine prop sprout green leaves underground.

They made their way through the town, past store windows bright with holiday shopping hours. The wind lifted snow from the rooftops. Under the street lamps, silver flurries fell like shards of metal, bright and industrial.

"I'm worried about Leonard," Ev said. "He

should have been back by now. I'd hate for him to hear it from somebody else."

"He's still at school?"

"He came home last night," said Ev. "He went to the bus station to pick up Lucy."

Up ahead, the traffic light turned from yellow to red. The car ahead of him slammed on its brakes. A moment later it went into a spin.

"Hang on," said George, pumping the brakes. The Cadillac slid, then recovered. "Whoops." He reached out a hand to brace her. She stiffened at his touch.

"Sorry," he said. "I do that when Arthur rides with me."

"That's okay," she said.

They crossed the bridge and joined the procession, a long line of cars barely moving in the snow. Engine noise, smoking tailpipes; a string of red taillights. It seemed that the whole town was driving to the Twelve. Here and there, cars had slid off the road. An old Plymouth had nosed into a ditch.

Finally they approached the tipple. A man

in a hunting vest stood inside the yard, directing traffic. George rolled down his window. "Any word from down there?" he asked.

The man studied him. "Are you relatives?"

"This is Evelyn Stusick. Her husband is down there."

"Gene's wife?" The man pointed out a narrow road that led into a forest. "Deer Run is thataway."

They followed the road, bumpy with red dog but cleared of snow, as though many cars had come before them.

"I should have packed him more food. I just put the one sandwich in his bucket. He's on a diet." Ev laughed, a choking sound. There was a tremor in her voice. "He put on some weight during the strike."

The road ended in a clearing, where a long construction trailer was parked. Lights on inside; outside, people milled about. George wondered how long it had been there, if it was kept at the ready for just this purpose.

They parked the car and went inside. Someone had set up folding chairs and card tables. Only a few people sat waiting.

Gene was the assistant foreman of the crew. Ev had been one of the first called.

George sat and removed his coat. The Salvation Army had set up urns of coffee. It was going to be a long night.

They were longwall miners, a crew of ten. A few had come over from the Two, mined out that summer; the rest from other sections of the Twelve. The strike had sapped their bank accounts, their confidence. A year ago they'd bought hunting rifles for Christmas, fishing gear, power tools. Now they watched every penny. They were grateful to be back at work.

All through autumn they had worked in low coal. At Deer Run the seam was three feet high. On their hands and knees they set the chock line, to lock the longwall in place. A deafening roar, a flash of lights: coal and rock clawed from the face. Behind the chock line, the earth crumbled; fast, crab-legged, the roof bolters crawled into place. Coal was loaded onto the conveyor. On their knees the men moved the chocks. Noisily the longwall was reset. Another block of coal was cut.

The machine was an old one, brought over from the Two. New longwalls were coming, machines that protected the miners under a shield; but at Deer Run, the roof still required bolting. Old-timers sang the praises of the old Lee Norse miner; but there was no arguing with the longwall's efficiency. The machine made cuts a thousand feet long.

The men were named Yurkovich, Yurkovich and Sullivan, Kukla, Randazzo and Quinn. Kelly and Kovacs were the roof bolters. The foremen were Bernardi and Stusick. A young crew, like a bone newly set, not yet fused. Their grievances were small. Stusick's humor grated on them. As a foreman, he was a stickler for details. Twenty minutes exactly for chow break, and at quarter past he started tapping at his watch. *Jesus, I hate that tapping,* Pat Randazzo complained once to Kovacs. *Just yell for me, why don't you? Or beat me like my wife does.*

Angie Bernardi did not tap. He clapped his hands in their yellow gloves; he shouted, he whistled, he called the men special names. Filthy names, some of them, but pronounced with such affection, such ringing admiration, you felt you'd done something remarkable to earn them. One day Joe Kukla had taken an enormous crap in the hole, and after that Bernardi called the guy Footlong. The men hooted with laughter; Kukla beamed with pride. Coming from Angie it seemed like the highest praise.

Aboveground, wives and mothers murmured prayers to Saint Anne. The Salvation
Army distributed sandwiches and sugar
cookies. Cots were unfolded against the
corrugated wall.

George smoked and paced. Periodically
he brought Ev sandwiches she didn't eat.
He drank Salvation Army coffee until his
stomach ached.

After a few hours they stepped outside
for a breath. The snow had stopped; the
sky was flat and starless. George marveled
at the absolute darkness, so unlike his sub-
urban neighborhood, where street lamps
glowed every fifty feet. The cold hit his brain
like a drug. Years ago, as a student,
he'd worked nights; he remembered the
jangly rush of energy that came at midnight,

the body, shaken from its usual routines, primed for crisis.

Ev leaned against the corrugated wall. Her skin looked ghostly under the floodlight. "I should have waited for Leonard before we left. The house is never empty when he comes home. He'll know something's wrong."

"I'm sure he went right to his grandparents'," George said. "He's a bright kid. He'll know what to do."

A man approached them, a silver-haired man in a plaid lumberman's jacket. "Mrs. Stusick?"

"Yes?"

"Oh, don't be frightened, dear. I'm nobody." He chuckled. "Actually, I'm Regis Devlin. I know your husband."

She smiled. "Mr. Devlin used to be the president of the local," she told George.

"Your Gene is a clever boy," said Devlin, patting her arm. "Don't worry, dear. Those men are in good hands. Gene'll bring them up safe." He smiled warmly, but George saw his eyes flicker.

"This is Georgie Novak," Ev said. "We went to high school together."

"Novak?" Devlin offered his hand. "Sure,

sure. Your brother Sandy was out in Cleveland with my boys. I hear he's in California now. Good-looking kid. He should be in the pictures." Gently he touched Ev's shoulder. "You look exhausted, dear. Go and have yourself a nap."

Ev watched him go. "I'm surprised he has a kind word, after that horrible election," she said. "You know how Gene can be."

George nodded.

"But he's right. Gene *is* clever." Ev hugged her coat around her. "I'm going to see if any of those cots are free. It might do me good to close my eyes."

George stared into the distance, at the lights of town on the other side of the river. This was Ev's whole world: Polish Hill, the Twelve, the eight blocks of downtown. Just a few hours ago he'd imagined taking her to New York. By then the explosion had already happened. Gene was already trapped underground.

He glanced across the parking lot. A man in a topcoat stood beneath the single floodlight. Beside him stood Regis Devlin, head bowed, listening intently. George thought of the way his eyes had flickered.

They're dead, he thought. *He knows they're all dead.*

Hours passed. Slowly the room began to fill. Old women in babushkas, in mantillas; young women in high heels, in pantsuits, holding babies. Men in Sunday clothes, fathers and brothers; wet-haired men from the Six, the Eight, just finished with their shifts.

Sometime after midnight a man entered the room. He wore a dark coat and hat. George recognized him from outside, the man he'd seen talking to Regis Devlin.

"Who's that?" Ev whispered.

Someone answered, "The secretary of mines."

The secretary stood at the front of the room. In an instant the crowd quieted.

"Thanks for your patience, folks. I know some of you have been waiting for hours." His voice was grave. "Here's the situation. At twelve-thirty this afternoon there was an explosion in the Deer Run section of the mine. We know that because the brattices have collapsed. They're solid concrete, and they've buckled under the impact."

Gasps, a stifled cry. Ev's eyes widened. She placed a hand over her mouth.

"At twelve forty-six, as best as we can figure, there was a second explosion. That's when the backup generator kicked in and restored power to the mine. What exactly caused that second impact, we don't know for certain."

A male voice mumbled something at the front of the room.

"Could have been a spark," the secretary answered. "Or an electrical fire. There's no sense in speculating on that now."

"Methane," said a deep voice. George turned to see who was speaking. A man had risen from his chair—an old miner, by the looks of him, stooped and unshaven. He wore a dirty red cap. "A spark isn't going to explode unless there's methane down there." He spoke gruffly, his breath short. His lower lip held a pinch of snuff.

"That's one explanation," said the secretary.

The man sat, shaking his head. "Jesus Christ, I hope you shut the power off."

"We're aware of the methane issue." The secretary had raised his voice slightly, to recapture the crowd's attention. "Ventilation is our primary concern." He spoke quickly, bluntly, a man used to giving orders. "We don't know what kind of air is flowing down there. The men have portable ventilation devices, and they're trained to use them in an emergency. That's standard equipment.

"Two rescue teams are down there right now, one from Iselin Collieries and one from Eastern Coal and Coke. We'll know more in the morning," he said.

"Morning?" George murmured. "Why is it taking so long?"

Ev sat silent, her hand still clamped over her mouth. Her other hand clutched George's arm.

The mine secretary knew why. So did Regis Devlin, and the old miner in the red cap. Blame the long success, the legendary profit and glory of the mighty Baker Twelve.

A mine is made by mining, and for seventeen years the Twelve had been mined hard. The Deer Run shaft was seven hundred feet deep. From it, tunnels extended for miles in all directions. Viewed from above, the Twelve resembled a snow-covered pasture, thousands of acres of rolling meadow. But beneath the surface, the layout was as elaborate as a honeycomb, an intricate network of rooms and corridors running parallel to the ground.

Even with their antiquated longwall, the Deer Run crew had progressed far from the shaft. Shift after shift, they cut a narrow corridor through solid coal. The corridor was now two miles long. How much of it had collapsed—behind them, around them—was impossible to say.

A little boy told her. Dorothy would remember it later like a dream. The implausibility of it did not trouble her; her life had been filled with strange totems. Birds. Nuns walking. There had been a Chinese woman in a mink coat, stepping out of a car long ago.

"Where did you come from?" she asked the boy. He was standing on her porch.

"Connecticut, ma'am. Before that, Philadelphia." He was very polite. His voice was clear and sweet as an altar boy's.

There had been an accident at a coal mine, he told her. Men were trapped. His father had taken the lady from across the street.

"Trapped?" she repeated. The connections eluded her at first, the series of deductions, like the solution to a math problem.

Gene Stusick lived across the street. Gene worked with Angelo at the Twelve.

"Do you have a car?" she asked the boy.

"I'm only thirteen," he said.

First she called Joyce, who had heard about it on the radio.

"I tried to call you earlier," she said. "Where were you?"

"Taking a bath." Dorothy hugged her housecoat around her. Gooseflesh rose on her bare legs.

"Angelo is down there," she said. "Can you come and get me? I need to get out there right away."

"Oh, honey, I'm sorry. Ed has the car this evening. He had a meeting after school." Joyce paused. "Are you sure you want to go out there? The roads are terrible, and the bridge traffic is jammed. They're telling everyone to stay at home. All but the immediate families."

Dorothy hesitated. It was true: he was not her family. He was something else to her, something she had no word for.

"Sit tight," Joyce said. "I'll call you in a few hours."

Dorothy hung up the phone.

She walked up and down Polish Hill in her old raincoat, looking for cars. None in front of the Poblockis', the Klezeks'—Ted and Bud were working Hoot Owl at the Six. Dan Wojick had sold his Chevy during the strike. Across the street the Stusicks' windows were dark.

Inside, the boy was sitting at the kitchen table, his hands folded in his lap.

"Your hair is frozen," he observed.

Her hand went to her head. Spiky tendrils at the nape of her neck, where her hair had gotten wet in the bath. She wasn't thinking clearly. She needed to compose herself.

She went upstairs and collected a wool sweater, a hat and gloves. Angie had left three pairs of trousers for her to alter; he had gained a little weight, and she'd offered to let out the waist. For a moment she considered wearing them—she'd never owned slacks, herself—but Angie's trousers would be far too big. She combed through the closet in Joyce's room and slipped on a pair of old corduroys Sandy had left behind.

In the hall closet she found her galoshes,

her long coat. She looked a sight, she knew, but that hardly mattered. It would be a long walk.

"Where are you going?" the boy asked.

"To the mine." She wound a scarf around her neck.

He eyed her a moment in her strange getup. "I'll come with you," he said.

They set out into the cold. Down the hill and across the tracks. Snow was falling nearly sideways. They walked in the middle of the road; it was impossible to find the sidewalk. All around them the snow swirled. Parked cars were shrouded in it, the white shapes looming like humpbacked beasts.

The boy walked a few paces ahead. A fierce wind smacked his left cheek. In the hall closet he'd found a red stocking cap Lucy had knitted. The tail blew out to the side like a wind sock. Dorothy hunched along behind him, her hands in her pockets.

"Georgie!"

He'd begun to doze off in his chair when his name roused him. His sister Dorothy stood in the doorway, her eyes wide with panic. Her coat was crusted with snow. Beside her stood Arthur in a red Santa hat.

"What are you doing here?" George took her arm and helped her off with her coat. He felt the tremor in her back, in her shoulders. "Arthur, are you all right?" The hat gave him an elfin appearance. His left cheek was bright red.

George guided his sister to a chair.

"Angelo is down there. Georgie, why didn't you call me?"

"The phones are out," George said. "Knocked out in the explosion. There's no way to reach anybody."

"I've been trying to get here for hours."
Her voice rose indignantly. Again the heads
turned. "I couldn't find a ride anywhere.
None of the neighbors were home."

"So how'd you get here?"

"We walked."

"You're joking." The route was six miles,
maybe seven, including a steep hike up
Saxon Mountain. In good weather the trek
would be rigorous. In the wind and snow, it
seemed nearly impossible. "All the way
from Polish Hill?"

"Halfway," said Arthur. "Then we hitched
a ride in a hearse." His eyes went to the
door. Jerry Bernardi stood there stamping
snow from his boots.

Other people noticed, too. A hush settled
over the room.

"Relax," Jerry said, to no one in particular. "It ain't business."

A few laughs; again people started talking.

"That's Angelo's cousin," Dorothy whispered. "The whole family is here." The
Bernardis had taken over a corner of the
room: his brothers and sisters, his father
and cousins. A small, pretty woman Dorothy

didn't recognize, her curly hair tinged with gray. *Julia,* she realized.

"Lucy's around here somewhere," George told her. "She and Leonard showed up about an hour ago."

"What do we do now?" Arthur asked, removing his hat.

No one answered. There was nothing to do but wait.

Lucy stood behind the trailer, shivering. Her frozen fingers curled around a cigarette. The other hand fingered a silver crucifix that hung at her throat. The cross was no bigger than a thumbnail, the Christ figure surprisingly detailed. Its hands and feet were sharp as tacks.

Angelo had given her the necklace the day she left for college. Joyce had bought her sheets and towels, a portable type-writer; but only Angelo had thought to give her a real gift. He'd wrapped the box himself, using too much Scotch tape. *I should have left it to the professionals,* he told her, grinning. She lifted her hair, and he clasped the delicate chain around her neck. She'd kept, but never used, the velvety box from Schoenberg's Jewelers. She wore the necklace to bed, in the shower, everywhere. In two years she'd never taken it off.

What the hell is that? she'd been asked more than once. Always by Catholic boys, she'd noticed, Italians and Irish, who found it dangling between her breasts when they unbuttoned her blouse.

Leonard emerged from the corrugated shack and handed her a foam cup. "Drink this. It'll warm you up."

She butted her cigarette.

"Where are your gloves?" he asked.

"I left them in the truck." The cup warmed her right hand. She shoved the left into his coat pocket. Inside she felt keys, a slip of paper. "What's this? Some girl's phone number?"

"Not likely," said Leonard.

She withdrew the paper: a tiny comic from Bazooka bubblegum. A smile tugged at her lips.

"There's another rescue crew coming," he said. "From West Virginia. They have better equipment, I guess." The floodlight cast a glare on his glasses. She could not see his eyes.

The waitress at Keener's had told them. They had sat in the booth a long time, Lucy smoking, waiting for Connie and Steven Fleck to leave. There had been an awkward moment at the cash register as they both reached for their wallets. Then the thought occurred to her: *He thinks we're on a date.* She'd stared at him dumbly, her face frozen in shock. Then the waitress asked him: *Aren't you Gene Stusick's boy?*

"Dad was sick this week," said Leonard. "Mom told him to stay home, but he wouldn't listen. He hasn't missed a day of work in twenty years."

Lucy fingered the crucifix at her throat.

"He gets a cold every winter. Then he gives it to the rest of the crew. Mom says he should stay home and keep his germs to himself." Leonard jammed his hands into his pockets. "I can drive you to Joyce's, if you want. You don't have to stay here all night."

Lucy slid her hand back into his pocket, curling her fingers around his.

"That's okay," she said. "I don't mind."

Through the long snowy night, the silent morning, rescuers dug. Another crew was bused in from Kentucky. A supply chain was started. Power lines were handed down, hydraulic drills, hardware, wooden roof supports.

They dug six men to a crew, air supplies strapped to their backs. On eight-hour shifts they inched forward, hammering in roof posts, rebuilding the corridor as they went. Periodically they tested the air. Carbon monoxide; methane gas. The rescuers sweated in the damp. They feared another explosion. A single spark would be enough.

The first man, Patrice Randazzo, was found four thousand feet from the mine face—nearly a mile from where the crew had been working, from where he should have been. He was carried that far by the impact. To the other families waiting aboveground, this was the worst news yet.

The men had been killed instantly. That's what the mine secretary said. No one had a reason to doubt it, though you had to wonder how he knew.

Found at the mine face, two miles from the Deer Run shaft, Baker Brothers Number Twelve:

One Lancashire longwall machine, circa 1951. Its back end had been hit by rockfall, but the chassis wasn't even dented. The longwall was perfectly intact.

Four mismatched mining boots. The force of the blast had blown them a hundred feet. Four men had died in their socks.

A pair of horn-rimmed glasses, mended at the temple with electrical tape.

Ten dinner buckets, firmly closed and tied with twine. In recent weeks, someone on the Deer Run crew had been stealing snuff from the other men's buckets. The wives had responded with security measures. The buckets were airtight. Two massive explosions hadn't blown them open.

Tip Kelly and Ab Kovacs, who had bolted roofs in the One, the Three and the Four. They were the oldest miners on the crew. They had each been married for forty years. They'd been partners for forty-one.

John Terence Sullivan, who'd once studied for the priesthood, and John Patrick Quinn. Joe Kukla, known as Footlong. Father of six blond daughters, one of them a Fire Queen.

One Yurkovich twin, Peter or Paul, whose mother had baked a hazelnut torte for their third birthday and sent it to Rose Novak's house instead. The other twin was found five hundred feet down the corridor, his body deposited there by the blast.

Eugene Stusick, once known as Eugenius. Husband of Evelyn, father of four. Past president of Bakerton Local 1450, United Mineworkers of America. Old friend and bookmark of George Novak, who now knows how it all turned out.

Angelo Bernardi, father of four, Friday companion of Dorothy Novak. An autopsy

would show his lungs black with pneumo-
coniosis. He was found wearing bright yellow gloves. Underneath them, his hands
were perfectly clean.

NINE

Everything froze.

Christmas came and went. A federal injunction halted mining at the Twelve. You didn't speak of what would happen next. You knew Randazzo from the Knights, Kukla and Stusick from St. Casimir's. You'd seen Quinn and Kelly playing cards at the Vets, the Yurkovich twins at the firehall dances, walking the Bakerton Circle. Kovacs's wife ran a press iron at the dress factory. Angie's uncle had buried yours. You knew them from the Legion, the ball field. There was no escaping all the ways you knew them. The ways they were just like you.

Funerals were held all over town. Stoner and Bernardi drove their hearses back and forth, back and forth. Classes were canceled at the high school. Some people attended three masses in one day.

The explosion had happened four days before Christmas, a fact the newspapers would emphasize. As though March or July would have been preferable, the timing a comfort: at least it didn't happen at Christmas.

For months afterward, mine investigators toured the Twelve. They interviewed employees and conducted tests. Reports were filed. Then public hearings were held.

Methane gas was a fact of miners' lives. Most days it escaped from coal seams at a minute trickle; the levels were influenced by atmospheric pressure, which fluctuated with the change of seasons. The pressure had dropped sharply that December, after four days of freakish summer temperatures. A flood of methane had been released.

Ten months of investigations, and that was the size of it: you couldn't blame Baker for the weather. Meanwhile the Twelve had been closed for a year. Production was off by eighty thousand tons. Enough to heat all of Bakerton that winter, as Gene Stusick might have said.

His widow attended the hearings, her son

at her side. She remembered the crocuses blooming in her front yard that December. For the rest of her life, the sight of yellow flowers would make her sick inside.

Every friday afternoon, Dorothy Novak walked to the cemetery. She visited Angie first. Then Nicholas Annacone, the boy crushed by a car as he chased a ball into the street. Buried seven years that October, the day Angie had first taken her for a ride.

Every week she left flowers on Angie's grave. His headstone was large and handsome, the name engraved in bold block letters: ANGELO FRANCESCO, 1916–1963. SOLDIER, HUSBAND AND FATHER. The family had refused the army's free headstone, believing Angie deserved something more impressive. His uncle had chosen the best his suppliers had to offer, a massive slab of pinkish granite. In the bottom corner a design had been added, the crude outline of a bat and baseball.

Angie had been recruited out of high school to pitch for the Bombers. *It runs in the family,* he'd told Dorothy: the famous

Ernie Tedesco was a distant cousin of his father's. The team went undefeated, and Angie was spotted by a scout for the New York Giants, signed to play for their minor-league club in St. Cloud, Minnesota. He spent a season with the team, traveling the flat states of Minnesota and Wisconsin and Illinois. *We were on a bus every night,* he told Dorothy. *Getting paid to play baseball. I couldn't believe it. I felt like I robbed a bank.* The money was lousy, half what he'd earned in the coal mines; but he'd have played for nothing. *Are you kidding?* he told her. *I would have paid them to let me play.* Finally Julia had laid down the law. She was jealous; she didn't trust him out on the road, drinking and carousing. They were engaged to be married. It was time he grew up.

Don't you wish you'd kept playing? Dorothy had asked him. *Don't you wonder what could have happened?*

Angie shrugged. Maybe later, after his lungs got bad, he had some regrets; but what was the use in thinking like that? The war would have put a stop to it anyway. In those years nobody played ball.

Now, standing at his grave, Dorothy couldn't shake the thought: If he'd kept playing baseball, he would have stayed out of the mines. There would still be an Angie in the world.

Some Fridays, she found another bouquet at his grave. She laid her own flowers beside it. The other half of his headstone was engraved with a name: JULIA MARIA, 1920– , the date to be filled in later. The place where his wife would someday lie.

Dorothy had recognized them at the funeral, sitting in the front pew: the son and three daughters who'd broken his heart, the wife, weeping, who had poisoned them against him. They'd pretended not to notice Dorothy, which suited her. None of that mattered anymore.

Walking home from the graveyard, she thought often of Nicholas Annacone. A weeping angel had been cut into his gravestone. An Italianate angel, with dark eyes and curly hair, how Nicholas himself must have looked. How Angie might have looked as a boy.

For a month, two months, she thought she might be pregnant. Her body allowed her to believe this. Since Joyce had moved out of the house, Dorothy bled only rarely. Angie had been careful, but mistakes happened. Lying in bed at night, she massaged her flat belly, and hoped.

Twice a week Joyce brought her a few bags of groceries, a casserole or a pot of home-made soup. *You've got to eat,* she pointed out. Dorothy's dresses hung on her. She seemed to be wasting away.

They sat outside in the long summer evenings, on the new porch swing Ed had hung. Behind them the house was dark. Dorothy used electricity sparingly, aware that Joyce still paid the utility bills. They never spoke of Angelo Bernardi. The sub-ject made Dorothy weepy, Joyce uncom-fortable and a little ashamed. She under-stood, too late, that her sister had lost the only thing she'd ever valued. That her own response to that thing, the disdainful way she'd treated it, had been obstinate and heartless.

Dorothy, always frail, now seemed bro-ken. When Joyce telephoned her each morning, she answered in a hoarse whisper, sounding slightly panicked, as if she ex-pected bad news. She wore ragged housedresses in summer; in winter, baggy men's trousers cinched at the waist with a belt. (*They're warm,* she explained when Joyce inquired. She liked to keep the furnace turned low.) Joyce offered to give her a home permanent, but Dorothy couldn't be bothered. Her hair was wound into a bun at the nape of her neck. In the past year, gray had choked out the brown.

The house, too, had fallen into disarray. The place wasn't dirty, just overrun with clutter. Magazines—*Silver Screen, TV Guide, Screen Stars*—were stacked in every corner of the parlor, arranged by size and date. The kitchen counters were covered with empty margarine tubs, or soup cans, or mayonnaise jars, which Dorothy had washed and arranged on towels to dry. In a cupboard Joyce discovered two large grocery sacks filled with empty prescription bottles. ROSE NOVAK, one of the labels read. OCTOBER 1, 1955.

"She doesn't throw anything away," she told Ed afterward. "She must spend the whole day organizing and sorting this stuff."

"Well, why not?" he countered. "It gives her something to do."

At one time the clutter would have driven

Joyce crazy. Now she understood how little it mattered, and held her tongue. She
entertained Dorothy with the latest town
gossip—births and marriages, illnesses
and deaths. Acquaintances or strangers, it
didn't matter: Dorothy's memory was ency-
clopedic. She could always conjure forth
the name of the groom's uncle, the bride's
cousin, connecting each new event to
someone they both knew.

You're alone too much, Joyce sometimes
told her.

I keep busy, Dorothy said. She had the
television; every afternoon she took a long
walk. Sunday mornings she went to church.
Joyce had offered a dozen times to teach
her, but she would not learn to drive. She
had always been a homebody. There was
no place she wanted to go.

Often, in the summer, Evelyn Stusick
crossed the street with a basket of Early Girl
tomatoes, a bag of the cucumbers that
grew faster than she could pickle them.
Every spring she planted too much, more
than one person could possibly use. Her

daughters were married now, with houses of their own. Leonard was in medical school and visited only on holidays. Like Dorothy Novak, Ev was all alone.

She sliced the vegetables in Dorothy's kitchen and sprinkled the tomatoes with sugar, the way Rose had liked them—a sweetly grainy, acidic treat.

"How is Nicholas doing in school?" Dorothy asked. "Isn't he almost finished by now?"

"Leonard," Ev corrected. "He has another year of medical school." She couldn't keep the pride out of her voice. In four years her son would be a doctor. It was as if she had raised a president, or a pope. Gene, if he had lived, would have felt the same way.

"I'll have to tell Georgie," Dorothy said. "He called this morning. He asked after you."

"He did?" Ev rose and arranged the extra Early Girls on the windowsill.

"He always does," said Dorothy. "You should write him a letter. Or call him some-time."

"I'll leave these green ones here to ripen," Ev said. "They'll be ready in a day or two. Don't let them wait too long."

She crossed the street to her empty house. She'd deny it if anyone asked, but the silence wore on her. *You don't have to stay there, Mom,* her daughters told her periodically. And she'd had offers. Some she'd talk about—Rebecca, her oldest, had invited her to come live in Maryland—and at least one she'd never mentioned to anyone.

The spring after the Twelve collapse, George Novak had asked her to marry him. Like his proposal—by her watch, twenty-eight years too late—Ev's answer was slow in coming. She was simply too stunned to speak.

There was the disrespect to Gene, dead just four months; a death so sudden and violent that no one—not Ev or his children or anyone who knew him—would ever recover from it. *He thought the world of you,* she told Georgie—after the initial shock, when she'd regained the power of speech. *He still called you his best friend.* Then there was the fact that Georgie, for all his talk, was still legally married. *Where are we, Utah?* she asked. *Excuse me if I don't know the proper etiquette. I've never been proposed to by a married man.*

Later, she realized that none of this was

surprising, that the proposal was perfectly in Georgie's character. He had always followed his heart, in whatever foolish direction that organ led him. Oblivious to the other hearts—hers, Gene's, his mother's—he broke along the way.

I love you, he told her. *Ev, I've always loved you.*

Oh, Georgie, she said, pitying them both. *The years go. You can't have them back.*

The Twelve did not reopen. In its heyday, most of its coal had been barged to Pittsburgh, processed into coke to feed the blast furnaces of American Steel. Now AmSteel had its own troubles. Its Pittsburgh plant had closed that summer. More and more, houses were heated with oil, with gas. The world could survive without Bakerton coal.

The changes spread outward, like an epidemic. Ten families had lost fathers, husbands. Nine hundred lost paychecks, and more would follow. Baker Two was mined out; the Four and the Seven nearly so. Out-of-work miners sat on front porches. There was nowhere for them to go.

Susquehanna Avenue had one empty storefront, then two. In a year, the whole block was dark.

*   *   *

People kept their heads down. They pretended not to notice. To Lucy, who had been away, the changes were astounding. It was as if a blight had settled, a deadly fungus passed from tree to tree.

She'd been gone four years, nearly five. Nursing school, then a bachelor's degree—school and more school, until the original purpose of her studies had been forgotten. Studies funded by Joyce, a savings account she'd fed for years with tens and twenties from her small paycheck. Started early, when she was still in the air force; still a young woman herself. In the selfishness of adolescence, Lucy had accepted this gift without question. Only later did she see how remarkable it was. At twenty, Joyce had already traded away her own future, invested everything she had in someone else.

The savings covered her first year's tuition. Then, scholarships and fellowships; somehow the money had always come. On school breaks, she worked—in the Student Union, in Pittsburgh restaurants and hotels. Summer jobs didn't exist in Bakerton. Waitresses, cashiers at the Quaker—they were grown people who needed the paycheck, adults with families to support.

It seemed to Lucy that she'd always been expected to leave—like her brothers, who'd roared out of Bakerton the first chance they got. It was the sisters who stayed: Joyce to care for their mother, Dorothy because she could not care for herself. They'd assumed Lucy would have no such limitations. The family's slim resources had been lavished upon her, with no other expectation than that she would succeed in life. That she would *go*.

She did her best to oblige, to do what was expected. She found a job the day before her graduation, at Presbyterian Hospital in Pittsburgh; she shared an apartment with two of her classmates. For nearly two years she worked. She had herself fitted with an IUD, a small copper device no bigger than a quarter. She bought a car, a '65 Ford Mustang, and every month or two she drove out to Saxon County for a visit. A boyfriend disappeared; another took his place. She grew older. Nothing changed.

She might have gone on that way for years. Instead she went back to Bakerton, the one Novak who truly wanted to stay. For a long time she'd fought the desire, through all her years of schooling, that extraordinary privilege that felt to her like a kind of exile. When she broke the news to Joyce, she did it apologetically: *There's something I have to tell you. I hope you'll understand.*

She found a job easily enough; she seemed to be the only one in Saxon County who could. After the war, during the coal boom, a new wing had been added to Miners' Hospital. The annex overlooked the Number Twelve, the rusting iron skeleton of its abandoned tipple. The top floor was devoted entirely to pulmonary care. The only thing, she told her college friends—late at night, by phone, after a long, exhausting shift—that Bakerton was still producing: old men who couldn't breathe.

Except they weren't old. Most were in their fifties or early sixties. A few saw seventy; invariably, they were the ones who hadn't smoked. Black Lung could take ten or twenty of a miner's healthy years. Black Lung plus cigarettes would cut them in half.

The lungs died by degrees, silently, inexorably, a slow erosion of tissue. In the end they collapsed completely; the men died gasping for breath, their eyes wide with terror. After a few months on the unit, Lucy was familiar with the process; she understood just how little she could do. She gave the men steroids and lectured them about smoking. The acute cases she placed in oxygen tents. More and more, she helped them with their paperwork. A law had been passed: if you were persistent, if you hadn't smoked, if you were smart enough to make sense of the forms and patient enough to spend hours filling them out, your widow might be awarded a small monthly check. The men wouldn't see a dime, themselves. They would all be dead before the money came through.

The men slept six to a ward, loud with the rush of oxygen tanks. The tanks breathed in unison, a sound like the rhythmic roll of the ocean. Weaving in between the beds, checking the men's vitals, Lucy imagined herself aboard a battleship, ministering to wounded soldiers at sea. Her patients were all veterans; she knew it from their stories, their bearing, the greenish marks tattooed on their withering biceps. Listening to them, she thought of the father she couldn't remember, the face she knew from a single photograph, taken on his wedding day. She recalled Angelo Bernardi's deep laugh, his cigarette kiss on her cheek, his breathing audible from the next room. The two men who'd loved her had disappeared from the world, without ever knowing the person she had become.

At the end of her shift she drove across the bridge, barely used since the explosion at the Twelve. She passed the abandoned tipple, the weathered outbuildings, the Towers still glowing in the distance, as though nothing had changed. Sometimes, driving into town, she passed Connie Kukla and Clare Ann Baran, still inseparable, walking home from their shift at the dress factory. Connie had married Steven Fleck, who worked for a strip-mining company in West Virginia and came home only on weekends. They shared a house with Connie's widowed mother, which made sense to Lucy. She couldn't imagine Connie being alone.

Of all the differences between them, it was perhaps the most profound: Lucy's life was solitary. She couldn't imagine it any other way. She'd tried living on Polish Hill with Dorothy, but the memories paralyzed her, and Dorothy's silence only amplified the emptiness of the house. Finally she'd rented

a small apartment above a flower shop, in
what used to be called Little Italy. The
neighborhood distinctions had disappeared; now people lived wherever they
pleased. More and more, that meant leaving
Bakerton entirely, for steady work in Maryland or Virginia or the eastern part of the
state. Next door to Lucy was the building
that had housed Bellavia's Bakery, its windows now dark. Across the street, the Sons
of Italy and Rizzo's Tavern still did a brisk
business. Above Rizzo's was the apartment
where her mother had lived as a girl. At the
end of the block was Nudo's Pennzoil station, its concrete wall stenciled with large
letters: TOUGH TIMES NEVER LAST. TOUGH
PEOPLE DO.

On warm nights, in summertime, the
neighborhood was still lively. Music spilled
through the open windows; voices and
laughter in the street. Infrequently, on a Friday or Saturday, Lucy had a drink at one of
the bars. When a man approached her, she
flirted out of habit; but always she went
home alone. The need that had once possessed her—to be watched and listened to,
noticed and approved—had simply vanished. She still felt hollow inside, cored like

an apple; she still hated sleeping alone. Yet she no longer believed that love would fill her. Each night she ate supper at the window, listening to the radio. And sometimes, after a particularly long shift at the hospital, she smoked a single cigarette.

It was summer when the motorcycle came. Dorothy heard it from her porch swing. She had visited the graves that morning, to avoid the heat. The afternoon stretched long before her. The late August sun was warm on her skin. Her eyelids fluttered, opened, fluttered again.

She heard a gentle buzzing in the distance, like the drone of a bumblebee. At the top of the hill, a hunting dog bayed. The buzzing became a great roar, the sound rising in pitch. Then the Poblockis' beagles joined in.

A motorcycle shot up the hill at a speed that seemed impossible, chrome blinding in the sunlight. It roared past Dorothy's house, then made a sharp U-turn, spraying gravel. She shaded her eyes with her hand.

The bike skidded to a stop. Tied to its sides were saddlebags and a scruffy bedroll. The rider was a young man in a denim jacket.

"My word," Dorothy said.

The rider stepped off the bike. He wore a scruffy beard and dirty blue jeans, torn at the knees. His helmet was decorated with the Stars and Stripes. He glanced around as if he were lost.

He climbed the porch steps and took off his helmet. "Aunt Dorothy," he said, offering his hand. "How do you do?"

Arthur moved into Joyce's old room. The room where his mother had slept, tranquilized, during her one visit to Bakerton, where Sandy had ironed his monogrammed shirts the winter of the strike. The mattress sagged, but compared to the places he'd slept recently, Arthur found it exquisitely comfortable. After dropping out of Swarthmore, he'd spent several months riding: as far west as Nevada, he told his aunt; then south and eastward across Texas. His aunt fed him and listened to his stories. She

seemed to enjoy them, although she sometimes looked at him strangely, as though
she weren't quite sure who he was.

For his part, he remembered her vividly—
the aunt who'd followed him through a
snowstorm, her face wrapped in a scarf, her
eyes tearing in the wind. His father's sister
who had never married, who'd lived in a
boardinghouse in Washington, D.C., until
she went crazy and came back to Bakerton
to live with her mother. She didn't seem
crazy now, just extremely quiet. Her house
was messy, in a way that comforted him. He
felt strangely at home.

She asked no questions, which pleased
him. He got enough of those from his father:
*When are you coming back? What will be-
come of you? For God's sake, have you lost
your mind?* Except for a couple of phone
calls from the road, Arthur hadn't spoken to
him in months. He'd tried to make the old
man understand that college was a dead issue. There was nothing he wanted to study,
and he didn't need the deferment. He'd
failed his Selective Service physical. His
asthma had bought him freedom, and possibly saved his life.

Away from school, the world opened to

him. There was plenty he could do. He knew everything about motorcycles, and he could fake his way around a lawnmower, a snow-mobile, any kind of small engine. In Allerton, Texas, he'd stopped to help a biker broken down on the highway. They had shared a joint; then the biker, a wild-haired, Injun-looking guy named Grif, had offered him a place to sleep. There was plenty of floor space in his trailer. A buddy of his needed help in his garage.

Arthur set up his bedroll in Grif's trailer. Each day he changed oil and rotated tires. At night he and Grif shared joints, road sto-ries and, oddly, books. *On the Road, Sid-dartha* and *Doors of Perception,* which Grif referred to, not unseriously, as The Oracle. Arthur read them all, glad his father couldn't see him. The old man would have been en-tirely too pleased, which would have ruined Arthur's enjoyment. That reading could be pleasurable was an astonishing discovery. He'd never voluntarily read a book in his life.

One night, a little stoned, he telephoned his father. He didn't mention reading, just rambled on about Grif, the desert heat, his job in the garage.

The old man had nearly dropped the phone. "A grease monkey?" he said.

"Don't knock it," Arthur told him. Cars, trucks, everything broke down eventually. A mechanic was like a doctor, or an undertaker. A steady stream of business was guaranteed.

He stayed in Allerton a full month, until Grif decided to drive the trailer down to Mexico. "You're welcome to come," he said, but Arthur was already safe from the draft. They said their good-byes and Arthur hit the road, with Grif's tattered copy of The Oracle stowed in his saddlebag. He crossed Texas in two days; then Louisiana and Mississippi, stopping to camp along the Natchez Trace. By August he was riding into Bakerton.

He explored the town. On hot days he climbed the hill to the municipal swimming pool, an old bath towel looped around his neck, The Oracle tucked under his arm. He borrowed other books from the public library—*Great Expectations, The Last of the Mohicans,* books he'd been assigned in high school but had never actually read. "How's this one?" he'd ask the pretty dark-haired girl who stamped them at the front desk.

"I liked it," she'd answer each time, but that was the most he could get out of her. Her reticence baffled him. He'd never had a problem talking to girls.

Finally he figured it out. "Will you cut my hair?" he asked his aunt. She sat him on the back stoop, an old bedsheet over his shoulders, and went crazy with a pair of kitchen scissors. His ponytail lay on the grass like a dead animal.

"Can you get it any shorter?" he asked, and she kept cutting. Finally, she handed him a mirror.

"You look handsome," she observed, and Arthur had to agree. His head felt curiously light, an agreeable sensation. He thought: *Now my brain can breathe.*

He liked talking to people. In the pool hall, the post office, the sidewalk in front of the fire hall, nobody was in a hurry. He was surprised when strangers recognized his name. *Georgie's boy,* they said, their faces lighting with recognition. *Mrs. Hauser's nephew.* Afterward they greeted him like a relative, these people he'd never seen before in his life. It was because of his father that he belonged here. The realization filled him with a strange gratitude. He found himself missing the old man—a feeling that had haunted his childhood, the long winters at school. He hadn't missed his father in years.

"Stay as long as you like," his aunt told him. She wasn't crazy, he decided; she just had trouble remembering his name. Depending on the day, she might call him Angie, Nicholas, Sandy or Chick.

In the evenings they ate together at the big table in the kitchen. She cooked piles of noodles, fried eggplant, an Italian soup he couldn't get enough of. "Have some more, Angie," she said, refilling his bowl. He had never eaten so well in his life.

She asked him, once, about his mother.

"She's fine," he said automatically. A moment passed before he understood the question. She hadn't asked how his mother was doing. She'd asked *what is she like.*

"You never met her?" he asked.

"Oh, no. She came once to visit, but I was living in Washington then. Joyce said she was a beautiful girl."

Arthur frowned. He would never have

called his mother *a beautiful girl.* In recent years she had grown fragile and desiccated, her thin shoulders slightly stooped. It seemed incredible that they were talking about the same person.

"They've been married, like, fifty years," he said. "Maybe not fifty, but a long time. It's weird that you never met her."

"Georgie has been gone for so long," his aunt said. "And so far away."

Arthur considered this. Philadelphia wasn't that far, maybe four hundred miles. He'd ridden twice that in a single day.

"She's a regular mother," he said. "She likes nice things. Like all mothers, I guess." As he said it, he realized it wasn't right. There were other kinds of mothers. In Bakerton, mothers—like everything else—were probably different.

"She likes art," he said. "She collects antiques. And she likes to travel."

"Like you," his aunt said.

"I guess." Arthur couldn't imagine his mother riding a motorcycle across the country. She spent every spring at a spa in Switzerland, breathing mountain air.

"You should phone her," his aunt said.

"Let her know where you are. She must be worried about you."

"She's in Europe. She probably doesn't even know I left home."

His aunt refilled his soup bowl. He cut them each a slice of bread. They ate the rest of the meal in silence, as they usually did. Then Arthur got up to clear their plates from the table. "They're getting divorced," he said.

His aunt colored.

"They should have done it years ago, if you ask me. I think they were waiting for me to grow up." He rinsed the plates at the sink, his back to her. Still she didn't speak.

"They think I'm upset about it, but I'm not. He's always working, and she's always gone. I don't think they even like each other. I can't figure out why they ever got married in the first place." He filled the sink with water. "They both changed. That's what my dad says."

"That happens sometimes," his aunt said.

TEN

The town wore away like a bar of soap. Each year, smaller and less distinct, the letters of its name fading. The thing it had been became harder to discern.

Whole neighborhoods went up for sale. School enrollment dropped. Every sort of job disappeared. There were fewer cars to service, fewer teeth to fill, no houses whatsoever to build.

The landscape softened. One by one the tipples fell. The conveyors were dismantled. Aging machinery was carted away: longwalls, mantrips, shuttlecars. Outbuildings were demolished and sold for scrap, or left to rust in the weather. Black scars were left behind, as though the earth had been burned.

In springtime a fleet of trucks climbed

Saxon Mountain, dieseling loudly: a low convoy of blunt shapes, their purpose unknown. Gary Poblocki saw them and spread the word on his CB radio. His brother Bernie, back from Vietnam, suspected the army. Bernie always suspected the army, but this time no one had a better theory.

The trucks funneled into the valley, their empty beds clattering. They circled the Towers and slowed.

The morning was still; there was no breeze to ignite the bony piles. In the April sunlight they looked like what they were: two eighty-foot heaps of mine dirt, brought over by the truckload from the Three, the Five and the Twelve. Dug by pick and shovel, by longwall, by Lee Norse and Wilcox machines; hauled by donkey, by conveyor, by shuttlecar. By English and Irish, Italian and Slavish, the hands and backs and lungs of four generations of men.

The Towers had proved that Bakerton was working. Their absence would prove the opposite. The piles would be leveled in three days and the dirt carted westward, to backfill a thousand acres of wetlands on the outskirts of Cleveland.

A crew was already waiting. The driver signaled. Gears grinding, the machine opened its jaws.

Lucy had been working at Miners' for three years when Leonard Stusick came home. She was trimming Dorothy's hedges on Polish Hill when he drove up to his mother's house in a U-Haul truck. The sight of the truck moved her in a way she couldn't have predicted. She was like a shipwreck survivor clinging to her raft; overhead, the rhythmic chop of helicopter blades. Crossing the street to greet him, she felt her eyes tearing. They both wondered what was wrong with her.

He had finished his residency that spring. Like Lucy, he could have gone anywhere; yet he, too, had chosen Bakerton. Months would pass before they spoke of why. First they would work together on the pulmonary ward at Miners'; dance together at the fire hall and watch the fireworks at Dago Day; then drink too much and wake up together, awkwardly, in Lucy's bed.

Later it would seem as if she'd always known it. The others had been mere filler:

the college boys, the men in Pittsburgh, the long series of thrilling disappointments, from Steven Fleck onward. All those years she'd been passing time, waiting for Leonard to grow up.

The wedding was held at St. Casimir's, where the bride had been baptized, where both sets of grandparents had been married. Joyce Hauser, visibly pregnant, was the matron of honor. Her husband gave the bride away.

George Novak paid for the wedding: the polka band, the hall rental, the three elderly cooks at the Polish Legion, who spent the morning stuffing cabbage at lightning speed. The whole affair cost half what he'd paid for his new Cadillac, and it brought him greater pleasure. It was the hometown wedding he'd never had.

The news had shocked him at first. Arthur was twenty-two, barely old enough to vote. *You're just a kid,* George had told him. *What's the rush?*

Come meet Susan, Arthur said bashfully. *Then you'll understand.*

And he had. Susan Jevic was lovely in ways George found achingly familiar: her intelligence and kindness, her sincerity and warmth. *Don't worry,* he reassured Marion, who had boycotted the whole affair. *Arthur will be fine.* Any boy would be fine, married to such a girl. George thought of himself at that age, the summer he had come home on furlough. The summer he should have married Ev.

They hadn't spoken in years, not since his foolish proposal. She had told him not to phone her; sick with shame, he had obeyed. Instead he made weekly calls to his sisters, angling for news of her. It was Joyce who'd told him about Leonard, that he'd been accepted into the medical school at Penn.

George tracked down the boy easily enough, took him out for a couple of steak dinners. Leonard was bright and earnest, serious and polite, without the stubborn streak George saw in his own son. For his part, he was grateful for the company. Since his divorce he dined alone at lunch counters or ate sandwiches standing over the kitchen sink.

He'd offered the boy a job at Quigley's, stocking shelves on Sunday afternoons, unloading trucks late at night. When the hours became too much for him, George had simply mailed in the tuition checks, a thousand dollars here and there, from the college fund Arthur would never spend. *It's nothing to me,* he told Leonard, and this was true. He could drive his Cadillacs for four years instead of three. The money meant nothing at all.

He did it for Ev, for Gene and for himself—the young man he'd once been, full of ambition, hungry to learn. *Your dad was my friend,* he told Leonard, who'd agreed not to tell his mother. *He would want me to help.*

A hundred guests attended the wedding. After dinner, they lined up for the bridal dance. The band launched into a joyful mazurka. The bride sat on a chair in the middle of the dance floor, and Joyce removed the bridal veil. The crowd clapped and whooped as Joyce replaced the veil with a babushka. She tied a lacy white apron at Susan's waist.

They danced together first, the teacher and her student. The guests waited, clapping in time with the music. The line wrapped twice around the dance floor.

Susan danced next with her sister Irene, grown gray and stout; then a long series of blue-eyed Jevics. She danced with George Novak, then Dorothy, then Arthur's handsome uncle Sandy in his white leisure suit. She danced with Lucy Stusick, with Leonard, some Scarponi cousins she couldn't name. Her co-workers from the library, then Jerry Bernardi, who'd driven there in his hearse. The Poblockis took their turns, the Wojicks and Klezeks and Yurkoviches. She danced with every man, woman and child on Polish Hill.

Each guest slipped a dollar into her lacy apron, then joined the circle around the floor. Spinning round and round, Susan didn't notice the commotion, the decorated monstrosity her brothers had brought in through the back door.

Her sister Irene danced first in the trough—her second-eldest sister, old enough to be her mother, as a few guests pointed out.

She was joined by Sandy Novak. A slight bending of tradition—Arthur was his nephew, not his brother—but Sandy felt entitled. When Lucy and Leonard had eloped, he'd lost his rightful chance.

In the spring the wagons came. Black wagons, small and square, their looping wheels delicately webbed. The men driving were paler than the Irish, quieter than the Polish. The women wore dark dresses. After the English and Irish, the Italians and Hungarians, the Poles and Slovaks and Ukrainians and Croats—after all these, came the plain.

Wagons on the back roads, to Coalport, to Fallentree. Horses were tied outside the A&P. Boys in dark pants chased one another through the parking lot. The plain weren't given to chatting, but if you were friendly and persistent—like Arthur Novak, in his plain-style beard, who made a good living repairing their farm equipment—you could sometimes have a word. Land was cheap in Saxon County; industry had moved into Lancaster, forcing the prices up. Back east, environmentalists had raised a fuss about farm runoff into the Chesapeake. Here, plain farmers would not be bothered. After a hundred years of bony dumps and streams running red, no one minded a little manure.

The plain built houses, or fixed what was there. In town they bought lumber and hardware, shingles and paint. Wheat grew, feed corn, acres of soybeans. The land grew over, softened and greened.

Each year the scarred places shrank a little. The green spread slowly, planted and harvested by the plain. The green covered, but did not fill, the dark world that lay beneath.